Stop Talking

by

Patti Gaustad Procopi

BLUE FORTUNE ENTERPRISES LLC

Lavender Press
an imprint of Blue Fortune Enterprises, LLC

STOP TALKING

Copyright © 2023 by Patti Gaustad Procopi

For information contact :
Blue Fortune Enterprises, LLC
Lavender Press
P.O. Box 554
Yorktown, VA 23690
http://blue-fortune.com

Cover design by BFE, LLC
Cover Artwork by Joan Loren Gaustad

ISBN: 978-1-961548-04-6
First Edition: December 2023

Dedication

To my husband
Greg
and my daughters
Allie, Elena, and Leah

Family is everything

Every time I thought I knew what was about to happen in this ultimately heartwarming story, Procopi threw me a curve, keeping me turning pages late into the night.

Linda Rosen, author of *The Emerald Necklace*

A compelling and satisfying family drama.

Grace Sammon, award-winning author of *The Eves* and host of *The Storytellers*

When the trials of a fractured family spiral into the depths of overwhelming tragedy and upheaval, oftentimes you reach a breaking point—the moment you just want to tell people to just *"stop talking"*. You can't bear to hear any more. Grief, loss, and alcoholism complicate the main character, Rose's emotional turmoil in the face of adversity. Her pain is real, richly drawn by Procopi's heartfelt prose which captures the essence of a mature protagonist whose ghosts of the past plague her through a deeply moving read.

Janis Robinson Daly, author of *The Unlocked Path*, #1 New Release for U.S. Historical Fiction, Kindle

A sequel to the much loved *Please… Tell Me More*, Patti Gaustad Procopi's *Stop Talking* continues the saga of sisters Rose and Ivy. Beautifully written, the author portrays her character's flaws and strengths so that her readers cannot help but fall in love with them. Even Thor, the giant wolf dog from Alaska, worked his way into my heart.

Stop Talking is the story of what we do for family, the cruelty of addiction, and the hope for tomorrow.

Barbara Conrey, USA Today bestselling author of *Nowhere Near Goodbye* and *My Secret to Keep*.

Dear Reader,

Like all my books, this is a work of fiction with some elements of truth tossed in.

When I finished *Please…Tell Me More,* I was exhausted and thought I had ended the book with all the characters in a good place. But when my oldest daughter Allie read it, she said she couldn't wait for the sequel. My thought was: never! But then the ideas started coming to me and after I finished writing *I'll Get By,* I started on this book.

I hope you enjoy it. If you haven't read *Please,* I think you will still enjoy this one but hopefully you will want to read the beginning of the story.

If you are so inclined, please leave a review on Amazon, Barnes & Noble and/or Goodreads. It's wonderful to get feedback from readers, and it helps others decide if they want to read it.

Please feel free to reach out and contact me. You can find me in a number of ways, including:

Website: pattiproauthor.com
Facebook: @pattiproauthor
Instagram: patti.pro
LinkedIn: patricia-procopi
Or email me at patti.pro@cox.net
I'd love to hear from you.

If you pick one of my books for a book club, I'd love to join in at the end for questions and comments, either in person or by Zoom.

Acknowledgements

- My book is dedicated to my husband Greg. I was luckier than Rose and Ivy. We've just celebrated 44 years of marriage, and I'm planning on at least another 44!

- I've also dedicated this book to our wonderful, incredible brilliant daughters. They were my first and best creation. In many ways, they have encouraged and inspired my writing. My books are fiction but there are real elements in them sometimes loosely based on things that happened to me or my kids. I think they've forgiven me for that!

- Much gratitude to my sister, who is my biggest fan but sometimes my sharpest critic. The Ivy to my Rose. Thanks for sharing the journey. And thank you for the beautiful cover that so beautifully depicts the bond between Fern and Thor.

- I also want to give a shout-out to The Chesapeake Bay Writers, my local writing group. My writing really didn't take off until I found my people. Writing is solitary but we all need support. And that includes a big thank you to my critique group who've read all my books and made them better: Peter Stipe, Dave Pistorese, Mark Green, Caterina Novelierre, Elizabeth Lee, Ginny Brock, Sandy Hicks, Diane Caron, and Shary Raske.

- Also want to thank my friend Dr. Sarah West, who I badgered with many questions to make my hospital scenes realistic. I ended up changing what happened to everyone at the hospital so didn't use many of her brilliant insights and medical advice, but I still appreciate her help.

- And of course thank you once again to my amazing editor and publisher Narielle Living of Blue Fortune Enterprises, who was the first person to say, send me your manuscript. She's been there with me from the beginning.

One of the themes of my writing is about the terrible toll alcoholism takes on individuals and families. If you are struggling, find your local AA group. They can help you turn your life around.

And my last message is: adopt don't shop. If you want a pet, please consider your local shelter. There are so many wonderful animals there just waiting for a loving home.

Patti

Stop Talking

Your words are like an avalanche of rocks
Breaking my heart
shattering my soul
I cover my ears and
shut my eyes to block the words
But they seep through my pores
Please stop talking
Give me hope
Give me comfort
Give me time to heal

Prologue

I don't know how long the phone rang. I was in a deep sleep. So deep it took a while for me to come back to wakefulness. Drifting up from the blackness, the ringing phone became a part of my dream.

In my dream, I couldn't find the source of the annoying, incessant beeping. "What is that sound?" I wondered as I wandered from room to room so I could turn it off.

Finally, I woke. My cell phone sat across the room, on my dresser, ringing. Why was it over there? Usually I plugged it in next to the bed in case clients called during the night.

Bolting upward, I looked at the clock. It was way past midnight. Calls in the middle of the night are never good news.

Probably a client. Another sweet soul departing this world with only me there to see her off. Those goodbyes always left me filled with sorrow.

Flipping on the light, Jack lay sound asleep next to me. Nothing, but nothing, ever woke him.

Stumbling out of bed, I ran to grab my phone. Fumbling, I dropped it. Take a deep breath. I bent over to pick it up.

"Hello!" I practically shouted into the phone. "Who is this?" Since I didn't have my contact lenses in, I couldn't see the screen.

Sobbing came over the other end of the line. "Oh, Rose," Ivy blubbered. "Oh, Rose." Her sobbing stopped her words, and she couldn't speak coherently. "It's… too awful…"

Phillipe, her massage therapist, was in the background. "Ivy, give me ze phone. Let me talk to Rose." Part of my mind wondered what he was doing there in the middle of the night and why he still used that phony French accent.

Ivy's crying grew fainter, though her shouting in the background was still audible. "No, oh no! It can't be true."

"Rose," Phillipe said, "this eezz Phillipe."

It was all I could do not to scream, "I know who the hell it is!"

"Ivy just got a call from Elaska. It eezz bad news. No, it eezz terrible news. I don't even know how to tell you."

Terrible news? From Alaska? Had something happened to William? Or Margie? Or God forbid! Not Fern. Please God! Not Fern.

Chapter One

Six Years Earlier...

$\mathcal{J}$ack and I left the cemetery and walked over to the closest coffee shop, with Fritz trotting happily between us. Here I was, going off with an almost complete stranger. I looked at Fritz and thought, *I am relying on your doggie instincts, Fritz. You seem to like Jack, so I am trusting you.* Fritz tilted his head as if to reassure me.

Ironically, we ended up at the same café Dad and I went to when we met at Mom and Lily's graves. Damn, almost five years ago. In some ways it seemed like yesterday, and in other ways it seemed a lifetime ago. So much had happened since then. Finding William, changing jobs, getting sober.

The same sour-faced waitress was still there. She took one look at Fritz and said, "You'll have to sit outside. No dogs allowed." Fritz settled happily under our table.

She poured us coffee, put down some menus, and marched off. She glared at me as she walked away. I wondered if she remembered me from my last visit and was still angry about her tip. How ridiculous. She must see hundreds of people in a week. Maybe several thousand since the last time I was there. I was not that memorable. She probably looked that way at everyone who came in. How did she keep her job?

"Have you been here before?" Jack asked.

"Only once, over four years ago, with my dad. It was the first time I'd seen him in over forty years and the last time I'd ever see him." Pausing. "That's not completely true. I did see him once more when he was dying." Jack grimaced. "Why do you ask?"

"The waitress appears to dislike you. Intensely."

"I think she dislikes everyone."

Jack sipped his coffee and looked at me. Normally, I'd be uncomfortable, but I was relaxed with him. As if I'd known him forever.

"Come here often?" I said with a sly smile.

"Trying that old pick-up line?" He laughed. "No. This is the first time. Usually, I'm not in the mood to do anything after I visit my brother Ricky's grave. In the past, I'd usually find a bar. Now I go to an AA meeting."

How quickly our lives start revolving around meetings. If you're upset—go to a meeting. If you're happy—go to a meeting. If you're lonely—go to a meeting. And most importantly, if you want, need, or think you're going to have a drink—go to a meeting.

Jack and I fell into an easy conversation. There were no awkward pauses or silences. If we ran out of things to say, the quiet moments were comfortable, not embarrassing. I've never been a social creature and am often tongue-tied in the presence of others. It was different with Jack.

"I'm still in awe of you standing up in front of everyone at the Tuesday meeting and spilling your guts, telling your life story to the group. Something I probably need to do," Jack said.

"It's not easy, but it must be done."

"I'm just so embarrassed by my behavior. All those years I drank. The things I did." Jack stared down into his cup, probably remembering the worst moments.

"You think there's anything you've done that anyone there hasn't? Remember the old saying about how to talk in front of a crowd: imagine them all naked? When you stand up at an AA meeting, imagine them all passed out drunk in a pool of vomit."

Jack winced. "Ew. What an image. But you're right."

After we finished our coffee, he asked me if I wanted to have something to eat. "I'm hungry," he announced. "And I'd love to share a meal with you. Eating alone is depressing."

I fiddled with the handle of my coffee cup. "I know what you mean. Usually I don't make anything for dinner because it makes me lonely. I try to have a big lunch and snack at night. Of course, back in the day, I enjoyed a liquid dinner."

"Oh, yeah," Jack said with a laugh. "I've had plenty of those nights myself. Way too many."

The waitress returned to ask if we wanted anything else. She implied if we weren't going to order something to eat, we'd have to leave. There wasn't a crowd of people waiting to be seated. Only one other table was occupied.

"Do you have any specials?" Jack asked. He smiled at me when he said this, and I covered my face with my menu so the waitress wouldn't see my grin.

"No," she said in an irritated tone of voice. "This isn't the kind of place for specials. The menu is the menu."

"We must come here more often," Jack said to me, trying to look serious as he scanned the menu. "There are so many choices, it's almost impossible to decide."

He ordered a hamburger, and I ordered a chef salad. What might my salad consist of? Wilted lettuce and soggy croutons?

"Why do women do that?" Jack asked.

"Do what?" I responded, confused by the question.

"Always order salad? Why don't you order a burger or a sandwich? Are you trying to convince the man you're with that you are a light eater or a cheap date?"

"Wow," I shook my head. "I never thought about it. Don't know why women often order salads. Probably because women think they need to be on diets or they want the people they're with to think they are concerned about their weight?"

"Most guys would rather you just order the burger! And the fries." Jack laughed. "What's that old expression? 'Life is short, eat the dessert? Eat dessert first?' or something like that?"

"I will probably regret ordering a salad in this place," I agreed. "And come to think of it, I remember many times I wanted the dessert but didn't want people judging me."

"Funny how we're so afraid of being judged, but it doesn't stop us from making stupid decisions like becoming drunks," Jack said sorrowfully.

"Sad but true," I agreed.

My salad was passable, barely. Jack said his burger was great. He was probably pulling my leg. I saw him slipping bites to Fritz, who was lying half-asleep under the table. We split the dessert.

Chapter Two

"Do you believe in love at first sight?" a client asked me once.

"I believe in 'lust at first sight,'" I replied. ("And what's wrong with a little lust?" I could hear my sister Ivy whispering). Though, I meant more of a physical attraction than actual lust.

Why do I continue to deny 'love at first sight'? I experienced firsthand evidence of it when Ivy and her second husband, Terry, met. The moment their hands touched, I knew they were in love. They knew they were in love.

And now it happened to me. I loved Jack from the moment he invited me to have a cup of coffee.

After our first date—lunch at the Unfriendly Café—if Jack had casually suggested we go to the courthouse and get married, I would've readily agreed. This was the man I'd been waiting for. The one I deserved. My soulmate. God took his sweet time fulfilling my deepest desire, which was someone to share my life with. Magnanimously, I graciously decided to forgive God for taking so long. Jack was worth waiting for.

After Jack and I parted ways, with plans to see each other Tuesday night at my favorite AA meeting, I headed home with Fritz. This was news I couldn't wait to share with Ivy. Unluckily for me, she was at an art show in Chicago giving a talk about her paintings, which is why Fritz was with me. When we got home, I picked up Fritz and gave him a big hug. "You little matchmaker, Fritzie! You helped me find Jack. Love at last. All thanks to you."

I was nervous and agitated because there was no one to talk to. Since Ivy wasn't available, I thought about calling my one and only friend Lauren. Checking the time, I knew she was probably still at work. I hated the time difference between the East and West Coast. Made it difficult sometimes to get in touch.

I was full of pent-up energy and started dancing around the living room and singing. Fritz loved this. He chased me around, barking. Grabbing him up, I swirled, singing in his ear, "I'm in love, Fritz!"

As usual, my mood quickly swung the other way. Jack hadn't asked for my number. Hadn't suggested getting together again other than saying, "See you at the Tuesday night meeting." There was no evidence he was in love with me. Or that he even liked me as more than an AA friend.

Looking at myself critically in the mirror, I saw an average woman, fifty-five years old, closer to fifty-six. As I turned my head side to side, I thought I'd aged well. Still no great beauty, but my hair was glossy, my skin almost wrinkle-free and since I'd finally gotten contacts, you could see my pretty eyes. And while I'm not thin—I'm never going to be thin—I'm not obese.

So, what if I'm in my fifties? Isn't fifty the new thirty? Cringing, I realized that was something Ivy would say. Actually had said when she turned fifty.

Even though I was on the hump, ready to slide down the slippery slope to sixty, I was still in my fifties. Mid-fifties. Jack was probably also in his fifties. At least, I thought he was. I agonized about it. Maybe he's only in his forties. Maybe he thinks of me as a big sister. Someone to talk to. Maybe he wants me to be his AA sponsor.

Flopping down on the couch, I pulled a blanket over my head. Why was I so confused? One minute happy and the next miserable. Is this love? If it is, I don't want it. I want to be happy, not wretched. Fritz jumped up next to me and whined, pulling the blanket off my head.

"Where is your mommy when I need her, Fritz? I need someone to talk to. You're a good listener, but you totally fail in the advice department." Fritz tilted his head, looking at me quizzically. Then he barked and jumped off the couch and ran to the door.

"Is that all you got? Let's go for a walk?" I laughed, and he ran back to me. "What I need to do is go to a meeting before I reach for a drink."

Could I survive until Tuesday night?

Chapter Three

$\mathscr{M}$y plans have a way of getting interrupted. Tuesday finally arrived, and I was filled with high hopes of seeing Jack. My outfit was selected, my hair done, and I even practiced some new make-up tricks.

It was not to be.

I only have myself to blame. I picked a job that doesn't have regular hours. When I was a therapist, working nine-to-five in an office, I was usually home by 6:00 with my feet up and my wine glass filled. Hopefully, I helped my clients, but I was blind to my own issues. "Physician, heal thyself" certainly applied to me.

As is often the case with drinkers, I came from a long line of alcoholics but convinced myself my drinking was different. I was a responsible drinker. Does such a thing really exist? I blamed my mother for being drunk when my beloved sister Lily drowned in the neighborhood pool. Though I blamed myself even more since I was supposed to be watching her. A six-year-old responsible for a three-year-old.

By the time I left home to live on my own, I barely spoke to my mother. Ivy often tried to get us together for lunches and dinners. When my mother told us she had cancer, something inside me shattered. How could I lose my mother? Especially with so many unresolved issues standing between us. It was the catalyst I needed to make some major changes. I quit my job to take care of her. She tried to talk me out of it, but this was my chance to finally lay all my demons to rest. Before the end, we reconciled and forgave each other.

The experience of being with my mother as she passed motivated me to become a hospice worker. Not simply a hospice worker. I hoped to help my clients achieve what I managed to do with my own mother. I wanted to help families reconcile before the end. It doesn't always work out, but when it does, it's such a gratifying experience.

Since I am my own worst critic, I began to doubt myself almost as soon as I started working hospice. I called Lauren to tell her I wasn't any good at this.

"What do you mean, you aren't any good at it? You haven't even given it a try yet," she said, as I moaned into the phone.

"I've made a mistake," I countered, continuing to complain. "I don't like all these people. Sometimes I'm not surprised their relatives don't speak to them."

"Did you like everyone when you were a therapist?" Lauren asked.

"Well, no… but this is different. These people are on the brink. With only days to live, and I want to help. I want to make a difference."

"You're never going to like everyone, and you're never going to save every family and turn a lifetime of regrets into a glorious moment where they fall into each other's arms while a choir of angels breaks into song as the clouds part. Some people aren't likable."

She was right. Still, I worried.

"As long as you don't let them know how you feel and you do your best for them, it's all they can expect," Lauren added.

I stared out the window. "Everyone acts as if hospice workers are some kind of angels. I am no kind of angel."

"People are delusional. Apparently, they don't know most of the angels in the Bible were kick-ass dudes with swords. Not sweet women with wings."

I laughed. Lauren could always get me to laugh.

"Even Jesus was not some milquetoast who sat around letting people slap his cheeks. He got filled with some righteous damn anger and broke bad on a lot of people."

"Your fundamentalist upbringing is showing with all your Bible knowledge." Lauren's parents were deeply religious. After she told them she was gay, they decided they should never speak to her again. According to them, the Bible said it was a sin. A mortal sin.

"Though it might have been me marrying a black woman that pushed them over the edge," Lauren said. "Gay is bad enough. Interracial is just too too much."

"Does the Bible actually mention interracial marriage?" I asked.

"Not in so many words, but if you are gifted with insight, you know these things. My parents have the gift." Lauren's sarcasm seeped through the phone line.

"And yet you don't hate them. You are wise and wonderful, my dearest Lauren."

Lauren snorted. She did not take compliments well. "Moving on. I'm curious, do you ever discuss the religious aspects of dying with your clients? Like what lies beyond?"

"Oh God, no!" I almost shouted. "If they want to discuss those sorts of things, they should call a minister." I paused. "If asked, I steer the conversation away. I'm there for the patient and the family. To make the end easier. Lessen the pain. And if I can help them let go of past hurts and find closure, so much the better. I am not there for religious counseling. However, if they ask me to pray with them, I'm happy to do so. I do believe in the power of prayer."

I stood, filled with nervous energy. In the past, I'd always had a large glass of wine next to me when I was on the phone. I needed to move around to squelch the urge to drink. "I admit to a certain curiosity about the afterworld. The idea of heaven seems incredibly boring to me. Everyone claims to be excited to be able to see their loved ones again, but aren't these the same people you argued with on earth? How's it going to be any different? Not to mention, isn't Heaven going to max out population wise, eventually?"

"Might be crowded," Lauren agreed with a chuckle.

"And sitting around on a cloud playing a harp? Seriously? Maybe if there was a huge library in Heaven or you could binge watch Netflix for eternity. I could get down with that."

"For sure," Lauren agreed.

"Reincarnation makes the most sense. I like the idea of souls being constantly recycled to keep trying to do better before you reach Nirvana. But let's say you're Hitler and you come back as a cockroach, because you have to start at the lowest of the low. How can you be a better cockroach? How can you move up? What's the criteria for being a good cockroach?"

I waited for Lauren to stop laughing over the idea of a better cockroach. She finally said, "If you're Hitler, you probably have to be a cockroach for eternity. Being hated, and squashed, and sprayed with poisons."

"Sounds fitting," I agreed. "Seriously, that's often what drives families apart. Differences in religious beliefs. Not to mention politics."

"So true. Look what happened with my parents," she said sadly.

"If I tried to work with you and your parents, either you on your deathbed or one of them, would they, could they, forgive you for your sins?"

Lauren was quiet for a moment. "No. You'd fail with us in the reconciliation department. When my dad was dying, I called and asked my mom if I could come to say goodbye, and she said it wasn't a good idea. She didn't want him reminded of his failures."

"Damn. I'm so sorry."

"In my line of work, I see the vilest things humans do to other humans. What they do to innocent children is the worst. Some people deserve hell for sure."

I could almost see Lauren shaking her head to dislodge the memories. "My dear Rose, I hope I helped. You are doing good things. Don't worry about loving your clients. Worry about helping them." After making her usual kissy noises, she hung up.

She was right. I didn't have to love my clients. My job was to do my best for them. If I'm able to help them reconcile with family members, with the choices they've made and the lives they've led, it's the reason I picked this job. And if I'm the only one there at the end, I hope I've helped them die with grace and dignity.

An hour before the Tuesday night meeting, I received a call about one of my hospice clients. According to the nurse on call, she was fading fast, and they needed me there. I switched gears from seeing Jack at AA to attending the death of someone.

This client was, unfortunately, one of those I found difficult to like, let alone love. She was not a pleasant person. Her husband originally called six months earlier to arrange for hospice when she decided she couldn't, or wouldn't, get out of bed anymore. It appeared she enjoyed having the family at her beck and call 24/7. She always became quite angry when I showed up. She didn't want any strangers in her house. I'd already been at her deathbed several times in the last six months. Each time she rallied, and I was dismissed until the next crisis.

She made me think of all the sweet people I dealt with whose relatives couldn't be bothered with them. Who died alone with only me there to hold their hand. This woman appeared to want to punish her nearest and dearest. I worried about her elderly husband, who was amazingly devoted to her and willing to cater to her every need and desire, no matter how much trouble it caused him. In the six months I'd been involved with the family, she hadn't changed much while he looked like he'd aged ten years.

Still, what choice did I have? This was the job I'd wanted, so off I went. As I drove to her house, I told myself the next time I saw Jack, I'd get his number. Would that be presumptive of me? All my doubts came back. Maybe I'm nothing more than an AA buddy to him. Why was I assuming I'm something special?

Arriving at the house, I found everyone gathered around the bed. They all appeared to be in various stages of grief and distress. Standing in the doorway, I quietly watched the scene. A small smile appeared to flicker across the woman's face. Probably my imagination. The family finally hired a nurse, over her objections, and the nurse was taking her vital signs. The nurse looked up at me; her face blank, and I couldn't tell if things were critical or if it was another false alarm.

I walked out into the hallway, and in a moment, the nurse joined me. "How does it look?" I asked.

She shrugged. "I'd say pretty much the same. Could be any moment or weeks from now."

The nurse and I agreed this woman was dying. When she broke her hip, and even after a replacement, she took to her bed and developed pneumonia. Now, she was covered with bedsores and her organs were shutting down. She held on by sheer willpower. If only she'd used her iron will to get up after she broke her hip, she might have lived a few more years. People are strange and there is no way to figure out why they do the things they do. Maybe she was waiting for her husband to go with her. Or go first.

Returning to the room, I sat next to her. The family decided to take a break. "Mrs. Sanders," I whispered. In the past six months of care, she never allowed me to call her by her first name.

When I whispered her name again, her eyes flickered open. She looked around the room, realizing we were alone. "Mrs. Sanders, Nurse Frances says things appear to be about the same. There's no predicting what might happen. Is there anything you'd like to talk about?"

She gave me a steely glare. "Where is everyone?" she muttered.

Was she upset they'd escaped for an instant? "I think they went out to…" To what? Get a drink? Take a pee? Flee for their lives? What should I say?

"Why are you here?" She glared at me and yanked her hand away.

"Remember, Mrs. Sanders, I'm your hospice aide. I am here to help you and your family during this difficult time." No matter how many times I came to see her, she acted like she had no idea who I was or why I was there.

"Waste of time." She glared at me. "They don't need any help. They're waiting for me to die. The sooner. The better. For all they care."

"They do care. They care very much. I've seldom seen such a devoted family. Your husband dotes on you. They need something from you before you're gone. Some acknowledgement? A blessing?" I was seriously at my wit's end.

"Acknowledgement of what? How about they acknowledge me? Being a good wife and mother is what I devoted my whole life to. I never got to do anything for myself. I never got to follow my dreams. It was always them. Them. Them. Them! Sucking away my life. Sucking the marrow from my bones." She was almost ranting now. "How about they say they're sorry?"

Looking up, I saw her husband standing in the doorway. Obviously, he'd heard what she said. He appeared devastated. Everything he'd done had not been enough. His love had not been enough. Her children's love had not been enough.

He came in, sat, took her hand in his and laid his head down and sobbed, repeatedly saying he was sorry.

In the kitchen, I found her children and talked to them about what their mom needed in order to let go. I didn't tell them their mom thought they'd collectively ruined her life. "When people get old and are at the end, they are sometimes filled with regrets about the things they wish they'd done. Often women who devoted their lives to raising their children and supporting their husband's careers imagine how differently things might have been."

They were, of course, shocked their mother had regrets. "She lived for us. And Dad. It's all she ever wanted!" they exclaimed. I was beginning to feel a little sorry for her. Maybe they didn't know her at all.

A long night full of tears, apologies, forgiveness, and love followed. The things I hope for in my job. A few hours later, Mrs. Sanders closed her eyes for the last time. Both she and the family were ready to let go.

Chapter Four

When I got home around five in the morning, I went right to bed, too exhausted to be upset about not seeing Jack the night before. Those regrets came later, when I woke up.

"There will be other Tuesday night meetings," I said to Fritz as I made something to eat. It didn't take the sting of disappointment away completely. Fritz looked confused. He no doubt was unhappy we hadn't been out yet for his morning walk. I'd let him out briefly when I got home in the early morning, which apparently didn't satisfy him. "You're right Fritz. We need a walk. It will be good for both of us." Fritz trotted happily to the door.

We walked for a long time. I was deep in thought. At one point, Fritz stopped and stared at me as if to say, "Are we done yet? I want to go home."

"Fritzie," I said, bending over to ruffle the fur on the top of his head. "I'm sorry. I forget you have rather short legs." Picking him up, we headed back.

Later, I was finally able to connect with Lauren. I'd left a message on her phone, asking her to return my call. The phone rang at ten. I was already in bed reading. Knowing it was her, I answered right away.

"Sorry to call so late, Rosie," she said. "Long day at the office. I'm working on a new crime documentary, and there is endless paperwork. People to interview, timelines to verify…. Don't want to bore you with the details."

My brilliant best friend was a well-known true crime reporter. She had her own television show. My mother had been quite impressed I knew Lauren Lowe personally.

"You could never bore me," I replied, smiling at the sound of her voice. Lauren is my oldest and dearest friend. Actually, my only friend besides Ivy, and Ivy has to be my friend because she is my sister.

"I've been dying to tell you my news. I might finally have met Mr. Right." Lauren had long been waiting for me to find someone, ever since she saved my life when I tried to kill myself in college over my stupid boyfriend.

"God, Rosie. Way to wait until you're ancient," Lauren said, laughing.

"You're the exact same age I am. So, if I'm ancient, so are you."

"I live in California. The Fountain of Youth. So even if I'm as old as you, I look better."

"Ummm. No. You only look better because you're covered with gobs of make-up and goo to help you look good in front of the cameras." I wasn't going to let her get away with calling me ancient.

"True. Forget it. Give me details. Who is this guy? Where did you meet? Is he handsome? Is he hot?" She bombarded me with questions.

"Why do you care if he's hot?" I laughed. "You don't even like men."

"Doesn't mean I don't appreciate a hot guy. Don't you like looking at pretty women?"

"Maybe," I said, shaking my head. Lauren always made me laugh. "Let me see… his name is Jack. We met at the cemetery." Lauren groaned. She hated cemeteries and dead people and thought I spent too much time visiting my deceased family members.

"Stop being such a drama queen. You really need to get over your negative attitude toward graveyards. He goes there too. He visits his younger brother."

"At least you have something in common. An unnatural attraction to dead people."

"We both suffer from guilt over our dead relatives. I blamed myself for Lily drowning. Jack blames himself for his younger brother, Ricky's death. I guess Ricky was trying to emulate the wild ways of his older brother and ended up dying of a drug overdose."

"Sad," Lauren said.

"Yes. Very sad. On the positive side, in addition to a fondness for our dead relatives, he's in AA."

"I'm relieved to know he's in AA. I'd hate for you to have fallen for a drinker and end up on square one after all these years of sobriety."

"There is one potential problem."

"What?" Lauren sounded anxious. "I've waited years for this and now you have a potential problem? What is the problem?"

I took a deep breath. "Even though I'm completely head over heels in love with him, I actually have no idea what he thinks about me."

Lauren was quiet.

"The thing is, we've only seen each other twice. Both times at the cemetery. After our second encounter this week, we went for a coffee and ended up having lunch. It was as if I'd known him forever. You know I'm not good in social situations, but I felt so comfortable with him. We said goodbye and agreed to meet up last night at the Tuesday meeting. Unfortunately, I got a work call and didn't make it to the meeting. And I couldn't call and tell him because I didn't have his number. And even if I did, I'm not sure I'd have called. It wasn't like we'd been on a date. We had lunch, said 'see-you-around,' and left. I have no idea how he feels about me."

"Rose. Calm down. If you sensed a connection, he must have too. He's not married or anything, is he?" Lauren sounded worried.

"No. He didn't mention a wife. No ring."

"Okay. This is the plan. Go to every meeting you can this week. Make sure you're lookin' fine! If and when he shows up, say you're sorry you didn't make the Tuesday meeting because you were called in to work. Tell him you're happy to see him again. Then the ball is in his court."

"You make it sound easy."

PATTI GAUSTAD PROCOPI

"It is. You'll see."

"I'll probably end up throwing up on him because I'll be so nervous."

Lauren laughed. "Not a good come-on. Keep your chin up and call me after you see him again." Lauren made her kissy sounds into the phone and hung up.

I stared at the phone for a long time before turning out the light and snuggling into bed. Is it really so simple? Maybe, I thought as I drifted off to sleep.

Chapter Five

*I*vy returned from her trip and stopped by to collect Fritz. I was glad to have Ivy home, but I was going to miss Fritz. Ivy constantly asked me why I didn't get my own dog.

"What if he/she/it doesn't like Fritz? Or Fritz doesn't like he/she/it? He'd probably be jealous."

Ivy rolled her eyes. "Why do you always make everything so complicated? Get a dog of your own!"

When Ivy walked in, I started to say I was excited she was back because I actually had something to tell her. Before I could, she launched into how exhausting her trip was. "Reminded me of those book tours I used to go on with Terry. Meetings with agents, gallery owners, museums, fans. It's all terribly draining. I'm sorry. I got your messages, but by the time I returned to my hotel room, I was worn out and didn't have the strength to do anything more than fall into bed. And the next day was a repeat of the same."

I needed to interrupt Ivy, because once she starts, I can rarely get a word in. "Yes, sounds awful. Must be terrible to be in demand. Eating fancy meals and staying in luxury hotels."

Ivy gave me a withering look. "Do you have Fritz's things packed? I need to get home."

"Can you sit down for a minute? I have some big news to share." Ivy looked doubtful. I never had big news. Ivy was the one who always had big news as an acclaimed artist traveling around to shows, talks, and other glamorous events.

"Big news?" She followed me to the living room. "I'm intrigued."

"I've met someone," I said, before she could even sit down.

"By someone, do you mean a guy?" Her face lit up. "A real honest to goodness guy? A potential?" Ivy rated men to see if they were potential mates—age appropriate, not married, and of course, good looking.

"Yes!" I exclaimed. "A bona fide potential."

"Where did you meet? I'm stunned, considering you've diddled around for years trying to find someone. Tell me everything," she exclaimed, flopping down on the couch and snuggling Fritz.

I started to fill her in on the details, suddenly realizing I didn't know much about Jack. "We met at the cemetery. We've both lost siblings we loved. Both of us felt responsible. After years of drinking, he's in AA, so we share that too." I quickly ran out of things to say.

"What's he look like?" Ivy prompted. I suppressed a grin. Of course, Ivy wanted to know those details.

"He's gorgeous. Salt and pepper hair. A bit shaggy. You'd probably think he needs a haircut and a shave." I laughed. "The most beautiful blue eyes I have ever seen…"

"Anything else? What does he do? Does he have a job? Where does he live?" The questions poured from her lips.

"Actually, I don't know."

Ivy gathered up Fritz and his bag of toys and treats and headed for the door. "Sounds like you need to get a little more information about this guy. Ask some questions the next time you meet." She looked at me sternly and left.

I am a failure at relationships. I have two friends. My sister, Ivy, who, as I said, has no choice since she's my sister, and Lauren, who saved my life. My dealings with men have all been disasters, starting with my dad, who walked out of my life when I was ten years old. At the time, I was almost relieved because our house had become a battleground between my parents. It set me up to be wary of men. Subconsciously, I decided men weren't reliable and couldn't be trusted.

In high school, I engaged in the usual shallow relationships. My boyfriends lasted about three months, because I was never willing to move past making out. Even high school boys want more after a while.

In college, I fell in love with a boy named Jason. I was head over heels and finally discovered why people enjoyed sex so much. However, he betrayed me because I believed we were going to spend the rest of our lives together, and he thought we were simply having fun. After catching him in bed with another girl and being told it was all my fault he wanted to break-up, I tried to kill myself.

Lauren was there to save the day, and we have been best friends ever since. Turns out, Lauren hoped we could be more than best friends. She was in love with me and thinking back, it might not have been a bad idea to switch teams, given my failure with men. Unfortunately, I'm not attracted to women.

This was followed by the episode of Franklin, the best man at Ivy's first wedding. He wanted to "fuck me," as he so eloquently put it. Turns out he only offered, since he said I was fat and ugly, as a favor to my new brother-in-law. I declined the invitation, which strangely made him extremely angry. Once again, I was appalled by men and their attitudes about women, sex, and relationships.

My next failure was even more laughable. On a cruise with Ivy, I fell for George, a great guy who was everything I wanted—smart, funny, and kind. Turns out, he was only attracted to men. Another kick in the pants.

A long time passed before I fell in love again. This time with someone even more perfect. Terry was a professor and author, and he was brilliant as well as also being funny and kind. I'm a sucker for kindness. However, when he met

Ivy, they fell madly in love, and I was left standing alone yet again.

That was the final blow. Afterwards, I gave up on men. A secret part of me hoped Terry eventually would come to realize I was the right one for him. He and Ivy would break up, and we'd be together forever. Sadly, Terry didn't get much of a forever. He died of Alzheimer's ten years after he and Ivy married, which broke both our hearts.

So, it seemed a celibate life full of wine (lots of wine) and books would be enough for me.

Then my mom died and that was a catalyst for me to finally make some changes and stop blaming everything on her and others. I changed jobs from a therapist to a hospice worker. I gave up drinking. Which brought me to Jack. Perfect for me in every way. Smart, funny, cute, kind, and sober. The rest didn't matter. He was sober.

But was he interested?

Chapter Six

*U*nbelievably, I wasn't able to make it to the Tuesday night meeting for the next three weeks. Work often prevented me from attending evening meetings. Many of my patients passed in the nighttime or in the early morning hours before dawn. I often wonder if the quiet of the darkness makes it easier to let go.

Ivy was, as usual, unhappy with my apparent inability to connect with the one guy I'd found in thirty-some years. "You're not moving this relationship along very quickly. Not to mention you know nothing about him," she snorted into the phone.

"Sorry, I am trying, but my job keeps getting in the way," I replied.

"Obviously, you need to quit working. Aren't you old enough yet for Social Security and Medicare?"

"I will remind you, my dear sister, you are older than me. And in addition, I'm not as financially well off as you. I need to work."

"Excuses, excuses," she muttered before hanging up.

Finally, I was able to get to the Tuesday night meeting. At this point, my hopes of ever seeing Jack again dimmed. I didn't try very hard that night with my makeup and outfit. I was pouring myself a cup of coffee, thinking about my patient from earlier that day, when a voice whispered in my ear, "Hi there." I was so surprised I almost threw my coffee up in the air.

I turned to see Jack grinning at me. "Have you been avoiding me?" he asked. "I've been to every Tuesday meeting for a month, and you haven't been here."

"No. I haven't been avoiding you." I was horrified, hoping I looked okay— was my hair messy? Was my make-up smeared? "Work has been demanding. This is the first evening meeting I've made it to in a long time."

"I'm glad to hear it wasn't me." Jack smiled. "I was going to call and see if you were okay, but I forgot to get your number."

My heart hammered. He wanted my number! I didn't even have to ask for his first.

We pulled out our phones and exchanged numbers. Connected at last. Since the meeting was about to start, we grabbed a couple of chairs next to each other. I could hardly concentrate because of his presence next to me. *He was sitting next to me! Finally!*

After the meeting, Jack asked if I wanted to go out and grab a bite to eat or something. Despite the fact I'd been waiting for this moment, I was completely exhausted and worried I'd fall asleep in my soup. Not to mention, I felt a bit grimy. I wanted our first date to be special. I wanted to be witty, charming, and need I say, beautiful!

"Jack, I'd absolutely love to go out, but I am asleep on my feet. I've had a long, arduous day. Maybe another time?" I said, with a hopeful lilt in my voice to let him know I really did want to see him again. And not just at a meeting.

"Sure," he replied. "I understand. It's short notice. Are you going to the cemetery this Saturday? We could go have lunch at our favorite café. The waitress there loves me, and they have a great menu."

I rolled my eyes and laughed. "She hates everyone. Sounds great. I'll be there."

Our first date.

Chapter Seven

I got to the cemetery early. Work had also kept me from visiting for a couple of weeks. I sat on the bench and said hello to my baby sister, Lily, my mom, my dad, and Ivy's beloved husband, Terry.

Ivy initially didn't want to bury our father here in the family plot, since he'd abandoned us when we were kids. I said he was family and belonged there. Luckily, her kids agreed with me, and since she was outvoted, she gave in.

"Hi Mom. Sorry it's been a while. It's funny how my life revolves around dead people—both in my personal and professional life." I imagined Mom laughing, but at the same time suggesting I needed to spend more time among the living.

"You're in luck. I have a new letter from William, well Margie, actually. Though, William scribbled a note on the bottom. Let me read you the news." After I finished, I folded the letter.

"Mom, did you notice the fellow who sat with me the last time I was here? Shaggy hair and the most amazing blue eyes ever?" I imagined Mom nodding. "He might be the one." I pretended to swoon. "Yes, I know. I've taken a long time fulfilling this wish of yours. Finding love. In my line of work, the men I meet are either dying or overcome by grief."

Continuing, I filled her in on the little I knew about Jack. "Today we're going to lunch, and I plan to discover more about this guy." I glanced down at Dad's name, adding, "We're going to the same awful café where you and I went for coffee after we met here. The same waitress is still there." Dad probably didn't remember the café, much less the waitress. It had been a rather overwhelming emotional occasion, since it was the first time we'd seen each other in forty years.

I met Jack at the Unfriendly Café at noon. Since Fritz wasn't with us, we could have sat inside. Jack said he preferred it outside. Remembering the interior, I thought it was a good call.

When our usual waitress appeared at our table with menus, she shot daggers at me with her eyes. I could almost hear her say, "You again?" Why did this woman dislike me so much? I tipped well.

"Any specials today?" Jack asked, looking up with a smile.

"No," she replied bluntly. "No specials today, no special tomorrow, no specials ever. The menu is what it is." And she turned and walked off.

"I love the vibe of this place," Jack said. I laughed out loud.

"You said the burger was good?" I asked.

"Maybe I lied," Jack said, looking at the menu with a smile curling the corners of his lips.

"Tell me again why we come here?" I asked.

"It's our place," Jack replied, and my heart went zing.

While we waited for our food, I decided to find out about Jack. I twirled my napkin in my lap and said, "Since I bared my soul in front of the Tuesday group, tell me about you."

Jack looked at me quizzically. "Like what?"

"The usual. Where were you born? Where did you grow up and go to school? Tell me about your family. You told me about your younger brother, Ricky. Do you have any other siblings? Mom? Dad? Dogs? Cats? A goldfish?"

Throwing back his head, Jack laughed uproariously. "My entire biography? Is that what you want?"

I nodded. "But first, what's your full name? In AA, all we ever say are our first names. What is your complete name?"

He snorted. "So, you'll know what to tell the cops when you call? 'He said his name was Jumping Jack Flash'. And they'd say, 'Oh yeah, we're quite familiar with that guy.'"

"No, silly. Because it's something friends know about each other."

Jack grimaced and sighed. "I hate telling people my name."

"Why? Is it Schicklegrubber or Hitler? Jack Hitler?"

"Almost as bad, but maybe not with all the negative connotations. My name is Jack Frost."

He looked like he was telling the truth. But what parents would actually name their son Jack Frost? "You're kidding? Right?"

"I wish."

I cringed. "It's a great name. A real ice breaker." Jack rolled his eyes. "Kids are probably in awe when they meet you."

"Moving on." Jack obviously was done talking about his name. "What's your full name? I can guess based on your family headstones, but maybe you kept the names of all your numerous ex-husbands, and your last name is some hyphenated monstrosity like Smyth-Jones-Grunewald. Or maybe Schicklegrubber-Hitler. Though Hitler-Schicklegrubber sounds better."

I took a sip from my water glass. "I haven't been married once, let alone a dozen times. So, my name is Bane. Like my parents."

"Ahhh… I've always loved that word 'bane.' Were you teased a lot at school about your name? Did kids say you were the 'bane of their existence?'"

"I don't think the kids I went to school with even knew that word or what it meant. We didn't live in the best neighborhood after my dad skipped out, nor did we go to the best schools."

"Another thing we have in common. I didn't go to the best schools either."

"All right, now we have been properly introduced—nice to meet you, Jack Frost. I still need to know more about you. So, spill the beans." I smiled.

He smiled back. "Nice to meet you too, Rose Bane. Where to start? My life hasn't been very exciting. The parts I remember. I was born right here in Richmond. Working class neighborhood. My dad was an auto mechanic. Owned his own shop. My mom was a typical stay-at-home mom. My dad was strict. No nonsense. My mom was sweet and loving. Both are gone now. I have one older sister who hasn't spoken to me in years. Everyone blamed me for Ricky's death. Rightfully so. I blame myself too."

The waitress arrived with our food and slammed our plates down before stalking off.

Jack took a big bite of his burger. "Pretty good," he said with a smile. I bite into mine. It was good.

Jack took a sip of soda before continuing. "I was a hellion from a young age. According to family stories, my dad's dad was a drunk, and my dad didn't allow any drink in the house. It became my personal mission to defy him.

"I didn't do great in school, no surprise, but I graduated. I worked in my dad's garage from about age thirteen on. After Ricky died, Dad fired me and threw me out. I wasn't even welcome at Rick's funeral. When my parents died, my sister sent me a letter telling me I'd been the death of them. She banned me from attending their funerals. Even though that hurt, it didn't make me want to stop drinking." He shook his head at the memory. "It was another excuse to drink more. The old 'fuck them' and 'I'll show them.' So mature."

"Ouch," I winced. "How awful. I'm sorry."

"Don't be. I wasn't. At least not sorry enough."

We both got quiet and finished eating our burgers.

"Want to split another dessert?" Jack smiled after he was done.

"Weren't we supposed to eat it first?"

Jack threw back his head and hooted. "True."

I loved his laugh.

Chapter Eight

Tuesday nights, I attended my AA home group, and Jack quickly adopted it as his too. Of course, we both still went to other meetings, some together and others separately. Work continued to interfere with my attendance. Sometimes I'd have to go to a daytime meeting.

My sponsor, Gwen, kept a watchful eye on me. One night, she asked if we could have a quick chat after the meeting. "Sure," I answered, wondering what was up. Sponsors have a sixth sense about changes in your life and want to be ahead of the curve.

Jack wasn't at the meeting, which made it easier to stay behind without having to explain to him Gwen wanted to talk. We grabbed cups of coffee before heading over to a table in the corner of the room. I sat down, waiting. Taking a sip of my coffee, I grimaced. It tasted burnt and lukewarm.

Gwen sat across from me, staring at me for several minutes. It was like being in a police interrogation, and she was waiting for me to break down and confess all. I smiled nervously. She took a sip of her coffee and shook her head violently.

"Oh, God! This is awful." I nodded in agreement, and we set our cups aside.

"I've noticed you and the new guy, Jack, are quite friendly," she finally started. "I don't blame you if you're interested. He's kind of cute."

"He's definitely that," I agreed.

Gwen sighed. "You're not going to make this easy for me, are you? Okay, you don't have to tell me what's going on, but I'm going to tell you why relationships within AA are discouraged, especially for people in the same home group."

I looked down at my hands while she continued. "Everyone thinks finding a new relationship in AA is a great idea. Especially if your former relationships revolved around drinking. You think, 'this is great! We can work on our sobriety together.' And it sounds like the beginning of a great new life.

"It isn't. We come to AA to get sober. For ourselves. To work the steps. To concentrate on the steps. You've been sober almost three years, but Jack is relatively new to the program. He's in the fragile state. Still committing to not drinking. Still working on issues he has to resolve. Steps to complete. His focus needs to be on the program, not on you."

I continued staring at my hands. I hadn't thought about what she was saying. Jack tried to quit many times before. He could easily slip again.

"Let's say one of you suffers a relapse. Which is a reality we all have to face in the program. I've known people who've been sober ten… fifteen years… and they fall off the wagon. It's hard to maintain distance when your partner cracks. And if your relationship doesn't work out, imagine how awkward it would be for the two of you to continue to meet up at AA meetings. It might push one to stop attending, which is a recipe for disaster."

Gwen stopped talking, and I finally looked up. "I hear everything you're saying, and it all makes sense. I didn't consider Jack only has a year of sobriety, actually not even a year yet. But, at this point, we're just friends. We meet up at AA meetings and at this café outside the cemetery where we both have family buried. That's really the extent of it. I certainly don't want to do anything to jeopardize his sobriety."

"I know you wouldn't want to do anything to cause him harm. As your sponsor, I needed to inform you of the downside." She took my hand and squeezed it. "And I've known lots of people who've met at AA and gotten married and been fine. But there are potential pitfalls."

"Thanks. To be honest, because I have to be honest with you, since you're my sponsor," she grinned back at me, "I am utterly madly, head over heels in love with Jack. But he seems to be happy to be friends. AA buddies."

Gwen stood up. "First thing, Jack needs a sponsor. If you're in love with him, it can't be you." We both laughed. "So you might want to encourage him to find one."

"Okay."

"And remember, take it one day at a time."

Chapter Nine

One day at a time is probably the most common AA slogan. AA is full of slogans. We need those little mantras to help us through some of the tough moments when we feel like we might be slipping.

Some people who come into AA complain about these 'cheesy' slogans or whine about AA being too religious with all that Higher Power and God stuff. They're just making excuses to get out the door and back to drinking.

One day at a time tells us we must focus on the present and not worry about the future. Don't worry about whether you'll be sober by the weekend, by next year or even in twenty years. Simply get through today. And tomorrow, focus on getting through that day.

Let go and let God is my personal favorite. I don't claim to be a deeply religious person. In fact, I have a rather complicated history with God. When I was a small child, my grandmother Meemee terrified me with her old school God, who was all fire and brimstone and smiting. I didn't want to do anything to incur his wrath. And I knew I needed to be good, so I could go to heaven and see Lily again.

Mom and Dad weren't big on church, though Mom liked to dump us at every Vacation Bible School during the summer to get us out of the house and out of her hair. So, I got a lot of mixed messages about religion and God from strict Baptists to feel good Episcopalians.

In middle school, I would have been voted most likely to join a cult. At the time, I decided I wanted to be a nun and started dressing in black and carrying a Bible around. I didn't want to be the kind of nun who was out in the world doing good works, but the kind who lived in a cell in an old-style convent. Something about being walled off from the world, wearing a hair shirt and flagellating myself, was quite appealing. I wanted to punish myself for what happened to Lily and prostrating myself on a cold stone floor while praying seemed like the perfect way to spend eternity. Not surprisingly, the other kids avoided me. About this same time, I started drinking, sneaking wine from my mom's stash, and decided that was a much better way to spend my life. So, my nun ambitions were abandoned.

Despite my checkered past with God, I do believe there is some force for good out there in the universe. When I'm stressed about something, often at night when I can't sleep, I use *Let Go and Let God* as a mantra to remind myself I am not in control of the universe. Once again, some people complain it's too religious. But God does not define the slogan. You can substitute another word, maybe Fate instead of God. The point is to acknowledge you aren't in control and remind yourself when you thought you were in charge, you were a drunk.

There are many other slogans to help someone in AA focus on the most important task of their lives, which is staying sober. None of the sayings state it so bluntly. It's not *Let Go of Drink and Let God keep you Sober*. It's implied. Another popular one is *Progress, not Perfection*. This is along the lines of Rome wasn't built in a day. As long as you made it through another day without a drink, that's progress. The only true failure is giving up.

Maybe I like these little sayings because I used something similar when I was a therapist. Pithy little words of wisdom that were easy to remember. Such as *Move on, the past is the past*, and even *Let go*. At the time, I didn't add *let God*. One I liked but didn't actually say was *Today is the first day of the rest of your life.* People roll their eyes and gag when you say those words, but it's profound. Each day we wake up, we have the chance to change our lives. We need to come to grips with our past. While it doesn't help to continually relive those worst moments, when we're able to forgive and move on, the chains of the past melt away.

Probably the most brilliant set of words in the entire English language is the Serenity Prayer. Everyone, not just people in AA, could benefit from these simple words which revolve around Serenity, Courage, and Wisdom. We all need to learn acceptance and to let go of the things we cannot change. I knew all this before I joined AA, but I wasn't able to do it. Maybe I got some hidden benefit from not changing things. It's one of those crazy aspects of humans. We'd rather live in the misery we know than risk trying to change.

If AA was nothing more than sitting around and telling each other we're alcoholics and repeating mantras, it would be pretty easy. Which is where the Twelve Steps come in, and some of them are very, very hard. Maybe the first three aren't so tough, but when you get to number four where you have to take a 'fearless moral inventory of yourself,' that's when the rubber hits the road. Not many people are prepared to look deeply at themselves and at their faults.

I've already completed all twelve steps, but it's a never-ending process. You have to keep looking and catch yourself before you end up at the same "full of yourself" attitude you had when you were drunk. You can never let your guard down. You have to keep working at it and keep sharing your experiences with others.

I love the meetings so much because you never stop learning. There's always someone new who comes in and shares their story and you're amazed and wowed all over again.

And I want to share the journey with Jack. I understood Gwen's note of caution. I will take it one day at a time, and if it's meant to be, I will let God take care of it.

Chapter Ten

"A car mechanic?" Ivy deliberately kept her tone neutral, so I couldn't tell if she was criticizing me for being interested in a working-class guy. Ivy likes to pretend she doesn't judge people.

"Yes. Isn't it great?" I replied, giving her a huge smile. "It's always difficult to find a good trust-worthy mechanic."

Ivy arched her eyebrows. "I'm not judging. However, I will point out, you have a master's degree in psychology, and he barely made it out of high school. Just saying."

I could have reminded Ivy she also barely made it out of high school. Now that she's a big-name artist, she forgets that fact. In the art world, it's more important what you paint, rather than where, when or even if you went to school. I went to college to escape my family. Ivy did the same by getting married as quickly as she could.

Our father was a college graduate. Our mother went to college to get her MRS. She was probably trying to escape her family. Both of Ivy's husbands went to college. Her first husband, rich boy Preston Van Dorn, was a financial genius. Though I only have Ivy's word on that. He probably got set up in business by his father, Preston the elder. Her second husband, the love of my life, Terry Berenstein, was a college professor with numerous degrees and a best-selling author. And Ivy's children went to prestigious universities and have good jobs.

I also kept my tone neutral. "You probably need to be pretty smart to figure out what's wrong with a car. There are lots of parts, you know."

Ivy was having a hard time not rolling her eyes at me as I kept talking. "There is nothing wrong with not going to college. Some incredibly smart people work with their hands. Including our own dear brother William, who is a homesteader, dog trainer, fur trapper, whatever, in the wilds of Alaska. He's quite happy."

"It's not like William needs a degree in electrical engineering to live in the middle of nowhere," Ivy snapped, no longer able to pretend to be neutral.

"Why Ivy, I do believe you are a snob." I grinned.

"I am not a snob!" The mask slipped further down. "I am the most accepting of people. People of all backgrounds. All shapes, all sizes... all... everything!"

I held up my hand to stop her from explaining any further. "Ivy, what difference does it make what he does? It's not like we're in our twenties, planning our future, and the future of our dozen children. He has a job. I have a job. We are both self-sufficient."

Ivy stared back at me.

"And it's not like we're getting married, or even dating at this point. I'm interested; however, he appears to be quite content being AA friends. On the bright side, even if he doesn't fall madly in love with me, if I ever need a mechanic, I know where to go." I tried to say this lightly, as if it didn't bother me our relationship was still stuck in neutral.

Ivy, who is rather intuitive sometimes, looked concerned. "Oh, Rosie. I'm sorry. I should be happy for you. Happy you've found someone at last instead of worrying about his profession."

"Yes, you should," I agreed.

Chapter Eleven

Lauren called on the weekend for an update on my man.

"There is no update," I sighed. "He ain't my man. Yet. We meet at the cemetery, have lunch at the Unfriendly Café, and meet up again at AA meetings. I should have known people don't suddenly find their soulmate at the age of fifty-five."

"The reason you can't find your soulmate is you are negative and defeatist." Lauren shot back. "Am I going to have to fly to Virginia and straighten the two of you out? You're not a teenager anymore. For God's sake, simply ask him what his intentions are. Stop beating around the bush and acting all, oh, I want to be your AA buddy, nothing more. How's he ever going to get the message you're interested in him?"

"According to my sponsor, AA romances are frowned upon for a variety of reasons. We need to focus on our sobriety, not fantasize about good-looking guys in the program."

"Same reason work romances are frowned upon. They want you concentrating on your job, not trying to figure out if and when you can sneak into the broom closet for a quickie. But guess what? Many adults meet their significant others at work."

"Step one, Jack needs a sponsor. Or I should say, my sponsor wants Jack to get a sponsor. And he does need one and it can't be me. I don't want it to be me! AA also frowns on different sexes sponsoring each other."

"Of course," Lauren said. "Men and women have different needs. Different communication styles."

"They are also worried about old men in the program creeping on young women who are new to AA."

"I totally understand. There will always be creeps trying to score in any situation. Enough. That's not your issue. Your issue is luring Jack into bed."

I laughed out loud. "Way to cut to the chase. Since you mention it, I'm terrified of getting him into bed. Do you know how long it's been since I've had sex? Don't answer!"

"Don't worry about it. Lust will handle the details." Lauren made little kissy noises and hung up.

Chapter Twelve

I arrived late for the Tuesday meeting. Work again. No wonder I couldn't manage a relationship with a member of the opposite sex. I saw Jack and Otto, one of the AA veterans, chatting over in the corner. Grabbing a cup of coffee, I found a seat. What was going on with Jack and Otto?

A few moments later, Jack plopped down next to me and gave me a dazzling smile. "So good to see you here. I always worry you might not make it." I smiled back, thinking what I really wanted to do was throw my arms around him and kiss him. Not appropriate behavior for an AA meeting, I reminded myself. And I doubted Gwen would approve.

"I was afraid I might miss the meeting. Fortunately, I got out of work sooner than I thought." I grimaced. "Often the reasons I get to leave early are not always happy ones." I changed the subject. "I saw you talking to Otto."

"Yes. He has offered to be my sponsor. I'm excited. I knew I needed a sponsor, but I've been afraid to ask anyone. Otto seems like a great guy."

"Otto is a great guy. He's one of the old-timers. Been in the program for thirty or forty years, maybe more. Full of good advice and good stories. And he isn't judgmental or holier than thou."

Jack nodded. "I definitely got positive vibes from him."

We stopped talking because the meeting was called to order. I smiled to myself. One hurdle jumped. Jack has a sponsor. Gwen should be happy. And he has a great sponsor, which was even better news. I glanced at Jack. He looked back, reached over, and squeezed my hand. Oh, my goodness. More than friends at last? Or was he simply happy he had a sponsor?

After the meeting, Gwen watched me as I grabbed my coat. She smiled and gave a thumbs up. What was that smile for? I smiled back.

Jack strolled over and helped me with my coat. "I feel legit now. Like I'm a real bona fide AA member. I have a sponsor. I'm cool."

I fluffed my hair, even though the jacket hadn't moved it. "I'm glad you're happy and feeling good. Which is the way to stay sober for sure."

We walked out the door into the cool evening air. I waited for him to say goodnight and walk away as usual. Instead, he stopped.

"I was wondering… do you like movies… or going to the movies… what kind of movies do you watch?" He was obviously nervous and on the brink of babbling incoherently.

"Jack. Take a deep breath. This is not complicated. Yes, I like pretty much all kinds of movies except those about macho men and noisy machines and gory murders. Comedies. Drama. Movies based on books I like, though I always think the books are better." I was scrambling because I hadn't been to a movie in ages, because for years I'd preferred to sit home and read while drinking my wine.

"Great! There's this one I've been dying to see, but I don't have anyone to go with and rather than start feeling sorry for myself, which is the slippery slope to drinking again, I thought—I'll ask Rose to go with me."

Was this a date? Or just a friend asking a friend to the movies? It's a start. "Yeah, sounds great. When?"

"How about this Friday? I know this great little Italian place, Luigi's, near the theater. We can go to dinner first and then to the movie. How does that sound?"

Sounded more and more like a date.

Chapter Thirteen

I didn't say anything to Lauren or Ivy. I didn't want to raise their hopes. Hell, I didn't want to raise mine. By the end of the evening, I'd know whether this was a real date. Then I'd call and share the news.

We met at Luigi's at six. Jack was waiting for me outside the door, and his face lit up when he saw me. He always appeared happy to see me.

"Have you ever been to Luigi's before? It's one of my favorite places." Once again, he was nervous to the point of descending into gibberish. I thought it was a good sign. Would he be this jumpy over a simple movie with a friend?

"I don't think so. I don't go out much and if I do, it's with my sister, Ivy, and I let her choose the restaurant because she's pickier than I am. She likes fancy places, and I don't mind because she always pays. She's quite generous." I was babbling too.

Jack held the door open for me and we walked in. It was small and charming, with soft Italian music playing. The walls were decorated with photographs of beautiful Italian towns and the tables were covered with traditional red and white checkered tablecloths.

The maître d', or possibly the owner, rushed up to Jack and shook his hand. "Jack," he said in his heavy Italian accent, "it has been too long. We have missed you. Please come in. Your table is waiting. A glass of wine, perhaps? Or a bottle for you and your beautiful lady."

Awkward! This must have been one of Jack's drinking spots. I assumed he mostly got drunk in bars, but a guy has to eat.

"Thanks, Luigi," Jack said, following the man to a table in the back. "Those days are over. No more wine for me. Or for the lady. You're seeing a new Jack."

Luigi didn't miss a beat. "Excellent news, my friend. Sometimes the wine has too much power over us. Please sit." He set menus in front of us and disappeared.

"I love the look of this place. And Luigi certainly is more charming than the waitress at the Unfriendly Café," I said, as I looked around.

Jack laughed. "True. The food is even better than the ambience. Well, maybe it's better. I wasn't much of a connoisseur in my drinking days."

We sat quietly, studying the menu. We ordered bruschetta for an appetizer. Jack ordered Rigatoni with beef, and I ordered the Tagliatelle with chicken. Luigi also brought a basket filled with warm bread. The smell was enticing. I am a sucker for good bread.

"No dessert," I announced when we were finished. "I can barely move as it is, and I want to have popcorn at the movies."

"You are a woman after my own heart. It's not the movies without popcorn."

A woman after his own heart. Be still my pounding heart.

The movie, a murder mystery with a love story thrown in, was good. Afterward, Jack walked me home.

"Would you like to come in?" I asked, standing in front of the door. "I won't offer a nightcap, however, there's the possibility of tea, coffee, water, soda?"

Jack leaned closer. "I'd love to come in," he whispered in my ear. "Maybe next time. I had a great time. You are wonderful." He kissed my ear and nuzzled my neck. Stepping back, he looked at me for several moments. "So wonderful." Taking my face in his hands, he kissed me softly on the lips.

I wanted to grab him in a full embrace and drag him into the house. Before I could, he said, "Goodnight Rose. I can't wait to see you again." And he left.

Chapter Fourteen

*F*inally, we were there. He liked me as more than a friend. There was plenty of news to tell both Ivy and Lauren the next day. "He kissed me! He kissed me!" I blubbered into the phone. "He was so sweet. It was so romantic. A perfect gentleman."

"Who the hell wants a gentleman at a time like that?" Ivy was miffed that all I got was a nuzzle and one chaste kiss. She liked to get to the action.

I paced as I talked, unable to contain my energy. "I want to take this slow. We're both new at this relationship thing. Well, new as sober people. I'm glad he's not pushing too quickly."

When I shared the news with Lauren, she had a different reaction. I could feel her smile over the phone. "Way to go, girl!"

We got there. In our own time and in our own way. We'd moved from our first kiss to making out and all the various types of foreplay. One night we were on the couch, half-naked, and Jack murmured into my ear, "Are you ready for the next step?"

I took his hand by way of my answer and led him upstairs to my bedroom. He sat on the edge of the bed and stared at the floor. Had he changed his mind? Sitting next to him, I held his hand and stroked his face. "What's the matter?" I whispered.

"This will be the first time I've ever had sex sober. And this won't just be sex. This will be making love, and I'm not sure I even know how to do that. All my relationships were shit. I was abusive. A complete asshole. I don't even know why women put up with me, though most of them were drunks like me. I'm glad I wasn't stupid enough to ever get married."

He looked at me, eyes glistening.

"Jack, same for me. In my case, not only have I never had sex sober, I haven't had sex in like a hundred years."

He laughed. "A hundred years? You must be older than I thought."

"Maybe not a hundred." I smiled, glad I'd made him laugh. "It's been a really, really long time. I'm for sure more nervous than you."

"It's like riding a bicycle." Jack grinned. "You never really forget."

He was right. I hadn't forgotten the mechanics; however, I had forgotten how absolutely amazing it was to share the moment with someone I loved.

"Just like a bicycle," Jack repeated with a huge smile on his face as we stared into each other's eyes.

"You survived that hurdle. Now you have to meet my sister." I could hardly suppress the smile tugging at my lips.

"Oh, no." Jack rolled over and groaned. "The whole 'meet the family' ordeal?"

"Yep. Love me, love my dog, or in this case, my sister's dog, though you already love Fritz. However, you still have to meet my sister. Ivy's an important part of my life."

Jack grimaced. "Another bullet I managed to dodge in past relationships. I never wanted my family to meet any of the women I hooked up with, and they probably didn't want to introduce a scruffy drunk to their families, either."

Rolling back to look at me, he said, "I do want to meet Ivy. Because she's important to you and I want to know the people you love. I want to be part of all your life."

Chapter Fifteen

*I*vy invited us over for dinner at her place. When Ivy was married to Terry, they'd lived in a huge old house. Several years after he died, she finally moved to a smaller, newer house, with all the benefits of a kitchen with modern appliances. Despite that, I was sure she'd ordered a meal in from one of her favorite restaurants. Ivy doesn't cook. Though honestly, I don't either. Because for years I drank my dinner.

Jack met me at Ivy's promptly at six o'clock, holding a huge bouquet of multi-colored carnations. He wore khakis, a light blue polo shirt, and a navy sports jacket. It appeared he'd gotten a haircut and a shave. He looked completely miserable.

"Khakis?" I said quizzically, rubbing his smooth cheeks. "Ivy might not recognize you with short hair and no beard, since I described you as a bit shaggy."

"I wanted to make a positive impact," Jack replied, still looking uncomfortable. Beads of sweat started to pop out on his forehead. "My dad always told us you only have one chance to make a good first impression."

"True," I agreed. "Ivy's going to love the flowers. That will help you get a positive reaction." I took a tissue out of my purse and blotted his face. "You're meeting my sister, not being interrogated by the Spanish Inquisition."

Before I could say anything else, the door flew open and Ivy was staring out at us. Fritz ran circles around us, barking and jumping on Jack. Ivy leaned down, grabbing Fritz. I introduced Jack and Ivy and as their hands met in a friendly handshake, I had an attack of nerves—more like PTSD. Years ago, when I introduced Ivy to Terry, who I was in love with, when their hands met, sparks flew, the heavens opened, and a choir of angels burst into song while fireworks erupted. Maybe it didn't happen that way, but it's the way I remember it.

Thankfully, this time, there was not even a glimmer of an ember being ignited. Jack handed Ivy the bouquet, and she smiled. I breathed an audible sigh of relief, and Jack looked at me curiously.

Ivy set Fritz down and reached for the flowers. Once his hands were free, Jack picked Fritz up. "Fritz, old boy, I've missed you."

Ivy smiled, thanking Jack for the flowers. "Come in." So far, so good.

After she took our coats, she went to get a vase. "So lovely, my favorite kind." Ivy really didn't know much about flowers and probably other than roses didn't know the names of any of them, but she knew they were beautiful and colorful and smelled marvelous, so they were all her favorite kind. I thought it was a brilliant attitude about flowers or about life in general.

Ivy brought the vase full of flowers out to the living room and set them on the coffee table. "What would everyone like to drink? I have hot and cold tea. Sparkling water, flavored or unflavored. Soft drinks, caffeinated, un-caffeinated, with sugar or without. And even plain tap water, if you prefer."

Jack asked for iced tea and I picked fruit-flavored sparkling water.

The evening was a great success. Ivy was a charming hostess, and Jack was a charming guest. After dinner, Ivy took us up to her studio to show us some of her recent work. Jack was, surprisingly, quite knowledgeable about art and made some insightful comments. This made a great impression on Ivy, and I could see his stock going up in her eyes.

As we walked back to my place after dinner, I snuggled up against his shoulder. "You done good. Ivy really likes you."

"I like her too. She's a fascinating woman. Her art is so... I'm not even sure I have the right word... deep. Moving. Touching. It's fascinating how she paints images of illness from what she pictures in her mind. I can understand why her work is popular."

"Probably every hospital in the country has an Ivy Bane Berenstein print in one of their various wings," I said.

Jack put his arm around my shoulder and kissed the top of my head. "I'm relieved it went well. I was terrified of meeting her. Afraid she wouldn't like me."

"What's not to like?" I asked. "You're cute, funny, and a great car mechanic."

"And I'm much more pleasant now I'm sober."

"Aren't we all."

Chapter Sixteen

I'd been nervous about introducing Jack to Ivy. I wanted/needed her approval. Though I'm sure I'd still have continued our relationship, even if Ivy didn't like him, it would have devastated me if my two lives and the two most important people in my life didn't merge seamlessly.

When Ivy married Preston, we hardly ever saw each other since she was living several states away, and it was like one of my limbs had been severed. When she married Terry, the three of us were best friends, and though it killed me sometimes to be around the man I'd hoped to marry, it would have been worse not to be with them.

Six months after the dinner at Ivy's, Jack and I got married. Ivy asked a bit peevishly what the rush was. "We're old, Ivy! No reason to wait." Even Gwen gave her approval.

Now I was getting married, and Ivy was single. She jokingly said, "I told you to get a dog, not to get married." She looked a little sad and wistful. "I hope this won't impact our relationship too much."

"Of course not!" I grabbed her and hugged her fiercely. "You will always be my number one. My very best friend. My hero." Holding her close. I whispered, "You're the only person I can share memories of our sister, Lily, with. We're the only people left who knew her." Choking back a sob, I smiled and said, "Not to mention memories of our mom and dad, who were not always sweet, but they were ours. And only we know the secrets of what we did to poor William when he was a child."

Ivy hugged me back. "Yes. All true. Thank goodness William forgave us."

I laughed. "I was afraid he would end up blackmailing us."

Jack walked in carrying Fritz. "Looks like I'm interrupting a moment."

Ivy wiped her hand across her eyes, and I blinked furiously. "Not at all," she said. "I'm giving Rose some pre-marital counseling."

Jack rolled his eyes. "Fritz and I are going for a walk. We can't deal with all these raging female hormones." We all laughed.

"Good idea," Ivy said. "Take your testosterone out for a stroll."

Lauren came the week before the wedding to check to see if Jack was worthy of me. They also got along really well. I began to get jealous over how well they got along. "You're supposed to be my best friend," I reminded her.

"I live in a house full of women—my dear wife Miranda, along with the three, or is it four daughters who are still home, various grandkids, even the dog is a girl! It's nice to be around a manly man," Lauren said.

"Speaking of all those women, why didn't Miranda come with you?" I'd met Lauren's wife Miranda a few times when I visited Lauren in LA.

"She said she needed some time alone." Lauren rolled her eyes. "She claims I'm extremely demanding, plus she said, 'Rose is your BFF, I'd be a third wheel.' I'll have to tell her Jack's my new BFF." Lauren leered at Jack.

"Oh, stop pretending you have the hots for Jack. You're a woman's woman."

"Like I said, I enjoy looking."

William, his wife Margie, and their little daughter Fern also came for the wedding. Fern was three the first time I saw her. I was shocked by how much she resembled Lily. Once again, I was overcome by the terrible loss of my baby sister. I briefly considered moving to Alaska to be close to Fern. However, William lives in a cabin deep in the woods with hardly any modern conveniences. I'm a modern, convenience needy person. At the very least, I require a flush toilet and toilet paper.

Fern was seven now. We tried to see William and family every couple of years. A trip to Alaska wasn't a simple flight to the airport, followed by an hour or two drive to his house. It was a day and a half trip to get to their cabin and required a four-wheel-drive vehicle.

William and Margie didn't have a lot of money, and I knew Ivy usually helped with their travel expenses. It was nice to have one person in the family with unlimited funds. Terry left Ivy financially secure, and her art career was quite lucrative.

The ceremony was simple. The men wore jeans and button up shirts. The women wore cotton dresses. My childhood dream of an enormous princess-style ball gown for my wedding dress wasn't appropriate at my age. Even though Ivy encouraged me, saying, "Go for it," I decided on a simple white cotton dress with a few lace accents to satisfy my ball gown dreams. Jack wore a white shirt, so we matched.

I felt sorry for Jack, who didn't have any family members on his side. Still, he'd made many great friends in AA, and his mechanic buddies and a few other old friends were there. Unfortunately, sometimes you lose friends when you stop drinking because they feel awkward around you. And you find out the only thing you shared was getting blasted.

Otto stood up as Jack's best man. Jack also asked William to stand up with him. "You're Rose's brother, which makes you my brother now." I loved Jack even more for saying that.

Fritz walked me down the aisle. Jack and I agreed he'd been instrumental in arranging our initial meeting.

Ivy was my matron of honor, and Lauren and Margie served as my bride's matrons. Fern and Ivy's first grandbaby, Little Ivy, were joint flower girls. Gwen officiated. I was thrilled to find out she was licensed to perform weddings, which really made it personal. I'd have hated to get a minister out of the phone book.

Ivy's grown twins, Cate and Alex, came with their spouses and assorted children. The only thing that would have made it perfect was if my mom could have been there to see I finally achieved her dream for me, which was to find love. There was a time I could barely stand to be around my mom. It still surprised me how much I missed her.

Of course, our reception was completely alcohol free. My brother William and Margie were also former drinkers who gave up the demon when they met. Fern was their gift for sobriety. My mom had struggled with alcoholism. Her father was a drunk, so it ran in the family, as it often does. Ivy liked to have a glass of wine, but she could take it or leave it. She was the only one spared the gene or whatever causes a person to become an alcoholic.

Our wedding night was at the amazing Jefferson Hotel. Our real honeymoon would be a visit to Alaska. Jack had never been there, and we convinced him it was worth the trip.

Chapter Seventeen

When "older" people marry, they often have way too many things to consolidate into a new joint life. That wasn't a problem for Jack and me. Jack had nothing. Of course, he had stuff, though apparently nothing he determined was worth saving or moving into our new home.

We had decided he should move into my townhouse. His apartment was over the garage where he worked. His furniture consisted of things he'd found at thrift stores and junk yards.

"Junk yards?" I asked incredulously.

"Yeah. You'd be surprised what people throw away. I found some great things at the dump."

"But nothing you want to move into our home?" Hoping he'd say no.

He looked a bit embarrassed. "Ummm…probably not." He looked around at my simple décor. "I don't think it fits in with your … color scheme?"

"Thank God you don't want to mess with my color scheme," I joked. "And don't worry about not bringing anything but yourself. Yourself is all I want." Which led to giggles and kisses, and we were momentarily distracted from discussing our house plans.

Jack had been living at my place for a couple of months before we got married. Once we were "official," he gifted his apartment and furniture to one of the other mechanics. All he brought to my place were two old suitcases with clothes, some photos, and books. "It's sad this is all I have to show for fifty years of life."

"Like I try to tell my clients, it's not the material things that matter at the end. It's the love you gave and shared. Remember the song: *the love you get is equal to the love you give* or something along those lines. I totally agree. It's not about the riches you acquire."

"Good to know," Jack exclaimed, "because I don't have any riches. But I have you."

Which led to more foolishness.

We fit together like a hand and glove.

In the six months before we married, we found out a lot more about each other. I confessed to him I hoped he wasn't looking forward to a cozy domestic scene with a wife who cooked and ironed his clothes.

"To be honest," I said, "I'm not much of a cook. Actually, I'm no kind of cook. Back in the day, I'd grab a granola bar and a coffee as I headed off to work. I'd usually have a salad or sandwich for lunch and at night I'd have some cheese and crackers and wine. Always wine." I winced at the memory. "So, I can make a mean microwave dinner, but that's about it."

"I'm quite distraught. I was hoping for a doting wife who waited on me hand and foot." Jack grinned. "I guess I can adjust. Truthfully, I wasn't much of an eater either. It was coffee for breakfast. Beer for lunch and hard liquor for dinner. You know, we can learn to cook together. And if doesn't work out, hopefully you have a local pizza parlor on speed dial and a good Chinese carry-out."

"Sounds perfect."

After Jack claimed his closet and drawer space, put his photos out and his books on the bookshelf, we were ready for a dog to make our family complete.

We debated what kind of dog to get. Jack wanted some macho type dog like a Bull Mastiff or Rottweiler. I wanted a Fritz type dog. Small. Cute. Easy.

"Fritz is the perfect dog," I reminded him. "Without him, we never would have met and fallen in love."

"That's not completely true," Jack retorted. "I fell for you the first time I saw you."

"Really? You took long enough letting me know!"

━━━⌒∞⌒━━━

We went to the local shelter to see what was available. We agreed that as cute as they were, a puppy was probably not a good option. Neither of us ever trained a puppy. "An older dog. A dog who's been dumped and is heartbroken. A dog whose life we can change."

We were not prepared for the reality. We fell in love with and wanted to save every one of the dogs at the shelter. After stopping at each kennel and gushing over every dog, the shelter worker took us to meet with a matchmaker. This is the person who lists all your needs and wants to match them with a dog's needs and wants.

They came up with a list of "potentials". I laughed, remembering Ivy's list of "potentials" when she was looking for a guy. Who knew the shelter had a similar list? I wondered if Ivy went through this same process when she got Fritz.

Ivy's list of possible potential men was much shorter than the shelter's list. Ivy's list only had three criteria: age appropriate, not married, and so good looking it made your teeth ache to look at the guy.

The shelter's list was much more detailed. The shelter agreed a puppy was not ideal for us. They also nixed super old dogs and special needs dogs since we were obviously new at the whole dog thing. They asked about our yard. Was it fenced? What were our work hours? Where would the dog stay when we were working? Did we plan to walk the dog? Were there children in the house? Other animals? I said we wanted a dog that got along with other dogs, since I knew Fritz would still be over for visits when Ivy traveled.

The list was narrowed to six dogs, and we were set up with sessions that were akin to speed dating. We went to a room. The dog was brought in so we could see how the dog interacted with us and how we felt about the dog. Then we took the dog outside for a short walk and threw a ball around. We even brought Fritz in to see how he behaved with the potential dogs.

We ended up with a dog I never would have considered if I'd walked in and picked it out on my own. He was a chihuahua pit bull mix, with a lot of something else thrown in. If I'd ever been asked about dog breeds and preferences, I'd have included chihuahuas and pit bulls on my list of least favorite dog breeds. Maybe it was the something else because Frito was incredibly charming and irresistible. He was small, about thirty pounds, and all white except for a large orange spot on his side, an orange tail and one orange ear and snout. And the world's best smile. The orange ear stood up, and the other flopped over. He would never win best in show, but even Jack, who wanted a "man's dog," fell completely in love with the little guy.

Our family was complete.

Chapter Eighteen

The year after we got married, we finally honeymooned in Alaska. Having Jack made the trip not only more enjoyable but also much easier. We didn't have to hire a guide to escort us into the wilderness. Jack was more than capable of driving a four-wheel-drive vehicle and could even repair it if we drove off the road or were involved in a moose stampede. Well, maybe not a stampede, but at least he could change a flat tire.

It was wonderful being with William and Margie and Fern. Fern was my heart. My sweet baby Lily returned to me. Looking at Fern let me know what Lily would have looked like if she'd lived longer than three short years. Fern was now eight years old and was the most charming and engaging child ever. She was also incredibly smart. Brilliant, in fact.

Fern was not exposed to any television or social media. She wasn't even exposed to school with its risks of bullying and other pressures. Margie homeschooled Fern, not that there was much of a choice given where they lived. They also belonged to a group of homeschoolers, who got together occasionally to give the children a chance to interact with other kids.

Margie was doing an amazing job, but she admitted she worried about how she'd manage Fern's education when she reached high school age.

"She's already too smart for me. I'm running out of things to teach her." She laughed. "I guess we'll cross that bridge when we come to it."

Joking, I said they could send her down to live with us to go to high school. I was only half joking since I'd have loved to have Fern live with us.

Margie replied she'd keep my offer in mind. She probably knew I was serious.

Jack absolutely loved it up at William's. It worried me a bit because I thought he might suggest we get a homestead next door. However, he knew my limits on "roughing it" and was smart enough not to suggest we move. There was still the flush toilet and toilet paper thing, not to mention being able to call for pizza delivery and pop over to the store if we needed something.

Every morning, we got up early and ate a massive breakfast, something I only allowed myself because Margie worked it off me with chores. William and Jack headed into the woods after breakfast, doing manly wilderness activities. When they took the dogs out for a run, Fern went along. She said she was going to be the first child to compete and win the Iditarod dogsled race.

Thinking about our silly little Frito, Jack laughed. "These are dogs. These are what dogs should look like and this is the life they should live."

"Not Fritz and Frito," I responded. "They have been molded by ten thousand years of sleeping next to their masters. First on a stone floor by the fire and finally up in the king-size bed."

After a wonderful visit, it was time to leave. Saying goodbye was always hard. William lived in the most beautiful spot on earth, but I reminded myself the world of flush toilets was waiting for me.

There were many hugs and kisses and promises of future visits. William and family had come east to see the extended family for Thanksgiving three years before. Even though they'd just been with us for our wedding, we convinced them they needed to think about coming again for Thanksgiving next year.

My longest goodbye was with Fern. I loved William and Margie, but it was always hardest to say goodbye to Fern. Being with her almost filled the ache in my heart over Lily. It shocked me to realize Lily would be in her fifties now if she had lived. Instead, she was three for eternity.

Chapter Nineteen

Jack and I quickly settled into domestic harmony. We thought we were too old to change, but we were soon doing things neither of us ever considered when we were single.

One day, Jack came home with some tomato plants. He planned to start a little garden in the corner of our backyard. It had to be little since the yard wasn't large. He made a fence to keep Frito out and proudly called me out to see his garden. The tomato plants looked sad and forlorn.

"They'll perk up soon," Jack announced. "They have to adjust to their new environment. I love fresh tomatoes. My mom used to have a little garden and the first tomato of the year was always cause for celebration. She made the best BLTs and club sandwiches."

The day Jack brought the tomato plants home, he also brought me a house plant. Plants were another thing I never had. I didn't want to be responsible for another living thing of any type.

"This is a ZZ plant," Jack said. "The guy at the nursery said you can't kill them. You can forget to water them for months and they're fine."

"That's certainly my kind of plant," I replied, "though I'm sure I'll still manage to kill it."

My ZZ thrived under my neglect, and I branched out, recklessly adding more plants. Soon I had a watering and fertilizing schedule. It amazed me how stress reducing it was to walk around and water my plants and turn them to face the sun.

Ivy, as usual, had been way ahead of the game. Some of her plants were over twenty years old.

"Plants are very peaceful and restorative," she told me. "You need something to help you stay calm given your line of work." Ivy never understood why I wanted to spend my days working with death. I'd explained to her that despite my job being stressful, it was also rewarding. We finally decided not to talk about it.

"I completely agree with you about plants. I should have gotten them years ago when I was a therapist. And suggested them to my patients."

The most surprising thing was Jack started to cook. After the tomatoes, he added more variety to the garden. When we were buried in a bonanza of squash and tomatoes, Jack looked up recipes online. I came home to find him happily chopping and stirring things in the kitchen. Of course, I soon joined him.

Our lives revolved around feathering our nest, attending meetings, and working. Ivy was a frequent guest for dinner and was impressed by Jack's gardening and cooking skills. She occasionally brought a man along, though there was never a serious relationship brewing. Ivy also always brought Fritz when she came over. Fritz and Frito were best buddies, as we hoped they'd be. We continued to keep Fritz when Ivy traveled.

After our Alaska trip, we went to California to see Lauren. She gave us a tour of all the well-known tourist sites. She also let us watch her tape an episode of her show. Jack felt like a movie star walking around the studios with her. Most of Lauren's children were grown and despite the occasional return, Lauren and Miranda were now empty nesters.

At dinner at her home, a small mansion as she described it, Lauren said, "I love my job but now the kids are out, making their own way, I'm seriously

PATTI GAUSTAD PROCOPI

thinking of retiring and moving to a small town in the Midwest."

"The Midwest?" I asked curiously. "Why not Alaska if you want remote?"

"I want my conveniences too. Besides, I could never get Miranda to move that far away from the kids, grandkids, and maybe some great grandkids I've lost track of."

Miranda laughed. "Lauren's never been good about keeping track of all our children. She's the breadwinner, which left me to be the domestic goddess-mommy-homemaker."

"And she's so good at it! God knows what I would have done without her." Lauren looked at Miranda and blew her an air-kiss.

"I wish Miranda wasn't too old to have another baby." Lauren grinned. "Wouldn't mind asking Jack to be a surrogate. Those blue eyes are gorgeous!"

Miranda rolled her eyes. "You can always trade me in for a young trophy wife."

"No, never. You are my everything." Lauren jumped up and ran over to hug and kiss Miranda.

"You two are too much." Jack and I laughed.

The day before we left, Lauren took me out for a one-on-one lunch. "We need to catch up without our spouses," she said.

We went to the most spectacular restaurant with an amazing view of the beach. I loved people watching. "I could live here," I said. "If I could afford a place like this."

"Yes. It's a great place to live if you have money," Lauren agreed.

We talked and laughed all through lunch. As we lingered over our coffees, Lauren asked, "Are you happy? I'm not used to a Rose that's not morose and eaten up with guilt and misery."

I was a bit taken aback. "Yes. I think I'm happy. Maybe finally happy for the first time. Which sounds stupid. I've had many wonderful moments in my life. Still, there's something about waking up each morning with someone you love that is fantastic. I have to pinch myself sometimes."

"I wanted to be sure because you seem like you've softened. You're not

70

quite the same old snarky Rose. I miss her, but if you're happy, I'm happy. I worry because you've been through so many changes in a short time." Lauren reached over, took my hand, and gave it a squeeze. "Your mother died, and you changed your job, then you got sober or maybe you got sober and then changed your job." Lauren laughed. "Then you met Jack and blam! Fell in love and got married after a week." She paused, then added, "You even got plants!"

"A week? I think it was a bit longer." I smiled at the memory of our rush to the altar.

"I know I'm exaggerating, but you know what I mean. It's a lot to handle."

"Agreed. I've been through the mill. Now the dust is settling, I feel I'm settling into a blissful state. In fact, I'm a little afraid. You know how the gods are always looking for someone to smite. At least that's the God my Meemee used to scare me with. I've always been afraid to be too happy. I wanted to coast below the radar. Maybe I should pretend I'm not happy at all. I worry about that smiting God."

We laughed, finished our coffee and, after one last longing look at the ocean, we headed to the house.

The next day, Lauren drove us to the airport. After a week, we needed to return to the real world. Back to our jobs, back to our dog, back to our home.

Chapter Twenty

*M*aybe the only hiccup in our lives was my job. Ivy continued to harass me and wonder why I wanted to do such a depressing job as hospice.

Jack wisely said nothing. He realized it wasn't his place to suggest what I should or shouldn't do with my life. And while not every moment in my job was wonderful, there were enough satisfying moments to convince me to stick with it.

One difficult part of the job was dealing with the families. Often the patient and family were confused about hospice. At one intake meeting, I had started handing out packets while explaining about hospice care.

The oldest son looked it all over in great confusion. "I need more details. You're here to monitor mom, and if there's a crisis, you'll call an ambulance and get her to the hospital to be taken care of, right?"

"No," I said slowly. "Once you sign up for hospice, you're accepting the end has come. I'm here to keep your mom as comfortable as possible until then. We will be stopping all other medicines from this point on except pain meds."

"Oh no!" He slammed the papers down on the coffee table. "This is not what we want. We haven't given up on Mom."

The mother interrupted, "Bill. I have inoperable cancer, and it's spread all over my body. I'm done with chemo. I want to die peacefully in my own bed."

A huge argument broke out, and no one listened or noticed the mother sinking deeper and deeper in her chair. No one but I heard her say in a pleading voice, "Please, can't we do what I want?"

The papers weren't signed. I have no idea what happened to the poor woman, but I doubt she got her wishes honored.

Another client, Cindy, reminded me of me when my mom was dying. She was also full of guilt and remorse. "My mom was not an easy person. She was super critical when I was young. I could never do anything right. When I had children, I hoped maybe I'd finally made her happy. Turns out she just had something new to complain about. She went on and on about my poor parenting skills and belittled my children to the point they don't want to be around her."

A tear slipped down her cheek. "I hate to admit it, but I started criticizing my mother to my kids. It was my way of paying her back for her meanness. I contributed to my kids not liking her. When I found out she was dying, I was so upset. I wanted us to start over. Make a better end. Unfortunately, it was too late for my kids by then. They won't even come over with me and sit with her.

"I'm heartbroken. I sit here alone, holding her hand, wishing we were all here together."

Her face twisted into a bitter smile. "And you know, she still criticizes me when I visit because the kids aren't coming over. She has no clue. And I get mad at her all over again, and I don't want to be mad. I want to hear her say she appreciates me. That I was and am a good daughter. A good person. I want her to say she loves me."

A few days later Cindy called, frantic, asking if I could meet her at the house. Cindy's mom passed away fifteen minutes after we arrived.

I stayed with Cindy for several hours, waiting for the funeral home to arrive. She was inconsolable. "I needed more time. I had so much more to say to her. I felt like we were on the brink of something and now she's gone and… I'll never have a chance."

Handing her a box of tissues, I patted her hand. "In my experience, there is never enough time to say everything you want."

She nodded, mopping her tears with a tissue.

"I went through the same experience with my mother," I said. "We also had a bad relationship built on mutual misunderstanding, blame, guilt, anger… I still miss her years later. Even now, I think of things I want to say to her. It was the worst right after she passed. I'd pick up the phone to call her or get in the car to drive over to her house and the grief would hit me again."

"Does it get better?" Cindy asked.

"It does. Though it takes a while. Don't be surprised by grief coming out of nowhere to overwhelm you." And knock you to your knees, I thought.

After the funeral home people left, I gave Cindy one more hug. "Call me. Call me anytime you need to talk."

She hugged me back. "Thanks."

When I walked outside, I was surprised to see it was already dark. We'd talked for longer than I realized. Climbing into my car, I headed home. Luckily, Jack was used to my odd hours. He might have gone to a meeting, but he always left me dinner before he took off.

I was reminiscing about my mom when I noticed I was lost. The neighborhood was familiar, but it wasn't the way home. An odd feeling crept over me as I stared out the window, trying to figure out where I was. The apartment building I was passing seemed oddly familiar. I gasped when I realized it was my mom's old apartment. The light was on, and someone moved behind the sheer curtains.

My heart said, "Mom!" but my brain said, "No." I pulled over and parked, peering up at the window, hoping against anything rational to see my mom. I almost jumped out of the car and ran up to the door of the building. Tears ran down my cheeks.

Do we ever stop missing our moms?

Chapter Twenty-One

*T*wo years after our honeymoon trip to Alaska, William and family came east for Thanksgiving again. We were almost too many to fit around a single table. All the under twenties were relegated to a separate table in a different room. They pretended to be upset, but they were secretly happy. After eating more food than was humanly possible, the women cleaned up while the men watched football on TV. We groused about being assigned the domestic chores, though we actually enjoyed time together without the men.

I especially appreciated hanging out with Margie. We saw each other far too infrequently. It still amazed me William had found such a bright woman to marry.

Of course, I was still amazed I'd found Jack.

As we worked together, Margie said, "I need to talk to you all about something."

That never is a good way to introduce a subject. We all stopped what we were doing and stared at her.

"Okay," Ivy said, her voice tentative.

Margie smiled at our sober faces. "Sorry, didn't mean to scare all of you. It's about Fern." We nodded encouragingly. Personally, I couldn't think of what

Fern could be doing that was worrisome. In my eyes, she was the perfect child.

"Fern is so smart. I want her to go to college. Be a doctor, an astronaut, a lawyer. She could be anything. But I don't think she's going to get there being homeschooled by me. We don't even have access to the internet, which has some advantages, but it hampers her education. I'm considering sending her to a boarding school where she can get a real education. Fern and William are of course totally opposed to this plan. Fern says she wants to stay on the homestead with us and raise dogs and compete in dog sled races.

"I keep trying to tell her there's a whole world out there for her to explore. It's one of the reasons I enjoy visiting here. I can take her to museums. Broaden her horizons. Show her all the possibilities.

"And she loves going to those kinds of places. She loves art and science and history, but she says she wants to stay with us. Forever." Margie grimaced. "I don't want her to miss out."

"Boarding school? Where?" I asked.

Margie sighed. "That's part of the problem. Alaska? Or somewhere on the West coast? Or the East coast? It's hard to decide, because I can't do an internet search except when we go to the library and use the computers there. I've been getting a lot of brochures in the mail and they all sound wonderful!"

We stood silently, uncertain what to say. The thought of Fern being thrust into a foreign environment far from her loving family was scary, but I certainly understood Margie wanting more for Fern than raising dogs in the woods.

Cate, Ivy's daughter, was the first to speak up. "When we were kids, Alex and I were sent to a boarding school. It was my father's family tradition that the children attend the same school they all had attended for generations."

I was glad to hear from someone who'd actually gone to a boarding school. Cate had insights the rest of us didn't.

"It was awful. Full of rich kids who were dumped there by their families. Or at least that's how most of the kids felt. There was so much drama and emotional turmoil. Drugs. Bullying. Like living out a *Lord of the Flies* remake.

Our first year there, a kid committed suicide.

"I was never happier than when Terry convinced our father to let us attend public school and stay at home with him and my mom. By then our father was remarried with new kids, so he completely lost interest in us and was happy not to have to pay for boarding school.

"I don't want to be such a downer, but the cliques and mean girls at a boarding school would eat someone as sweet and innocent as Fern alive."

Margie looked down and shrugged. "That's what I'm afraid of. I'm going to have to come up with a Plan B."

"Maybe some super cool summer camps? Something to get her interested in the outside world," I suggested. "I've heard of space camp. Must be lots of educational programs for kids along those lines. She could spend the summer with us. There are lots of fun and educational things for kids to do in the city. And she'd have her cousin Little Ivy to hang out with."

"Yeah. Maybe I'll start with something like that. Can I ask you all to help me do a little more research? Not this coming summer, but maybe the summer after? She'll be in seventh grade then. That's a good time. Thanks guys."

"Group hug!" I smiled. Everyone came together for a big, warm embrace. I glanced out the window and saw Fern alone, playing with the dogs. The men were watching football and the other kids were no doubt playing video games. I couldn't decide if it might be better for Fern not to be exposed to the supposed modern world.

Chapter Twenty-Two

After Dad died, Ivy and I curled up in bed together, reminiscing. She told me about Meemee dragging her off to church and singing the hymn *When Will our Sorrows Cease.* She said she asked God when they would. Or if they ever would. At the time, we had no idea there were a host of sorrows yet to come.

Apparently, God wasn't quite done with us and our sorrows. We thought we'd all reached our well-deserved happy place. Ivy had an amazing career, and all her children and grandchildren were happy and healthy. I was sober and married to a great guy, and our long-lost brother William was back in the family circle along with his wonderful wife, Margie, and his incredible daughter, Fern.

And then the phone rang in the middle of the night and our lifeboat tilted again and sank.

After taking the phone from Ivy, Phillipe told me the Alaska State Police had called and told Ivy that William, Margie, and Fern had been in a bad car accident. They'd all been taken to the hospital. The details were sketchy.

I told Phillipe to calm Ivy down, slap her if necessary, and put her back on the phone.

Ivy hiccupped into the phone, trying to stifle her sobs. "Ivy. We have to fly to Alaska first thing. Start packing. I'll let you know what I've booked."

I hung up the phone and Jack woke up. He looked at the clock and then at me quizzically. "What's up? Who are you talking to?"

"Ivy called. William, Margie, and Fern have been in a car accident. They're all in the hospital. Ivy's going to try to find out which hospital. We're flying to Alaska today."

The color drained from his face as he digested the news. "Wow. I hope everyone is okay."

"Yeah. Me too."

Chapter Twenty-Three

When we met at the airport, Ivy said she called the Alaska State Trooper back to find out which hospital they'd taken William and family to. He told her they'd all been medevacked by helicopter to a trauma center in Fairbanks.

"That sounds serious. We can probably take a taxi to the hospital from the airport instead of a trip into the wilderness," I said, relieved that we wouldn't have to add a long drive to our long flight.

"It does sound bad. The trooper said all he could add was they'd all been alive when they were removed from their vehicle."

"That's something positive, at least," I said. "Did you find out any more about what happened?"

"I asked, but all the trooper said was another vehicle was involved. He also added a moose had something to do with the accident. He couldn't give me any more details since they weren't finished with their investigation." Ivy turned to me. "A moose? A moose was involved?"

I shook my head. "Only in Alaska."

We sat quietly, both lost in our thoughts. Hoping and praying everyone was fine. The moose part of the report worried me. William once told me running into a moose was one of his biggest fears. "Those things are huge.

It's like hitting a tank, and they can come over the hood of your car and crash through your window." Is that what happened?

I wondered why they were out driving at night, and suddenly had a thought, "Wasn't last night Fern's Spelling Bee competition? It would explain why they were on the road so late."

"You're right," Ivy agreed. "I'd forgotten about that."

Our flight took over thirteen hours with two layovers. At each layover, Ivy called the hospital to get information on their condition. Each time she was told they couldn't give information over the phone. She became increasingly upset.

"We are flying from the East coast to Alaska, and we won't be there for hours. Can you at least give me some idea how my brother and family are doing?"

They repeated that as sympathetic as they were to our situation, they simply could not discuss patients over the phone since they couldn't verify we were really relatives. Ivy wore them down and they finally told us that the family had been admitted the night before but that was all they would say.

By the time we'd get to the hospital, it would be almost twenty hours from when we received the initial phone call. I needed to distract myself from fear and worry. I turned to Ivy. "Why was Phillipe at your house so late?"

Ivy stared back at me. "Why do you think, Rose? I needed a massage in the middle of the night? No. I needed some companionship, and I enjoy Phillipe's company. In more ways than one." She arched her eyebrows, giving me a knowing look.

"You know he's not really French," I said.

"You know I don't really care," Ivy responded. She shut her eyes and tried to sleep.

Chapter Twenty-Four

*W*e landed in Fairbanks at 3:00 in the afternoon Alaska time. My internal clock was totally turned around. We had left Virginia at 6:00 in the morning, so how could it still be the same day and only nine hours later after flying for over fourteen hours? I don't do time changes well.

We hurried off the plane and out of the airport to the taxi stand. Ivy had suggested we pack everything in carry-ons, so we didn't have to wait for our luggage. It helped to travel with someone who was a frequent flyer who knew the ropes.

Jumping in a cab, we told the driver we wanted to go to Fairbanks Memorial Hospital. When I started to look up the address, the cabbie indicated with a hand gesture he knew the location. I put my head back and shut my eyes. If we weren't in such a rush to check on William and family, I might have asked to go to our hotel first. We'd been up for hours and only managed to grab a few snatches of sleep on our various flights, which only made it worse.

Forcing my eyes open, I glanced at Ivy. She looked bad, and Ivy never looked bad. I assumed I looked worse. I sent a quick text to Jack. *"We've arrived. OTW to hospital."*

"Let me know how everyone is as soon as you can," he answered. I replied with

a thumbs-up emoji.

Thirty minutes after we got in the cab, it pulled in front of a massive block of a building. It looked exactly like a hospital, nondescript and clinical. "I hope they have competent doctors," Ivy muttered.

The cabbie spoke for the first time. "Don't worry. This place is amazing. Good doctors and skilled staff." I paid him for the ride, and he said, "Good luck," as we climbed out.

We walked in the front door, and I let Ivy take over. Striding over to the information desk, she said, "Hello. We're here to see our brother and family. They were medevacked here last night after a traffic accident. His name is William Bane. His wife is Margie and their daughter's Fern."

Ivy pulled out her driver's license, showing her name as Ivy Bane Berenstein. I handed mine over too. I hadn't changed my name after getting married. It was easier professionally to keep my name.

The receptionist looked at our IDs and started typing on her computer. She picked up the phone and called someone. She spoke softly so we couldn't hear the conversation. Looking up, she smiled. "Someone is coming to escort you to the trauma wing. It's a big hospital, and it's easy to get lost."

I could tell Ivy was about to explode and say something about how she was competent enough to follow signs in a hospital. I squeezed her hand, and she thought better of it. A few minutes later, a middle-aged woman in blue scrubs arrived at the desk. "Hi. My name is Peggy. I'll take you to the family waiting room in the trauma wing. Dr. Prescott will meet you there."

I'd assumed we'd be taken right to William's room. However, it might be good to hear from the doctor first. We walked through a maze of corridors and went up two elevators before we finally arrived at the trauma wing. I was glad we had a guide since we surely would've gotten lost.

Peggy opened the door to a small room which had a couch and several comfortable-looking chairs. It was painted in soft colors in an obvious effort to calm waiting family members. There was also a coffee pot. The coffee smelled inviting. It struck me I was starving as well as exhausted. "Dr.

Prescott will be right in." Peggy smiled and shut the door.

"Thank God," I muttered as I poured myself a cup of coffee. "Maybe this will perk me up."

Ivy looked grim. "This doesn't sound good."

Gratefully, I sipped my coffee. "Ivy, it doesn't sound like anything. It's nice the doctor's coming to talk to us."

Let go and let God, I repeated to myself over and over while looking around the room. "Ivy! Look, they have one of your prints here in the waiting room."

Ivy turned and stared at her own artwork. She walked closer to inspect it, straightening it. "This is a really early piece," she said. It was black with explosions of colors, almost like fireworks. "Trauma," she muttered. "Might need to paint a new version after this."

The door opened and a silver-haired man in a white coat walked in. I glanced at his name tag. This was Dr. Prescott. He put out his hand and introduced himself. We gave him our names. He suggested we sit down, and he pulled a chair across from us.

"Has anyone spoken to you about the accident?" he asked.

"No," Ivy said, a hint of anger in her voice. "I got a call from the Alaska state troopers around midnight last night, or maybe it was the night before. I don't even know what time it was here. They said there'd been a bad car accident and another vehicle and a moose were involved." Ivy grimaced when she said *moose*. "Since then, we've been trying to get here. We've been up for about twenty hours. I called the hospital several times, but they said they couldn't talk to me on the phone."

"Yes, hospital policy, I'm afraid. We have to verify we're really talking to family members. Also, it's better to get the news in person…"

Something about the way he said "get the news in person" made me sick to my stomach. My heart started pounding.

Ivy had the same reaction because when she spoke, it was barely a whisper. "What news? What are you trying to say?"

Dr. Prescott glanced down briefly before sighing. "There's never an easy way to say this. I am sorry to have to tell you your sister-in-law, Margie, has passed away."

My hands flew to my face, and I covered my eyes. Like a little child thinking, if I couldn't see the monsters, they couldn't see me. I wanted to cover my ears too and scream, "Stop talking!" Ivy gasped and began to sob.

Dr. Prescott continued. "She was alive when she arrived. The team did a great job getting her here as quickly as possible. However, her injuries were too severe, and we couldn't save her."

I lowered my hands. "William?" I choked out. "And Fern?"

"Thankfully they are doing okay. Your brother William broke his right arm. It's a very bad break. We had to do surgery last night to piece the bones together. He's also cut and banged up, but given what happened, it's a miracle he's not in worse shape. Your niece, Fern was in the back seat, apparently asleep, and she rolled off the seat into the footwell. She is also banged up and bruised. A sprained wrist. Her injuries are not life threatening."

How could Margie be dead? How could such a sweet, loving spirit be extinguished and no longer with us on this earth? I couldn't imagine how William would take the news. And Fern... my beloved Fern... she was fine... she was safe.

I heard Ivy's voice as if from a great distance. "Can we see our brother?"

Dr. Prescott's voice floated through the fog. "Yes, but you need to be prepared. You might not recognize him because of his injuries."

Chapter Twenty-Five

*D*r. Prescott walked us down the hall to William's room. We walked in and were assaulted by an array of machines with flashing lights and beeping sounds. I recognized the heart monitor and blood pressure machine.

William looked small in the bed. He was hooked up to the various machines and had an IV in his left arm. His right arm was bandaged and lay across his chest. Bandages covered half his face, including his eyes. The exposed part of his face was horribly swollen and disfigured. Ivy clutched my hand and gasped.

"It might not look like it but your brother was lucky. Sometimes in car accidents, the driver makes it through when the passenger doesn't, but I'll let the police tell you more about what happened when they talk to you."

I walked to the left side of the bed and took William's hand and squeezed it. "William? It's Rose. Ivy is here too. Can you hear me? If you can, squeeze my hand." There was no reaction.

"Your brother is heavily sedated. We'll be reducing the pain medication so he'll begin to wake up and be able to communicate. Hopefully by tomorrow."

We stared silently at William's still form. All I could think was when he woke up, we'd have to tell him about Margie.

"Can we see Fern now?" I asked, looking at Dr. Prescott.

"Of course." We followed him out of the room and down a long hall. Fern's room was much quieter in comparison. The lights were low, and there was only one beeping machine. She also had an IV in her arm.

"She's really doing well. As I said, she escaped serious injury. We're being a bit overly cautious. We'll be reducing her pain medication as well and she'll no doubt be awake by tomorrow.

I was struck again by the thought that when she woke up, she'd have to be told her mother was dead. I leaned over and kissed her on the forehead. She felt warm compared to William. I whispered, "Ivy and I are here, honey. Don't worry. We're going to take care of you."

"You'll probably see some improvement when you return tomorrow," Dr. Prescott said, holding the door open for us. Obviously, he thought we should leave. I hated to agree, but I really needed a hot shower and some sleep.

"We'll be back first thing in the morning," Ivy said as we walked out.

Ivy let me take the first shower. When she was in the shower, I called Jack. I dreaded calling him. I didn't want to tell him the news.

He picked up on the first ring. "How are you? I've been worried sick."

"Oh, Jack…" was all I could manage at first. He waited. "It's bad. It's really bad," I choked. "Margie is dead. William broke his arm. He's pretty banged up. I hardly recognized him, his face was so swollen. Fern got away with just bruises and a sprained wrist. She was sleeping on the back seat and rolled over onto the floor instead of going through the window."

"Rose. Oh my God. I can't believe it. Margie is dead? Sweet Margie?"

"Yes." I could barely continue. "I'm dreading telling William and Fern. The doctor said they'll be awake tomorrow."

"Poor William. Poor Fern. How will they manage without Margie?" After a moment, he asked, "Have you learned any more about the accident?"

"No. The doctor said the police will be in touch. We're going to try to get some sleep now. We want to get up early tomorrow and head back to the hospital."

"I love you, and I'm praying for William and Fern."

Chapter Twenty-Six

*I*t surprised me that I actually slept. Total exhaustion, not to mention stress and worry, sometimes prevents me from unwinding enough to sleep.

We grabbed a coffee and a muffin from the hotel restaurant and took a cab back to the hospital. We went in a different door and were able to take an elevator up to the trauma unit. At the desk, Ivy asked the nurse if Dr. Prescott was available. She said he was on rounds.

"Can we see our brother, William Bane?"

The nurse typed on her computer before looking up and saying we could. "Do you know what room he's in?"

"Yes. We were there yesterday."

We walked in and were once again blinded by the bright lights and the noises. William looked slightly better today. The bandages had been removed, except for a large one on his forehead that covered a gash. The swelling had gone down. The area around his eyes was bruised, but it was nice to see his whole face.

Ivy and I sat on opposite sides of the bed. I held his one free hand while we talked to him. I flashbacked to the memory of Ivy and I doing the same thing at our father's bedside in the hospital after his heart attack. He only woke up in time for us to say goodbye before he passed away. Hopefully the doctor was right, and William had nothing worse than a broken arm.

Dr. Prescott walked in and we stood in case he had some news for us. He didn't suggest we sit down, instead he motioned us out into the hallway. "William should be fully conscious by this afternoon. Do you want to go see Fern? She's starting to recover and is awake, though still groggy.

"Do you know if there are any wishes for your sister-in-law's remains? Burial? Cremation? And the police want to talk to you at some point. Can I tell them you'll be here for the rest of the day?"

"Yes, you can tell the police we'll be here. We want to find out what happened. Sorry, but we have no idea what Margie and William wanted in the way of burial." Ivy and I glanced at each other. "I'm thinking cremation." I thought about how they often joked about just walking out in the woods and waiting for the bears when they got old. "We'll have to wait for William to wake up before we decide."

We headed to Fern's room. I said I'd be right in. I wanted to update Jack. Though there really wasn't anything new, I needed to hear his voice.

Once again, he answered on the first ring. "Hey honey. Anything new? How are William and Fern?"

"About the same. They said Fern is waking up. We haven't seen her yet." For the first time, I almost broke down sobbing. I took a deep breath. "And we might see the police today." It occurred to me maybe William had been at fault and he'd be charged with a crime on top of everything else.

"It will be good to find out what happened. I know it doesn't change anything but..." Jack stopped talking. Maybe he had the same thought I did.

"I'll try to call later. It might be late."

"Don't worry. Call."

When I got to the room, the nurse told me Ivy was talking to the police. She directed me to the waiting room.

Ivy looked up when I walked in. "Oh good, my sister's here. Now you can tell us what happened."

The police officer stood up and shook my hand, introducing himself as Sergeant McNally. He appeared impossibly young for the job he had.

We sat down, and he pulled out a notepad. "The accident involved two vehicles and a moose. It was a terrible scene, and it took us a while to sort it all out. Apparently, your brother and family were returning late from a school event. They were heading west. Another truck was coming east. A moose ran in front of your brother's truck. Your brother must have seen it but figured it was already halfway across the road. If the other truck hadn't been coming, it would have been fine, but the moose got spooked, turned back around, and your brother hit him. It happened fast."

Sergeant McNally looked down at his notes again as if collecting himself. "The other driver swerved off the road but was not hurt. He was able to call 911." He paused. "Your brother didn't have time to react. The moose crashed through his windshield.

"Having a moose come through your windshield is not a good thing. I guess your brother was lucky it was a young moose instead of a bull moose. Those guys can weigh over a thousand pounds and with the antlers…" He stuttered to a halt. I looked at Ivy, who was giving him a death ray stare, as if to say we couldn't care less about the size of the moose.

Sergeant McNally blushed scarlet red. He cleared his throat but stopped again, as if overcome by the memory of the accident. "It was a terrible scene. Emergency vehicles arrived quickly. We got your family out of the vehicle and on to the helicopter."

He looked down at his notes again. I could tell it had been very upsetting to him. "I was very sorry to hear that your sister-in-law didn't make it." He looked up at us with teary eyes. "It wasn't anyone's fault. Just one of those things that happen. Wrong place. Wrong time."

He stood and handed each of us a card. "If you have more questions, or if your brother has any when he wakes up, contact me at this number."

Ivy and I sat, lost in our thoughts.

"A fucking moose," I said.

"Only in Alaska." Ivy shook her head in disbelief.

After Sergeant McNally left, I called Jack and told him about the accident. "No one's fault. Just one of those things."

"A moose? Seriously?" Jack asked.

"Yes. Seriously."

Chapter Twenty-Seven

We went to Fern's room. Her eyes were closed but when I said her name, they fluttered open. "Rose? Ivy? Why are you here? What's going on? I hurt all over." She moaned, looking around groggily.

"You're in the hospital, sweetie. There was an accident when you were coming home."

Her face changed. She looked frightened. "An accident?" She struggled to get up and glanced around frantically. "Where are my mom and dad?"

The nurse stepped to her side and tried to soothe her. She fiddled with the IV, maybe putting more sedative into Fern.

Ivy and I sat on either side of Fern and held her hands. It was now or never. Did we tell her? We couldn't lie and say everything was fine. I looked into her eyes. Did I want to rip the Band-Aid off or try to make it easier? Was it possible to make it easier?

Tears ran down Fern's cheeks. "Something bad happened. I know it. I can tell from the way you're looking at me."

"Do you remember anything?" I asked.

Fern shut her eyes. "We were coming home after the spelling bee." She briefly smiled and looked at us. "I won. First place." I smiled and nodded.

"We were all singing. I was tired and lay down on the back seat. Then I heard Dad yell and Mom scream and there was a crash, and I flew off the seat." She looked around. "What happened? Are Mom and Dad all right?"

I couldn't put it off any longer. "Fern. Honey. Your dad is in a room down the hall. He's banged up and has a broken arm. You'll be able to see him later today. Your mom…" I paused before continuing, "I don't know how to tell you this except straight. Your mom was killed in the accident."

An unearthly cry of grief erupted from Fern. She curled into a ball and cried and cried until she fell asleep while Ivy and I hugged and kissed her.

"That was god-awful," Ivy said as we stepped out of the room.

"Worst thing ever," I agreed.

Dr. Prescott met us in the hallway. We told him Fern was awake and that we had told her about her mother and father. He nodded grimly.

He asked us to follow him to the waiting room again. We seemed to spend a lot of time there. Once there, he suggested we sit down.

For a long moment, he stared at Ivy's painting on the wall. I almost said, "You know that's one of my sister's paintings. The famous artist Ivy Bane Berenstein is sitting right here in the room with you." I wanted to stop him from talking.

"Your brother is probably going to need some rehab, home care, basically someone to take care of him when he gets out of the hospital." We nodded. "It's my understanding that your brother and family are homesteaders, living in the wilderness." We nodded again. "If he can manage on his own, can he manage his daughter as well?" It was a good question.

It was only lunch time, and we had already been through so much. Ivy suggested we take a break and get something to eat. We'd hardly eaten since we'd arrived. We went to the cafeteria and even though I was starving, nothing appealed to me. The thought of eating anything made me nauseous. Finally, I decided on chicken noodle soup and saltine crackers. Childhood comfort food.

After eating, we returned to William's room. His eyes opened when we walked in. "What... happened?" he muttered. He closed his eyes. "I think there was a car accident?" His eyes shot open. "Where are Margie and Fern? Are they all right?" He tried to get out of bed. We pushed him gently back down.

"Yes, you're right. There was a car accident." He looked at us. He knew something was wrong. "William, Fern is fine, just bruised and banged up. But..." I could barely get the words out, "Margie was killed."

William shrieked in anguish. "What am I going to do without Margie?" He started blubbering and covered his face with his left forearm since he couldn't move his right arm.

Ivy and I hugged William and told him we loved him and we would do all that we could. The door opened and the nurse rolled Fern in. "There's someone here who wants to see you," the nurse said in a cheery voice. We were all feeling far from cheery, but it was good for Fern and William to be together. Fern climbed awkwardly onto William's bed, avoiding wires, tubes, bandages, and William's cast. They didn't speak, just held each other and cried. After a half hour, the nurse returned and helped Fern into her wheelchair. "You'll get to visit each other again tomorrow, but right now, you both need to rest and eat dinner."

We hugged Fern before they wheeled her away. She hardly acknowledged us. We waited until they brought William's dinner. The nurse said she could help but Ivy had already taken over. For dinner, he was given a small steak, peas, and mashed potatoes. The steak had not been cut up. I wondered how they expected a man with his right arm in a cast to feed himself. Ivy chopped up the steak into bite-sized bits and fed him.

William's voice broke through my haze. "Thanks. I think I've had enough to eat." Ivy patted William's mouth dry with a napkin and put the tray of food on the table.

Then we left for the hotel. I was starving again. The bowl of soup I'd had at lunchtime hadn't been very filling. Part of my brain chastised me for being hungry. How could I think of eating at a time like this? Ivy was also hungry, and we headed straight to the hotel restaurant.

The waitress handed us the menus while reciting the daily specials. She took a second look at us. Something in our faces obviously gave away the fact we hadn't had the best day. "Would you ladies like to see the drink menu?" she asked, placing it prominently on the table.

A drink. Oh, how badly I wanted a drink. To savor a glass of Merlot. I could feel the first sip sliding delectably down my throat. Just one. One wouldn't be so bad, I told myself. I needed it. I deserved it.

"I'd like—" I started, but Ivy interrupted me.

"Nothing to drink, thank you." Ivy stared at me before looking down at the menu.

If she hadn't been there, would I have slipped? Would I have "fallen off the wagon?" I remembered the AA saying, one drink is too many and a thousand are not enough. "Thank you. For a moment…"

Ivy smiled but said nothing.

After dinner, I called Jack. He picked up on the first ring. "Tell me," he said.

"Oh Jack. It's terrible. Both William and Fern woke up today, and we had to tell them Margie was dead. They brought Fern down to William's room. They were both devastated. I don't know how William will manage without Margie." I choked up and couldn't continue.

"The best plan is for them both to come home with you and stay here until William is better," Jack said.

"I was hoping you'd say that. You are the best man ever. How did I get so lucky to find you?" I paused and whispered, "I love you."

"I love you too. And I was just as lucky to find you." Jack hung up before I could tell him I'd almost had a drink. Well, truthfully, I'd thought for a moment about having a drink. Was it the same thing? We're all only one step from a fall.

Chapter Twenty-Eight

The next morning, Ivy and I got up later than usual. As much as I wanted to see Fern and William, I was exhausted by grief and worry. Despite my job, I wasn't used to saying goodbye to healthy, younger people. Most of my clients were elderly. They'd lived long lives. Which wasn't true of Margie. I was also concerned about talking to William and convincing him to live with me and Jack until he fully recovered. That didn't seem like something William would want to do. He was fiercely independent.

Walking into the hotel lobby, I saw a man stand up from a chair and start walking toward us. I gasped with sudden recognition and grabbed Ivy's hand before I ran and flung myself into Jack's arms.

"Jack, oh Jack. How did you get here so quickly? Oh my God, it's good to see you."

"After we talked yesterday morning, I decided you needed some moral support. I felt like I needed to be here. When you called last night, I was already at the airport about to catch my flight. When I told them what was going on, they got me on the first flight out. Everyone was great. I even got bumped up to first class." He grinned.

Ivy walked up, and Jack wrapped his arms around us both. We stood in his warm embrace for several moments.

"I'm just here for support. You guys need someone to take care of you. I'll be your back-up so you can focus on William and Fern. I've rented a car so I can drive you. I'll arrange meals, run errands. Whatever you need."

Both Ivy and I whispered a thousand thank-you's into Jack's ears. "This means so much," Ivy said.

Jack placed a kiss on each of our foreheads. "My first mission is to make sure you're eating, sleeping, and keeping your strength up." He handed each of us a bag. "There's a coffee and a muffin and a banana in there. If I know you both, you're not eating. You need something. The human body can't run on empty. And now, let's head to the hospital."

When we arrived, Jack said he'd hang out in the waiting room. "I don't want to get in the way of you talking with William and Fern, but," he warned us, "if you don't come back by lunch, I will hunt you down. You need fuel!"

He glanced at the painting and walked over, bending down to read the signature. I smiled at him as we left the room.

We headed to William's room first. Dr. Prescott was already there. "Ah, here are your sisters. I've already spoken to them about your condition. We are concerned about you managing in the wilderness with one arm. You'll have to come to the hospital at some point to have your cast removed. You'll need physical therapy. You have a bad break, and it's not going to be all better in a week. You need to make a plan." Dr. Prescott nodded at us before walking out.

Once again, Ivy and I took up our stations on opposite sides of William's bed. The facial swelling was down and the bruising was fading to red, light purple, and brown.

William grimaced. "Apparently my arm is badly broken. I guess I'll set off metal detectors in the airport because I've got all kinds of metal piecing my arm together. I'll be in this cast for months. My knee hurts, and so does my right ankle. I feel like I'm a hundred years old."

"You'll recover from all of that," Ivy said. "Before you know it, your cast will be off and you'll be back to normal. It will take time."

"Yeah. I guess." William laughed bitterly. "What are the chances we'd be at that exact spot at the same time as a moose and another truck? Usually, we drive hundreds of miles and never see another vehicle, let alone a moose."

It reminded me of how I felt when Lily died. All the what-ifs and wondering how it could have ended differently. I worried for years about fate and what might happen if you left your house five minutes earlier or five minutes later, could you have avoided the accident that destroyed your life? It all came down to wrong place, wrong time, as Sergeant McNally said.

William sat up straighter and took a deep breath. "As the doctor says, we have to figure out what to do. Most importantly, what to do with Fern."

We talked until noon when the nurse brought in William's lunch. It was a sandwich and chips, and he said he could manage. "I'm going to have to learn to eat left-handed for a while. Might as well start now."

Jack was waiting for us in the cafeteria. I caught him up on the latest news. "We're trying to make a plan for Fern. William thinks he'll be able to manage on his own if Fern is with us. I told him I'd be happy to be Fern's guardian, but I needed to check with you."

"Of course, we'll take her," Jack said. "William should come with us, too. He's too stubborn and too proud to ask."

"Thanks. I appreciate your support. It will be a big change for us."

"You think?" Jack laughed. "Becoming parents or guardians or whatever we will be, in our sixties is definitely a big change."

"We've had a chance to practice with Frito and we didn't do too badly."

Picking at my salad, I ate the croutons first. "William says he has a 'doomsday' plan written up already. It's at the cabin outlining what to do with the cabin and land. If he's unable to return for a while, his two neighbors will manage it for him. I'm not sure of all the details. It's a bit overwhelming."

I glanced at Ivy. I was worried she was hurt that William hadn't asked her to care for Fern. After all, she'd been a mother and raised two children. I hadn't. In the motherhood department, I was a zero.

"What do you think about the plan?" I asked tentatively.

"It's great. The best thing for all concerned. With my travels, I'm not really in the position to have Fern. Of course, I'll help all I can. But I am quite angry with William and his foolish belief that he can manage on his own with one arm. If Fern was with him, she could help, but she can't stay up here without her mom."

I was relieved that Ivy was fine with us taking Fern. I also agreed with her about the William situation. "You're right. But how can we convince him?"

"Maybe he'll listen to Fern? She won't want to come without him."

I nodded. "True. Hopefully that will work."

"Thanks for lunch, Jack. We're going upstairs to take Fern to see her father. He wants to prepare her for what might happen." Jack gave me a quick hug before turning to clear the table.

Fern was already in the room with her father. She looked grim. Her arms were crossed over her chest. She glanced up at us when we walked in the door. "Aunt Rose, can you please tell Dad he's being ridiculous. He's going to be fine. We'll both be fine, and then we can go home."

William looked at us sadly. What a terrible conversation to have with your child. Their lives had been completely turned upside down. "Fern, we all hope and pray your dad will be fine. He thinks it will be better if you come home with us for a while. Go to school in Virginia for a year," I said, sitting and patting Fern on the shoulder.

Fern objected to everything we suggested, including coming to live with us. "I don't want to live there. I want to live in our cabin and raise my dogs. I can't compete in the Iditarod from Virginia. I can't even train down there."

I tried not to be hurt by Fern saying she didn't want to live with me. I reminded myself it wasn't about me. It was about losing her mother and her father and her entire life. "It's temporary. Your dad needs time to recover. You might both have to come to Virginia for a while."

"But I can help him," Fern insisted. "He needs me 'til his arm heals."

Ivy glanced at Fern. "He does need you. He needs us." Then she gave her full oldest sister look at William. "You cannot manage on your own. How will you even open a can of soup? Come home with us until your arm is healed. It will be so much easier to see doctors in a town. To get physical therapy instead of having to drive back and forth to Fairbanks."

William's face darkened. He spoke through clenched teeth. "Who are you to tell me what to do? Oh yes. My older sisters, who tormented me when I was a child and then finally decided to find me to make amends after forty years? I've managed just fine all by myself since I left home. I don't need any advice from you two about how to manage the next forty years of my life. Fern and I will be fine."

We sat in stunned silence. The Bane family ghosts were rearing their ugly heads. Maybe the past is never quite buried or forgotten. I could tell by the set of Ivy's jaw that she was angry. Very angry. We had put our lives on hold to fly up to care for our baby brother and his daughter. We had offered our homes to them to recover in. And all William got out of it was that we were trying to boss him around like we had done when we were children.

Ivy might have launched into a tirade, but Fern started to cry and William laid back on his pillows, exhausted.

Ivy glanced at me and then stood up. "I think this is too overwhelming, considering all that happened. Hopefully, you'll think about Fern and what's best for her."

We went to the waiting room and collected Jack before heading to the hotel. We grabbed dinner and filled Jack in on William's reluctance to come home with us or even to listen to us.

"Give him a little time. I'm sure he's overwhelmed and in pain and traumatized."

Going to the front desk, Ivy booked another room for herself. Jack objected, saying he could get a rollaway cot, but Ivy said we all needed to be well rested for what was ahead. I couldn't disagree with that.

The next morning, William looked almost normal, aside from the cast and the bandage on his forehead. Jack came into the room with me. "Look who's here. Jack surprised us by flying up."

William actually smiled as he started to reach out to shake Jack's hand. He'd forgotten for a moment his right arm was in a cast. Instead, he fist bumped Jack with his left hand. "Good to see you, brother."

"Good to see you too, but I wish it wasn't in a hospital. I'm sorry about Margie. She was one in a million."

"She sure was," William agreed, his face twisting with grief. "I can't wrap my head around it. We were so happy driving home. Fern won first place. I saw the moose and thought he'd run into the woods but then the other truck came around the curve and spooked it. When it turned around, it was too late for me to do anything. I hit him and he came through the windshield. If only I'd had more time to react." He closed his eyes, probably seeing it all again. "How does everything turn to shit so fast?"

"I don't know, man. Rose and I will be there for you. Ivy too. We're family. Whatever you need. We'll take Fern while you're recovering. I hope you'll consider staying with us. Whatever you need. Don't be afraid to ask."

Dr. Prescott walked in, and I introduced him to Jack and they shook hands. He picked up William's chart. "If all continues to go well, you can probably check out tomorrow afternoon or the next morning." Dr. Prescott smiled and left.

The nurses brought Fern down, and we spent all day talking. Fern slowly began to accept the fact that her father was not going to walk out of the hospital in perfect shape. It also became apparent to William that Fern would not leave without him. That helped him decide. I was so happy Jack had come. William didn't think of him as a bossy big sister, so was more willing to listen to him.

We also talked to William about his wishes for Margie. It was a difficult conversation. I suggested cremation. "You can have an urn of her ashes at the homestead, and we can bury an urn at the family plot." He nodded and signed the papers.

After William and Fern had dinner, we returned to the hotel. Before we left, Jack reassured William once more we'd be there for him in any way he needed. "We got this, buddy. After you're discharged, we'll head up to the homestead and meet with your neighbors and make all the arrangements."

At the hotel, we enjoyed a nice meal. The only nice meal we'd had since we arrived. We went to our rooms as soon as we had finished eating. Tomorrow would be busy.

In the morning, we checked out. Jack went outside and I spotted Ivy in the lobby, finishing up a phone call. She shoved the phone in her purse as I walked up to her. "I made a call to my publicist. I told him to cancel my next two month's events."

Ivy had been scheduled for a major talk and exhibition in Chicago next week. "Oh Ivy, that sucks. I know you were looking forward to that exhibit."

"Yes, I was. However, I can hardly speak to a group of people like lah-de-dah, nothing's wrong, hope you like my paintings. This will take a while to get over." She paused. "Not that we'll ever get over it. I'm going to spend a couple of months in the studio, painting. I have some ideas for new pieces."

Jack walked in from outside. "Your chariot awaits, my ladies." He'd traded in the car he rented for something more practical to drive to the homestead. A huge four-wheel-drive SUV. Once again, I was grateful for Jack because there was no way we could have driven to William's cabin by ourselves. William couldn't drive either.

I hugged Jack. "I'm glad you came. For many reasons, among them that we don't have to hire a driver."

"Is that all I am to you, ma'am? A driver? A capable mechanic?"

"No. You are so much more." I held on to him and hugged him tighter. "You're a great comfort to me. A very great comfort and support. And the love of my life."

Chapter Twenty-Nine

The drive was long, though better than it had been the last time we visited. They had paved some of the roads and we could make it up to the homestead in a day rather than stopping halfway there.

William sat in the front with Jack. Ivy and I were in the back with Fern. She didn't say a word. William and Jack were quite chatty. Jack was telling William how much easier it would be for him to come with us until he was fully recovered.

"Pack the stuff you need for a couple of months for both of you. Your neighbors can keep an eye on everything while you're gone. You can skip the long cold winter and come back fresh and healed in the spring." William was nodding along. Seemed like he agreed with Jack's suggestion.

We got to the cabin late, but since it was summer, the sun was still up. Another reason I couldn't live in Alaska. Sun all day in the summer. No sun in the winter.

We pulled in and walked up to the front door. It was unlocked. William never locked his door. There was a note on the table from the neighbors saying they'd be over in the morning. Fern went to her room.

William's mood began to change shortly after we arrived. Memories of

Margie were everywhere in the cabin. He went into their bedroom and his face twisted in misery. "I can't sleep in there. I can't live without her." He sat on the couch, crying silently, his entire body shaking.

Jack suggested Ivy and I sleep in the bedroom. He said he'd sleep out in the living room with William. We didn't really want to sleep in Margie's bed either, but there wasn't any other option. William and Jack argued about who'd get the couch and who'd have to sleep on the floor. Ivy finally got annoyed with them. "Stop acting like children. William, take the couch. You just got out of the hospital."

That settled the matter. William took the couch and Jack slept on the floor. I fell into a deep and troubled sleep filled with dark dreams about searching for Fern and other members of the family in a huge building. The hospital, I assumed.

I woke to the sound of banging dishes and wondered why someone was in my hotel room making such a racket. I opened my eyes and stared up at a knotty pine ceiling and was completely disoriented. Did my hotel room have a wooden ceiling? Groaning, I rolled over and it came back to me in a rush. I was at William's cabin.

Ivy wasn't in bed. I heard dogs barking and voices outside. Was I the last one up? Ivy was in the kitchen making coffee. She turned when she heard me.

"Good morning sleepyhead."

"What the hell time is it? I feel like I only slept five minutes, but you can never tell what the time is when the sun is always up."

"It's early. Fern was the first one up, along with William, which must have woken Jack and when I heard him, I got up."

"Where is Jack?" I looked around the small cabin.

"Outside with William talking to the neighbors, Zac and Luke. Everyone wakes up early here."

I rubbed my head. "Probably because there's nothing else to do."

"Don't be cranky. You better get dressed. They'll probably be coming in for coffee in a minute."

Grabbing my bag, I headed to the bathroom. As I shut the door, I heard the front door open. I'd made it in the nick of time. It would have been awkward to meet the neighbors wearing my pajamas. Quickly, I scrubbed my face, brushed my teeth, and pulled on a shirt and pants before opening the door.

Two shaggy men stood in the living area as Ivy handed out mugs of coffee. They were clones of William. Lean and muscular with long hair and beards, wearing flannel shirts (it's summer, for goodness sakes!), boots and jeans.

They turned to me as I walked toward them and put their hands out to shake mine. "You must be William's sister Rose. We always hoped to meet you all when you visited, but I think the last time you were here we was guiding some hunters into the wilds."

They looked at each other and laughed. "City folk. Don't know shit about huntin', but the money's good."

I immediately forgot which one was Zac and which one was Luke. They were practically identical twins. They even wore identical plaid shirts.

"Are you twins?" I asked, which caused them to punch each other and laugh as they fended off each other's blows.

"What makes you think that?" Zac, or maybe Luke, said.

"Must be 'cause we look alike. Hell, even our own Ma can't tell us apart half the time."

We sat at the table. Zac and Luke looked serious as they sipped their coffee. "We sure was sorry to hear about Margie. She was something else."

William stared into his coffee mug. Jack, Ivy, and I nodded in response. There was really nothing to say.

"And little baby Fern. Losing her momma. Breaks our hearts."

Jack jumped in before we all started crying. "We've been outside talking. Luke and Zac are on board with taking care of things while William and Fern recover with us."

"We're gonna take some of William's dogs and sell the rest. Folks'll love gettin' one of his dogs," Zac, or possibly Luke, said.

The door flew open and Fern ran in. When she saw Zac and Luke, she ran to the table and gave them both a hug.

"Oh honey, oh honey…" they muttered as they hugged Fern. After a moment, she stepped away. I could see she was fighting tears. "We're gonna take care of the place while you and your daddy get better. Keep an eye on things and make sure it's kept up. Maybe find someone to rent it, short term. It'll all be waitin' for ya when you guys get better."

"What are you going to do with the dogs?" Fern asked. She loved the dogs. They were her team.

"Well, we can't keep 'em all. We only got so much room at our place. Can't leave 'em here. We'll keep the best of the lot and have to sell the rest."

"What about Thor?" Fern asked, looking them in the eyes.

The brothers squirmed a little. "Thor? Thor's gettin' old, honey. Might be time to…"

Fern turned her gaze to look at me. "We have to take Thor with us. I'm not leaving without him."

William finally spoke up. "You can't take Thor to live in a house in the suburbs. He wouldn't like it."

Jack and I looked at each other. Who the hell was Thor?

"If he's with me, he'll be happy," Fern responded, setting her jaw with fierce determination.

Fern and William stared at each other for a few minutes, neither willing to back down.

Finally, Jack said, "Well then, shall we go meet Thor?"

We all walked outside to the dog pens. The dogs started jumping and yapping as we approached. Not all of William's sled dogs were gigantic beasts. And they weren't all huskies. They were bred with different sled dog breeds and mostly looked like the average shaggy mutt. Though compared to Fritz and Frito, they were huge.

"Which one is Thor?" Jack asked, looking at one of the smaller dogs.

"He's down here at the end. The other dogs annoy him," Fern said.

We walked down to the last pen where a mass of black fur lay in the corner.

"Thor," Fern called out and rattled the chain-link fence.

A creature the size of a grizzly bear stood up, stretched, walked up to the fence, and licked Fern's fingers. I gasped.

Okay, Thor was not the size of a grizzly, but he was the size of a timber wolf. I think he was a wolf. Not a dog at all. He had that wolfish demeanor. I really didn't know anything about wolves or their demeanors but remembered watching a special on why wolves don't make good pets even if raised from pups. They have a wildness in their genes which doesn't go away. Thor had that wildness.

No way could that wolf—I mean dog—live in a townhouse in a small, civilized neighborhood.

Jack glanced at me before looking at Fern. "He's beautiful. What kind of dog is he?"

I could hear the doubt in Jack's voice when he said "dog." He probably also thought Thor was a wolf.

"Dad said he's a husky-malamute mix."

Zac, or Luke, snickered. "With some wolf thrown in. That's a one-of-a-kind dog."

"Wolf? Really?" Ivy's voice trembled. No doubt she was worried about bringing a wolf into our lives.

Fern gave the brothers a dirty look. "You know that's not true. Dad wouldn't keep a wolf around. Mom wouldn't let him." She turned to us. "He's a dog."

We all looked at William. He didn't say anything. I could imagine William climbing into a wolf's den and bringing Thor home, thinking, "I'll tell Margie he's an oversized husky." That was something William would do.

"How old is Thor?" Jack asked. I assumed he hoped Thor was old and feeble, despite appearances to the contrary. Zac and Luke had indicated he was past his prime.

Fern replied, "He's twelve. Same age as me. We grew up together. He's getting a bit too old to be pulling the sled, but he was dad's lead dog for almost nine years."

"Twelve?" Jack asked again. "That's old for a dog, isn't it?" He seemed more hopeful with every question.

"Yeah. A bit old, but huskies can live to fifteen." Fern replied. I did the math. He could be with us for three more years. I pictured Thor swallowing Fritz and Frito whole before going after all the neighborhood cats. And then the children.

Fern scratched Thor behind the ears. He reacted like a normal dog. "I'll bring him out so you guys can meet him."

Luckily, Fern didn't notice our combined looks of horror at the thought of the beast being released from its cage. I stifled my urge to scream.

Unlatching the pen, Fern let Thor out. He walked forward warily. He probably didn't see many strangers. Fern led him to each of us and introduced us, encouraging us to let him sniff our fingers. She then announced we could pat him on the head. I thought Ivy might faint from fright. Who am I kidding? I thought I might faint from fright.

Jack crouched down and ruffled the fur on Thor's neck. "What a magnificent dog," he said. I remembered Jack wanting a manly dog when we first went to the shelter. His eyes were glistening. They said, "This is the dog I always wanted."

"Uhhh, Jack," I said, trying to get him to see how this was not going to work. "Do you think Thor, who's used to running through the woods, would be happy in our small house and small yard? Not to mention he might not get along with Frito. Our dog, Frito. Remember him?"

But I had already lost Jack to the call of the wild.

Chapter Thirty

*A*fter breakfast, Zac and Luke left. They lived about five miles away. Ten if they came by road. They had ridden over on ATVs, which they said was the best way to get to William's since they could cut through the forest.

Ivy and I focused on packing things for William and Fern while Jack drove to the Last Outpost. When we had first visited, the sign over the Last Outpost said *The Last Outpost of Civilization*, which had seemed very appropriate, but over the years, the end of the sign had fallen off. Now it just said *The Last Outpost*. It was a combo store/post office/bar/communication center and was truly the last spot of civilization before entering the wilderness. Jack needed to make arrangements for all of us to fly to Virginia with a huge wolf dog. This trip was getting progressively more expensive and complicated, but nothing mattered other than getting our family home.

I offered to help William pack. His mood darkened again, and he yelled, "I'm not a child. I can pack for myself."

"Yes, I know you can pack your things, but since you only have one arm, I thought you could point to things you want to take and I could put them in the suitcase for you."

William didn't respond, just stormed to his room, kicking the door shut.

While I cleaned out the refrigerator of expired food, he opened doors and drawers and then slammed them shut. It didn't sound like much progress was being made.

Ivy helped Fern pack. I overheard her gently suggesting to Fern things that she didn't need to take. "I don't think you'll need your fur-lined parka in Virginia. It rarely gets below twenty degrees. Or those heavy boots..." I couldn't hear Fern's responses, just whiney and complaining sounds.

When Jack returned, he walked up and hugged me. I was at the sink washing up and putting away all the dishes. "How's it going? I think I've got all our flights worked out. We can leave the day after tomorrow. And then we'll all be home." I could tell he was trying to be positive, but he obviously sensed the tension in the air.

Stopping what I was doing, I looked at him. "It's very difficult for Fern and William to leave their home. I doubt they've completely processed Margie's death." Jack nodded. "I offered to help William pack since he basically only has one arm. He got furious and accused me of treating him like a child." The sound of a drawer slamming or being kicked echoed out of William's bedroom.

Jack glanced at the door to the bedroom. "Yes. Sounds like he's not dealing well with this." He squinted at Fern's bedroom. "Hopefully Fern's packing is going better."

"Hopefully, but it also doesn't sound like she's listening to Ivy. I hear lots of resistance. Ivy's been trying to suggest what she needs and what she can leave behind, and she doesn't want to hear it."

At lunch, we gathered in the main room of the cabin. No one was smiling. Ivy looked frazzled, Fern looked miserable, and William looked sullen. "Hope everyone's hungry. I've made soup and grilled cheese sandwiches for lunch," I said with a forced smile.

Everyone sat staring at their lunch. Neither Fern nor William spoke.

"How's the packing going?" I asked the top of Fern's head. "We can ship larger things, like your books, personal items, and knickknacks to Virginia.

They probably won't all fit in your suitcase."

Fern shrugged and continued to stare at her soup. Ivy glanced at me and rolled her eyes.

"Jack has some good news." That actually got William and Fern to look up and glance at Jack.

Jack cleared his throat nervously. The tension in the room was draining. "Yes. I was able to use the phone at the Last Outpost. We're all booked on a flight to Virginia day after tomorrow. Thor too. We'll have to leave early in the morning, so we have today and tomorrow to finish packing."

"Are you managing okay with your packing, William?" I asked. I knew I shouldn't have said anything, but sometimes I can't help myself. When he'd come out for lunch, I saw clothes thrown all over the bed and floor, but it didn't appear anything had been added to his suitcase.

William jumped to his feet, sending his chair crashing to the floor behind him. "No. I'm not. I'm not going. I've got too much to take care of here. Insurance, medical claims, getting a new truck. Stuff like that. Plus, I have to go to the hospital for this damn arm. Getting the cast off. Physical therapy. Stuff. Damn shit and stuff."

He turned to go. Fern jumped up and grabbed him, burying her head in his chest. "If you're not going, neither am I!" she declared.

William used his left arm to hold Fern, bending down to look her square in the face. "Yes. You are. You have to. I can't take care of you. I'll have enough to do managing myself." His voice caught.

Ivy stood up. "William, please be sensible. You can't stay here. The doctor said your arm could be in a cast for up to three months. Even after that, it won't be completely normal. Come home with us. You can get all your treatments in Richmond, and then you and Fern can come home after you're healed."

"No! I've made up my mind." William roared and then stormed out of the cabin. Fern ran after him, and I went after her. William jumped on his ATV and disappeared into the woods. Seemed like a dangerous thing to do with only one arm. Fern tried to follow, but I stopped her. "Leave him be. He'll come around."

"No. He won't," Fern cried. "Once he makes up his mind, he doesn't change it." She ran into her room and slammed the door. Jack, Ivy, and I stood in the living room with a sense of doom settling around us.

"And we thought the dog was going to be the hard part," Jack said.

William didn't come return that night. The next morning, we heard the sound of engines and saw Zac and Luke with William on one of their ATVs pulling up outside. They stood around for a few minutes talking and William shook his head adamantly to something one of them said. Then they came inside.

"Just in time for coffee and breakfast," Ivy said brightly, trying to smile and pretend everything was fine.

"Thanks," Zac (or Luke) muttered, and they all sat at the table. I helped Ivy pass out coffee and plates of food.

No one spoke while they ate. Finally, William pushed his plate away. He looked terrible. I could tell he was in pain. Probably driving miles one-handed on an ATV had not been a good idea. "I've talked to Zac and Luke. I am going to stay here. They're going to help. I'll be fine."

Fern started to speak, and William stared at her sternly until she sat still. "You are going to Virginia with your aunts." Fern wiggled in her seat. Her eyes filled with tears, but she didn't speak. "This is non-negotiable. I can't school you and take care of the place. Your momma wanted you to get a good education. Spend the year there and next summer you can come home."

This was such a bad idea on so many levels. Not Fern coming with us, but William staying on his own. None of us said anything. My one positive thought was that at least we didn't have to take Thor with us.

Chapter Thirty-One

*H*ope springs eternal but then dies a withering death. Fern knew she couldn't change her father's mind. She reluctantly agreed to come with us; however, she insisted that Thor come along too. I continued to think it was the worst idea ever, but Jack said, "Fern's lost her mom and now her dad. You're going to tell her she can't take her dog?"

He had me beat with that argument, but I still tried. "Thor's not going to be happy in Richmond."

"He'll be with Fern. He'll be happy."

Ivy was mum on the subject. I'm sure she also thought shipping a wolf to Virginia was a bad idea but agreed it would be too much for Fern to lose her dog along with everything else. She and Fern finally made peace over the packing. The suitcases were filled. We were able to use William's as well since he wasn't coming with us. There was also a pile of items that needed to be shipped. Zac and Luke said they'd take care of that.

The brothers came over early on the day of our departure. There were hugs and tears all around. "It'll be okay, honey. We'll keep an eye on your dad," they said to Fern.

Fern hugged William as if she would never let go. "You write me. Write me every day. Call me when you can." William hugged Fern back but made no verbal promises about keeping in touch.

———

Arriving home, we collected our luggage and Thor, who appeared to be sleeping. So much for worrying about him becoming hysterical. It had been a long flight, and Fern wanted to let him out of his cage to stretch his legs and relieve himself. Jack suggested Thor could last another half hour until we got home. Thank goodness Jack had driven his truck to the airport. He loaded Thor's crate in the back, and Fern jumped in the passenger seat.

Ivy and I found my car which I had driven to the airport... a week ago? More? I couldn't even remember how long we'd been gone. I winced when the total parking bill flashed up as we exited the garage.

We drove in silence. There was so much to say, but if we started talking, we'd start crying. It felt like it had all been a terrible nightmare that I was going to wake up from and laugh about. But it wasn't a terrible nightmare. It happened. Margie was dead. William was alone in the great wilderness. And we had a wolf.

I felt a momentary stab of guilt remembering how much I had wanted Fern to come live with me. And now she was here, but at what a terrible cost. What's that old saying—be careful what you wish for?

When I pulled into Ivy's driveway, she got out and grabbed her bag from the trunk. "Don't bother to stop. You need to get home."

"Wait!" I shouted and turned the car off, jumping out of my side, I ran around to Ivy. I hugged her fiercely. "Don't leave me. Please God, don't ever leave me. I couldn't stand it. I can't stand the thought of losing you ever."

She hugged me back and whispered, "Don't worry. I'll never leave you."

Chapter Thirty-Two

When I arrived home, I found Jack, Fern, and Thor on the first floor of the house. Frito was locked in our bedroom upstairs. I could hear him whining and scratching at the door. No doubt he could smell Thor. Fern took Thor out to relieve himself in the yard, but Jack told her to bring him in. The fence was only four feet high, and Thor could clear that height without any trouble.

Thor walked around, sniffing everything, his tail sweeping things off tables and chairs. He appeared completely baffled.

"He's never been inside a house before," Fern informed us. Great, I thought, he's not house broken either. Problem number… what number was it? I had begun to lose count.

At that point, I was too exhausted mentally, emotionally, and physically to deal with Thor. I told William I would take Fern and raise her. The question of also taking a wolf home hadn't come up.

Jack and Fern carried her suitcases upstairs, and I showed her the two spare bedrooms. One was set up as a guest room and the other I used as my office. "You can have either of these rooms. The light in the front room is nice, but the other one looks over the backyard."

Since she wasn't used to traffic noises, Fern decided the room that looked over the backyard was a better choice. "Seems more like home. The tree branches remind of the forest, and I can keep an eye on Thor when he's outside."

Jack looked around. "We'll get it set up properly when the rest of your stuff arrives. Right now, let's move the desk out and the bed in."

Moving things didn't take too long since we only had to switch the bed and desk, add a bedside table and a lamp. We ordered pizza for dinner. Fern was amazed that there were people who brought food to a person's house. "Mom had to drive twenty-five miles to go to the store. She planned like two weeks of meals when she went. If we ran out, we had to wait until the next trip. This is pretty neat to have food brought over if you don't want to cook."

We'd only cooked or gone to restaurants when William and family visited, so Fern hadn't known about food delivery.

While munching on our pizza, I decided we had to talk about Thor. Fern had taken him outside again before dinner. So far there had been no accidents, but I wasn't optimistic.

"Fern, we have to come up with a plan on how to manage your dog." Fern tensed up and stopped chewing.

She set her pizza down and looked at me. "What do you mean, Rosie?"

I paused, choosing my words carefully. "While you're home, you can take him for walks. I don't think we can just leave him in the backyard since he can probably jump the fence. He needs a collar, a leash, a name tag, a vet…" I ran out of steam when Fern's face crumpled. "And we have to introduce him to Frito. I'm sure they'll get along." I thought there was actually no way in hell that would happen. Maybe Frito could move in with Fritz and Ivy if he survived their initial encounter.

Jack jumped in. "Yes. There's a lot to do to prepare Thor for city life. We'll introduce him and Frito tomorrow. I think Thor's had enough changes for one day." We'd all had enough changes for one day.

After dinner, Fern said she wanted to go upstairs and read. She took Thor with her.

Jack and I stared at each other. "A child is one thing. A wolf is quite another," I said.

Shaking his head, Jack said, "Thor is not a wolf."

"Do you have his DNA results?"

"Do you think your brother would bring a wolf into his house with his child and wife?"

"Maybe not. But Thor might as well be a wolf. He's wild. He's used to living in the great beyond. Chasing the caribou, pulling a sled. Not living in a small house in the city. Did you catch the part about him not being used to living in a house, which means he's not even housebroken? Can you imagine the size of one of his poops?"

"I saw one earlier today. They're the size of a watermelon."

I sagged on the couch. "Can't wait to see the neighbor's reaction."

Jack came over and sat beside me. "We'll make it through this." Then he hugged me and kissed me and wiped away my tears.

Chapter Thirty-Three

The honeymoon was over. Jack and my simple life, with the two of us doing what we wanted, when we wanted, came to a crashing halt. We couldn't go out without taking Fern because we didn't feel comfortable leaving her by herself. She refused to have a babysitter. We probably couldn't have gotten one anyway because everyone was afraid of Thor. I guess we shouldn't have worried about leaving her alone with him because he could certainly scare away or devour anyone who tried to hurt her. But I was still worried she might decide to go out with him, and he'd take off or hurt someone. Our only other option was dropping Fern off at Ivy's, but Ivy wouldn't allow Thor in her house, and Fern didn't want to leave Thor alone. I didn't want to leave him alone either, for completely different reasons.

Everything was an adjustment. Fern had to adjust to the loss of her parents and moving thousands of miles to what amounted to a foreign land to her. We had to adjust to becoming parents in our sixties. Frito had to adjust to Thor and Thor had to adjust to living in suburbia.

We decided divide-and-conquer would be the best approach. Jack was in charge of Thor, and I was in charge of Fern. Thor was a physical challenge. Fern was an emotional one.

Each day we took on a "Thor issue." First on the agenda was introducing Thor and Frito. Jack and Fern worked out a plan to familiarize the dogs with each other. I bit my tongue since I knew I didn't have anything positive to say about their plan.

Fern held Thor by his collar. She couldn't have stopped him if he lunged at Frito. I don't think an army platoon could have held him back. Fern told Thor to sit, and Jack walked up slowly, holding Frito. Frito seemed incredibly eager to make friends with Thor, which shocked me. Didn't he realize what he was up against? Luckily, Thor seemed completely indifferent to Frito.

"He's been around other dogs his whole life," Fern said, stroking Thor's head. "Even puppies, so it's not like he's going to hurt Frito."

If Frito began yipping in a high-pitched sound, would he sound like a prey animal in pain to Thor? Would that arouse Thor's predator instincts? I closed my eyes. I couldn't watch.

I heard Jack murmuring to Frito and Thor in an encouraging way. Then Fern said, "Look, I knew they'd be friends."

I opened one eye and peeked. Jack squatted in front of Thor, holding Frito by his collar. Thor sniffed Frito, whose tail was wagging so hard I thought he might actually knock Jack over. Shockingly, Thor did not eat Frito, which he could have done quite easily. And that was that. From that moment on, Frito adored Thor and followed him everywhere. Thor appeared to tolerate this hero worship.

Next, we had to Thor-proof the backyard. Jack put up a six-foot privacy fence. It made our yard look so small. It was small, but now it looked tiny. Thor adjusted to his new circumstances a lot better than Fern did. Of course, he only had to adjust to a new home, not to the loss of everything he loved. As Fern said, as long as she was there, Thor was happy.

Also, despite never having lived in a house, Thor never had an accident. He never chewed or destroyed anything. He slept in bed with Fern. The minute she woke up, she'd take him out to drop one of his watermelon bombs in the backyard before coming in for breakfast.

After breakfast, Jack and Fern took Thor and Frito for a long walk the neighborhood. Fern could have walked him by herself, but Jack along to protect them from the neighbors. Our neighbors would pick up their little children or grab small dogs and cross the street when they saw Thor coming.

One morning before Fern came down, I told Jack a petition was being circulated in the neighborhood to have Thor declared a menace, a wild animal, a wolf, to have him removed permanently.

"I don't think they can do that." Jack said, sipping his coffee. He stopped, suddenly looking concerned. "Can they?"

"The scene from the Frankenstein movie comes to mind when the villagers are storming the castle trying to kill the beast," I said. "I'm imaging our neighbors grabbing their pitchforks and marching on our house."

"Lucky for us, most of them don't have pitchforks. Not too much reason to own a pitchfork in the suburbs." Jack grinned. "They'll probably attack with their Ninja blenders and Keurigs."

"It's funny but not really. People won't even talk to us anymore. Some woman I didn't recognize cornered me when I was leaving for work and started screaming about her children not being safe. And someone else said they were going to demand we have Thor DNA tested to prove he's a wolf."

"Do we have any neighborhood covenants that prohibit wolves?" Jack gave me a wicked grin.

"Jack. You have to take this seriously."

Fern walked in with Thor on their way to the backyard, so we stopped talking.

On weekends, Jack took Fern and Thor up to the mountains. They would find a deserted spot and hike deep into the woods then let Thor loose. Jack told me Thor would sniff the air and then take off running like the wind. Jack and Fern would find a comfortable place to sit and wait. Thor would pop in and out of the trees, checking back in with Fern. After an hour, he'd return, happily exhausted.

"What do you do while you're waiting? Do you talk?"

Jack's smile turned off. "No. I've tried but I'm afraid I've had no success getting Fern to talk. I try different topics, but all I get is silence or one syllable responses."

Which was also my experience with Fern. She didn't talk to me. Once I saw her on the back porch sitting with Thor. She had her arm around him, petting and stroking him while she talked to him. He'd occasionally look up and lick her cheek. I opened the screen door to see if maybe she'd let me join the conversation, but she turned and when she saw me, her face changed to a dark mask.

Where was the little girl I loved, who had loved me? Who had once told me I was her "favoritist" aunt ever? The little girl who wanted me and only me to read her a bedtime story and stay with her until she fell asleep? That child had been replaced by this sullen creature who acted as if we were the ones who'd ruined her life.

I knew she needed time to grieve. I understood that, but when Ivy and I grieved, we did so in each other's arms. Crying and comforting each other. I did not understand why Fern didn't want to be hugged and soothed, kissed and cuddled.

I showed up each night with a book asking if she'd like me to read her a story. She'd shrug and look away. I'd sit in a chair across from her. I wanted to perch on the end of her bed, but Thor took up most of the room. I wasn't going to try to move him. I'd read until I thought she'd fallen asleep. Leaving, I'd turn out the light and shut her door. Then I'd hear her whispering to Thor.

Chapter Thirty-Four

A few days after we got back, I called Lauren to fill her in on everything. She was stunned. Speechless. Lauren was never speechless. After a long silence, she croaked out, "Oh my God. I don't even know what to say. What a horrible tragedy. What a terrible loss."

"It is. When I wake up and remember what happened, I'm devastated all over again."

"How is Fern dealing with this? I can't even imagine how she feels after losing her mother and then her father sending her away. It's a double blow."

"Yes it was, and no surprise, she's not handling it well. She has become this remote, sullen child who only speaks to Thor."

"Thor?"

I took a deep breath. "Yes. Thor. The dog she insisted on bringing with us. And I use the term 'dog' very loosely. This creature is the size of a grizzly bear and looks like a full-blood wolf, though Fern claims he's a dog. You've seen our house. Can you imagine a wolf living here?"

"No. What do the neighbors think?"

"They are horrified and angry. But what could we say? Fern lost everything. How could we say she couldn't keep her dog?"

"How is Jack handling this? Becoming a father and a wolf tamer? And you? I know you always wanted children, but you're a bit old to be a first-time mother."

I laughed. "Yes, motherhood is not for the elderly, for sure! Jack has been amazing. He's taken charge of Thor and since Thor has yet to eat any of the neighbors or their pets or children, he must be doing a good job."

Pausing, I sucked in a deep breath. Exhaling slowly, I said, "I feel so guilty. A secret part of me always wanted Fern to come live with me. I thought I could offer her so much more than living in a cabin in the wilderness. Open up the world to her. And now she's here, but at what cost?"

"Rose, stop with the damn guilt! I thought you had finally gotten over blaming yourself for every bad thing that ever happened to your family. You do not control the universe. You did not cause this accident."

"I know. But it feels like it sometimes."

"Call me when you need to chat. Give Fern time. And lots of love even if she seems reluctant to receive it. She has a lot to deal with."

On Tuesday, I asked Jack if he could watch Fern and Thor. I wanted/needed to go to a meeting. I needed to talk to Gwen. I had to tell her how much I had been craving a drink, actually several drinks, over the last weeks.

Arriving early, I looked around for Gwen. She was usually the first one there, setting up, making the coffee. As soon as she saw me, she set down what she was doing, rushed over and threw her arms around me. "Oh my God. I heard what happened. How are you?"

"Not well," I murmured into her ear, hugging her back. "You don't know how badly I've been wanting a drink. I could taste it. I could feel the warmth seeping into my bones, easing my pain."

"Oh, I do know." Gwen led me over to some chairs in the corner. "I've had my slips back in the day."

"You?" I was shocked.

Gwen laughed. "You may think of me as a saint but none of us are saints. We're all just one step from the fall. Now tell me everything."

After the meeting, I felt better.

Chapter Thirty-Five

*T*wo weeks after we got home, Fern's boxes arrived from Alaska. Jack carried them up to her room, and I started to help her unpack. She looked at me with a mix of embarrassment and anger. "Please, Rose, I would like to unpack my things by myself. Okay?"

"Of course. I understand. Just let me know if you need any help." I stepped out of her room and shut the door. I didn't really understand. I thought this might be a chance for us to bond. To unwrap each item and talk about it and maybe discuss her parents, which she had refused to do up to this point.

When she came down for dinner with Thor, as always, on her heels, her face was red and splotchy, and her eyes were swollen.

Forcing a smile, I said, "Get it all done?" Fern nodded and sat down. She didn't say a word during dinner.

When I came up to say goodnight, I looked around. She had done an amazing job putting everything away. Her bed and chairs were covered with the quilts Margie had made. Her clothes were hung in the closet. Books and knickknacks were on the shelves.

The only thing still to do was hang the prints and photos. "I'll need Jack's help to hang those," she pointed to the items leaning up against the walls.

There were photos of the cabin, the woods, the dogs and another one of her and her mom. She'd propped a photo of both her parents on her bedside table.

I knew she could have hammered the nails herself, and she would have done it but she knew she had to ask permission to use Jack's tools. Over the weekend, he helped her hang everything.

Ivy continued to come for dinner every Sunday night. She didn't bring Fritz along, which made Frito sad. She still insisted Thor stay locked in Fern's room while she was there.

"You know, you're eventually going to have to bring Fritz over to meet Thor," I said.

Ivy raised an eyebrow quizzically. "Why?"

"Because if and when you get back out on the road, I'm guessing you'll want us to keep Fritz. So, the sooner they meet, the better."

Obviously, Ivy hadn't thought about that. Maybe, like me, she hoped Thor would disappear. "Let's not worry about Fritz and Thor right now. We have more pressing concerns." She was right. Fern was our main concern. Ivy was saddened by Fern's sulkiness but had no doubt endured similar episodes with her children during their pre-teen and possibly teen years. But she knew we were having a hard time.

Luckily for her, she was distracted by her current work. When we returned from Alaska, she threw herself into painting, cancelling all her engagements. The shows went on, but she wasn't there, much to the disappointment of her fans. A sign at the shows simply said, "Ivy Bane Berenstein has been struck by her muse and is busy creating new work."

A month after we returned, a box arrived from Alaska. I was mystified at first until I saw the return address and then my heart sank. It had been sent by the funeral home. This box contained the urn with Margie's cremated remains. How would Fern react? I thought it might have been nice for William to send a note, to give us a head's up. Fern wrote letters to her father almost every day. So far, she'd received one short note from him saying everything was fine. No details, just everything's fine.

I put the box in a closet until I could talk to Jack. We decided to ˑ Sunday dinner with Ivy to tell Fern about the arrival of the urn. I plannˑ on getting a headstone for Margie for the family plot. I hadn't been to the cemetery to visit since we'd returned. A foolish part of me felt bad. I hadn't gone to tell Mom what happened. Surely, she already knew Margie was dead. If there was a heaven or a better place, Margie would already be there with the rest of the family.

It occurred to me Fern had never visited the family plot. Not really the thing to do with a young child on a family trip.

Before Sunday dinner, Ivy, Jack, and I debated what to tell Fern. Should we go to the family plot first? Should we let her see the headstones of the other family members? Should we involve her in the choice of the stone for her parents? Jack and I agreed to let Ivy take the lead on this. Since she wasn't around all the time, Fern seemed less angry with her.

Ivy decided the best thing to do was visit the cemetery with Fern and talk about our family buried there. She broached the subject at dinner. "Fern, you know about our baby sister Lily, who died when we were children."

Fern nodded, though she didn't seem particularly interested. Ivy gamely plowed ahead. "When she died, my parents bought a plot at a cemetery for her grave. I guess they decided to get a family plot so we could all be together in death, if not in life." Fern looked baffled by this. No doubt, she, like her parents, held the opinion burying people was foolish and they should be left to nature to sort out at the end of their days.

"So," Ivy forged ahead, "we want to add a headstone at the cemetery for your mother." Fern's lip trembled. Ivy had decided not to mention receiving the urn until after Fern visited the graves and understood what we were talking about.

The next Saturday, Ivy, Fern, and I headed to the graveyard Fern had wanted to take Thor, but we said it wasn't the sort of place a dog would enjoy or be welcome. I could only imagine one of his bombs being unloaded on someone's grave.

At the family plot, we sat on the bench, and I told her about everyone there. "As Ivy said, when Lily died, our dad decided we should buy a plot for the whole family."

Fern finally reacted to this idea and screwed up her face in disgust. "That's gross."

"No, it's not Fern. Dying is a part of life. We all die. It was nice Dad wanted us to be together forever. Even though Dad and Mom got divorced, now they're back together. Ivy's husband Terry is here, and one day Ivy will join him. There are two spots left. One for your dad and mom and the last for me and Jack." There was a time I thought I'd end up alone under my tombstone. Thank God for Jack. For saving me from loneliness in this life and in the next.

Tears rolled silently down Fern's cheeks. Ivy started crying, too. We hugged Fern between us. "So, we wondered if you might like to pick out a headstone for your parents. And decide on the inscription for your mom."

Fern nodded. "I'd like that."

Chapter Thirty-Six

The summer was quickly coming to an end. Fern needed to be enrolled in school, but I had no idea where she'd attend. I called the school office and they told me they'd need her records from Alaska.

"She's never been in a school before," I said.

All I heard was silence on the other end of the phone, before a rude voice asked, "Come again? How old is she?"

"Twelve. Her mother said she'd be going into seventh grade."

"Based on?" This woman began to really annoy me.

"Based on the curriculum her mother used. They lived in a cabin in Alaska, and her mother homeschooled her. She is a very bright child. I'm sure she'll be able to keep up."

We went round and round, the woman sounding more incredulous with each passing moment. I knew people homeschooled in Virginia, so I didn't understand why she acted like Fern had dropped in from outer space. Finally, she said she'd have to talk to someone and call me back.

The next day, I got a phone call from a pleasant and helpful woman. I explained the circumstances of Fern's arrival in Virginia.

"Oh, the poor thing. How awful. We'll try to make her transition as easy as possible." She explained Fern would have to take aptitude tests in several subjects to see about grade placement.

The day I took Fern to take the tests, she acted more miserable and moody than usual. She dragged all the way to the school and almost bolted when we got to the front door.

"Fern, you're just taking a test. I know you've done that before. There's nothing to worry about."

Suddenly Fern's face twisted into a knot of anguish, and a howl erupted from her lips. "Yes, I've done that before! I've taken many tests. I took them with my mom, at my house, with my dad there." She collapsed on the sidewalk, sobbing. "I want to go home. I want my mom."

I sat next to her and pulled her closer, trying to comfort her. Her body stiffened, resisting my touch at first until she fell against me, finally unleashing the agony of grief she'd been bottling up. It was a breakthrough.

We walked home together, and I called to reschedule the tests for next week. We all went to the mountains for the weekend to let Thor run. Fern walked next to me and when we stopped for a break, she sat by me and leaned her head on my shoulder. I kissed the top of her head and smiled at Jack, who gave me a big grin.

Fern did extremely well on her tests and was admitted to seventh grade. Originally, I hoped she and Little Ivy would be together. However, Cate and her family moved up to Northern Virginia. Fern would have to brave school on her own.

The week before, we went shopping. I had gotten a list of all the notebooks, pens, pencils, and other paraphernalia required for seventh grade. Ivy came along and treated us to lunch. Fern continued to be amazed by the variety of restaurants in our area.

"Now, young lady, we need to take you for the very best part of back-to-school shopping: clothes." Ivy loved clothes and loved to shop for clothes. "I couldn't wait to pick out my new outfits. I'd try them all on and look at myself in the mirror, deciding which one to wear on the first day. Something that was sure to get me noticed." Ivy smiled at the memory of waltzing in on the first day, turning the heads of all the boys and angering all the girls.

I piped up. "A note of caution here, Fern. Ivy cared a lot about clothes—however, she didn't pay much attention to her studies."

Ivy gave me a withering look. "Despite that, I didn't do too badly for myself. Let's head over to the new outdoor mall. I've been told it's where all the young girls shop."

Fern didn't seem quite as enthusiastic as Ivy, but she dutifully followed us to the car. At the mall, she went from store to store, watching Ivy pick outfit after outfit. Ivy extolled the virtues of each one as she held them up to Fern. "The color of this blouse will bring out your eyes."

Fern had her mother's fair coloring and light reddish-brown hair, which contrasted to the rest of us with our dark brown hair. Ivy's gorgeous mahogany mane, mine a dull muddy brown with some gray appearing at my temples.

Ivy continued showing off various outfits. "This fabric is so soft. Very stylish, don't you think?" The sales ladies agreed with Ivy, rushing off to find similar clothing.

The sales lady took Fern to the changing room while Ivy and I waited. I was stunned at the volume of clothing. "Twenty outfits? Didn't we usually get three?"

"It's not like we're going to buy them all. Just the ones she likes best. Plus, we always had clothes from previous years. Fern has nothing except flannel and fur."

Fern came out and showed us each outfit as the sales lady exclaimed how absolutely darling she looked. I could see Fern wince. Ivy told Fern she could get her favorites. Fern stared at the pile of clothes. "I don't really need anything. I brought my clothes from Alaska…"

Ivy winced at the memory of Fern's Alaska clothes. "Of course, I know you have clothes already, but it's always fun to get something new. Makes you feel powerful on your first day." Ivy smiled.

Trying to be helpful and supportive, I chimed in, "Even I, who was not quite the fashionista Ivy was, enjoyed having a new outfit to wear on the first day of school." It didn't appear to help.

Ivy seemed completely oblivious to the fact Fern didn't want any new clothes. Walking to the pile, Ivy picked up two blouses, five t-shirts, a sweater, a hoodie, two pairs of leggings, and two pairs of jeans. "I liked you in these the most. Which ones did you like?"

Smiling slightly because she didn't want to hurt Ivy's feelings, Fern nodded. "Yeah. Those were my favorites too." Ivy paid for everything and we left.

"Now for shoe shopping," Ivy announced, and Fern's shoulders sagged.

Chapter Thirty-Seven

*T*he night before the first day, I don't know who was more nervous, me or Fern. We went through her new clothes and picked out one of the t-shirts and paired it with the leggings, the jeans, and then tried on the other t-shirts. Fern turned and looked at herself in the mirror. Obviously, she didn't like what she saw.

"Honey, you'll look great in anything. Don't overthink it." I tried to smile, hoping it didn't look like a grimace. I wasn't worried about the clothes, I worried about her fitting into this new experience.

"Now, get your pajamas on. It's time for bed. You have to get a good night's sleep so you'll be bright-eyed and bushy-tailed for tomorrow." Wow, those words came out of the distant past. Our mom used to say those words to us every night, before she became depressed and remote. I gave Fern a quick hug and a kiss and tucked her in.

Turning out the light, I closed the door. I heard Thor jump up on the bed. It would be a new experience for him as well. A day without Fern. I walked downstairs and plopped on the couch next to Jack. He turned and smiled. "Everything okay?"

"I don't know," I said, overcome by dread and foreboding. "This is not going to be easy for Fern. She's not a bubbly, outgoing kid. She's not used to being in a noisy building with hundreds of other kids. I'm afraid she'll be lost in the tide of humanity. I hope no one is mean to her."

"It'll be fine. She's tough. I'm sure she's faced bigger challenges."

"This is not the same thing as wrestling bears and training sled dogs." I tried to keep my tone neutral.

Men are so naïve, I thought. They don't understand the social pecking order of middle school. I remembered Cate saying the mean girls would eat Fern alive. She was referring to boarding school, but it was probably equally true here. When I worked as a therapist, some of my clients talked about things that had happened to them in school which they never recovered from. There was no way Fern would fit in. She had nothing in common with these kids. She didn't watch movies or TV. She knew nothing about social media. Or music. Maybe I should just let her stay at home until she went back home.

The next morning, I got up early. Knocking on Fern's door, I said, "Time to get up. First day. So exciting." I hoped I sounded enthusiastic.

Fern came down the stairs and took Thor out for his morning watermelon dump. He stayed with me while she went back up to get dressed. I made breakfast and packed Fern's lunch. Since she'd never eaten a meal in a cafeteria, I'd let her check it out first before trying a meal there. I remembered the food being awful, though it could have improved.

A few minutes later, she clumped down the stairs. Why did her new sneakers sound so clunky? Weren't you supposed to be able to silently sneak up on people? Hence the name.

When Fern came into the kitchen, I was stunned by her appearance. I tried to cover my surprise, but I don't think I managed it very well. Instead of the trendy t-shirt, jeans, and brand-name sneakers, Fern wore a pair of her old overalls, covered with an enormous worn-out flannel shirt which must have belonged to William. Instead of her sneakers, she wore her work boots, which appeared to be beat up old army combat boots.

"Oh," I squeaked out. "I thought you were wearing the light blue t-shirt with your new jeans."

Fern slumped in her chair and started shoveling cereal into her mouth. "I don't like those clothes. I like my clothes."

"I understand, honey, but you know what they say—when in Rome do what the Romans do." I cringed at my own words.

"What?" Fern screwed up her face and looked at me as if I'd lost my mind.

"Your clothes were perfect for Alaska. Alaska weather and the woods and outdoor things. Here, you might want to blend in with the rest of the kids. Don't you think?"

"No." Fern glowered at me. "Why do I have to go? to school? I'll be going home to Alaska. Until then, I can read and do workbooks. No big deal."

"You might be surprised." My fake smile hurt my face. "You might enjoy it. After all, you like learning. And your dad wanted you to go to school. I don't want to disappoint him. Do you?" Wow. What a low blow. I should have been ashamed of myself.

Fern didn't answer. Jack walked in and glanced at Fern, taking in her outfit before looking at me with a questioning look. I shook my head, saying nothing and indicating he shouldn't say anything either.

"Time to head to the bus stop," I said, with what I hoped was an eager, upbeat tone.

Jack leaned down and kissed Fern on the top of the head. "Don't worry about Thor. I'll take good care of him today." In truth, after all my fears about living with a wolf-dog, he turned out to be fairly easy to manage. He just ate and pooped and slept most of the rest of the day. He'd no doubt miss Fern, though.

A tear slipped down Fern's cheek as she knelt and hugged her dog long and hard. I carried her lunch bag as we walked to the corner. There were three other kids at the stop, a boy and two girls all around Fern's age. They stared at Fern. Not surprisingly, the girls were dressed in t-shirts and jeans and cute sneakers. Even the boy dressed in what appeared to be a brand-new t-shirt and jeans. None of their parents were there. I hoped to make small talk with another adult while I waited.

I could feel Fern fidgeting next to me. She realized I was the only parent who'd walked their child to the bus stop as if she was six instead of twelve. "I guess this is the right spot to catch the bus. See you later." I wanted to bend down and hug Fern and tell her not to worry. Fortunately, I stopped myself. I handed over the lunch bag, turned, and walked away.

When I got to the house, I slipped behind a tree and peered down the block. The other three kids were chatting happily with each other. Fern stood about five feet away, staring at her feet. A moment later, the bus pulled up to the corner and they all climbed on board. Fern got in last. I breathed a sigh of relief, fearing at the last moment she wouldn't get on.

Jack and the dogs were in the kitchen finishing breakfast. He looked at me. "What the hell was Fern wearing? Didn't Ivy buy her a whole new wardrobe?"

I slumped against the counter and picked up my coffee cup. "She did. And Fern picked out an outfit last night. I guess she wanted to wear something familiar."

"She probably wanted to feel closer to her parents."

I sighed. "Can you imagine how the other kids are going to react when Paulette Bunyan walks into their midst? I could see the look of horror on the faces of the three kids at her bus stop."

Jack took the dogs out for their morning walk while I cleaned the kitchen and tried not to worry about Fern.

I don't know how I survived until the afternoon. I half expected to get a call saying Fern was sitting in the hallway, refusing to go to class. Standing by the window, I watched for the bus. Finally, I heard the creak and squeal of the brakes and the engine rev up again as it continued down the street. I saw Fern walking toward the house, and I ran to the kitchen so she wouldn't know I'd been spying on her.

The front door opened and slammed. I called out, "Hey, Fern. Come into the kitchen. I'll make you a snack." She didn't respond. Her boots pounded heavily up the stairs, then her bedroom door slammed.

As hard as it was, I forced myself not to follow her.

Jack got home around 5:00. He walked in the back door and gave me a hug and a kiss. He looked around for Fern. Raising an eyebrow, he mouthed, "Where is she?"

"In her room. She's been there since she got home. Ran up the stairs and slammed her door. I haven't seen her or spoken to her."

Jack grimaced. "Doesn't sound like it went well."

Chapter Thirty-Eight

Fern finally came down in time for dinner, with Thor following her. He probably needed to go out, which might be the only reason she came down. She'd changed out of her overalls and had her pajamas on. She walked outside and clomped in as I pulled dinner out of the oven and set it on the counter. It amazed me how much noise she could make since she was quite petite. Pretending I didn't notice her glum mood, I asked her to help me carry dinner to the table.

We sat down. The silence was oppressive. Fern hunched over her plate with her arms on the table. Before I could stop, I heard myself say in my mother's voice, "Elbows off the table."

Fern jumped up, almost knocking her chair over. She started for the stairs and this time Jack stood up and said, "Come to the table. Now."

Thor followed Fern from the table and even he stopped and turned at the sound of Jack's deep voice. Fern hesitated, probably considering how far she could push Jack. I was a pushover. She already knew that.

She stomped to the table and flopped down. "Sit up straight." Jack said. I could tell he was furious. "Your aunt made us all a great dinner and you need to appreciate her hard work."

Fern still hunched over her food, but she made an effort to keep her arms off the table.

"How was your first day?" I asked, fearing the worst, but I wanted her to know I was interested and cared. "Do you like your teachers? Are your classes interesting?"

Shrugging, she said, "Yeah. They're fine."

Jack joined in. "I guess it's different being in a classroom with other kids compared to being by yourself. Did you find it hard to concentrate?" Jack was trying to be nice. "I remember my first day of middle school. Having to change classes every hour was confusing."

Fern nodded. "Yeah. The noise in the hallways scared me." She sat quietly before adding, "And all the kids, pushing and shoving. I didn't like it."

Jack continued, "I bet. You're not used to being around so many kids. But you'll get used to it."

I smiled with what I hoped was an encouraging look. "The first day is always the hardest. Did you check out the cafeteria food? How did it look? I remember it being kind of gross."

Fern pulled a paper out from the pocket of her pajamas. "Here's the monthly menu. Some days don't look bad. They have pizza."

"Pizza. Sounds good. Let me know which days you want to eat in the cafeteria."

We chatted a bit more and then Fern excused herself and went up to her room. Jack went to the living room, and I called Ivy.

"How did it go?" Ivy asked. "Which outfit did she wear?"

I hesitated. "Truth is, she wore her old overalls, one of William's flannel shirts, and her boots."

"What?" Ivy almost shouted. "Why?"

Why indeed. Why do kids do the things they do? I never worked with kids as a therapist. They were a complete mystery to me. Even Ivy's kids, Alex and Cate, baffled me until Terry came along. My childhood was hardly normal, and I couldn't relate to children.

I walked to the kitchen. "Maybe she thought she was honoring her mom and dad. Honoring her roots. Taking a stand."

Ivy snorted. "That is seriously the worst thing for her to do. To separate herself from the herd on the first day. Preteens pretend they're on the cusp of adulthood and independent, but they are the most conformist group on earth. It gets better by high school, but at her age, everyone has to adhere to the unspoken rules, which includes what to wear, what to say and how to act." She spoke with the authority of a parent who'd been there. "Don't you remember? Even for us in the dark ages that's the way it was."

What I remembered was Ivy and my middle school experiences were light years apart. "What do I do now? I already made my first mistake by walking her to the bus stop. Like she was six." I winced at the memory. "You should have seen the looks on the other kids' faces when she walked up dressed in those clothes. I imagine it only got worse through the day."

"You need to go up there and talk to her and explain you understand how hard this is and how she wants to honor her past, but for now, she needs to fit in. Slide in softly. Not be making bold statements."

"I'll try. All the progress we made this summer is gone and she's back to being sullen. I'm beginning to think private school might be the answer. At least they wear uniforms there. Though apparently they're wearing uniforms here too, it's just far more subtle, and it's determined by the kids, not the adults."

Hanging up, I walked out to the living room. Jack glanced up at me. "What now?"

"I'm going to try and talk to her."

"Good luck."

I knocked on Fern's door. I heard a muffled, "Come in." All the lights were off. Fern and Thor were in the dark.

"Hey honey, mind if I turn on a light?" I heard a muffled response, which I decided was a yes. I turned on the lamp next to Fern's bed rather than the bright overhead light. Fern was curled up against Thor with her back to me.

"I wanted to check to see if you're okay."

A sob escaped from Fern. "Why would you think I'm not okay? Just because today was almost the worst day of my life."

I sat on the edge of the bed and put my hand on Fern's shoulder. "I know it was hard. Still, it will be easier if you try to fit in instead of standing out. I talked to Aunt Ivy, and she confirmed seventh grade is all about fitting in."

"I'm never going to fit in. The girls are… I don't even know how to describe them. They look so sophisticated. They wear make-up!" Fern said this with such outraged horror as if they were all wearing sexy lingerie.

"They're practicing for high school. Figuring out the look that will make them popular."

"Did you do that?" Fern turned over and sat up, looking at me.

Thinking about my own dreaded middle school days. I shuddered, recollecting my goth looks and gloominess. "No. I was a failure at your age. And high school. Since I followed Ivy, I remained a failure all through school. She was pretty and popular, which were the only important things. I decided not to even try." Pausing, I remembered some of the weird things I did. "I actually considered dropping out and becoming a nun."

Fern sat up straighter. "What? A nun? Why? Were you super religious? I never got the feeling from Dad that you guys were raised that way."

"No, we weren't, though we did have a terrible mean grandmother who was kind of super religious. She was the worst kind of religious. She didn't believe in a religion of love but in one of punishment. She liked to talk about hell more than heaven." A shiver went down my spine thinking about Meemee.

"So, why did you want to be a nun?"

How much of this did I want to get into with Fern? I had some pretty messed up thoughts when I was a kid, complicated by guilt that I let my little sister drown and anger at my mom for accusing me of not watching her. Which was not exactly true, I mean the bit about my mom accusing me. It was convoluted.

"We told you about our little sister Lily, who died when we were kids. I blamed myself for her drowning. Ashamed that I'd let it happen. I decided I should spend the rest of my life locked in a convent repenting." Fern looked at me with shock and awe. "But I figured out I didn't really want to do that when I found out nuns don't eat pizza!" I was joking about the pizza, since it was discovering wine which made me decide not to join a convent, but I didn't need to share that with Fern.

Fern laughed, and I reached over and tickled her. "This year will be over before you know it. Your parents would want you to enjoy school. Especially your mom. She wanted you to be a lawyer or a doctor or an astronaut! Do your very, very best to honor her and her dreams for you. You might even discover dreams of your own."

Fern buried her face in my neck and hugged me. "Thank you, Rosie."

The next morning, Fern came down to breakfast wearing the outfit we originally picked out. After she let Thor out the back door, she wolfed down her breakfast.

"I need twenty bucks to put into the cafeteria account. They can charge me if I get lunch there instead of having to take money every day. Also, if I forget my lunch, I'll still be able to eat."

I grabbed my purse and handed over twenty dollars. I was sending off a completely different child this morning. Maybe I did know how to deal with sulky, moody pre-teens.

Fern grabbed her lunch and headed out the door. I snuck out a few moments afterwards and positioned myself by the tree to see how the bus stop went today. Fern walked up to the other kids, and I could see she greeted them. The two girls smiled and started talking to her. It was going to be fine.

142

Chapter Thirty-Nine

$\mathcal{T}$hings improved. Fern seemed to be adjusting. Her first quarter report card was full of As and praise from her teachers. I beamed as if I could take credit for any of it. Truth was, I'd finally gotten back to work and was often gone. Sometimes, I came home late to find Jack and Fern had eaten dinner and many times Fern was already in bed.

Both Jack and I assumed she did all her homework and the report card confirmed that. Margie had been right about Fern being smart and capable of doing anything in life.

When the weather got cold, Fern dragged out her Alaska clothing. She had one of those trapper-style hats with floppy side panels. It looked like it was lined with some kind of fur, which appeared to have been gnawed on by rats. It had seen better days. She also had a coat that looked like one of those things old mountain men wore. I based that on my extensive viewing of mountain man movies.

I remembered Ivy specifically telling her not to bring her sub-zero clothes to Virginia, since the weather rarely got that cold. As often happens in Virginia, the weather had been mild through winter break and turned miserable in January. On the first really cold day of the year, Fern came down in her mountain man clothes.

When she got ready to walk out the door, I bit my tongue so I didn't scream, "What the hell are you wearing? No, no, no! Don't slip backwards." Instead, I calmly said, "That coat seems a little large on you. It's probably not Alaska cold outside. Do you think you need such a warm coat and hat?"

"Yeah. I've been waiting to wear these down here, but it's been way too warm."

It will be okay, I told myself. She's already been accepted by the kids. They'll just laugh it off. I couldn't help thinking all she needed was an old- time musket and burlap satchel to complete the look.

When Fern got home, I was waiting. The door opened and slammed, and Fern ran up the stairs to her room. That door slammed as well. Maybe the mountain man look hadn't been a hit. I wasn't too concerned. A little teasing was part of growing up.

It surprised me when Fern came bouncing back down the steps for dinner with a big grin on her face.

"How was school today?" I asked passing around the food.

"Great. I found out there's going to be this assembly called 'My Dream Job' where you get to dress up and talk about what you want to be when you grow up. The kids were kidding me about my clothes today, and I told them I was trying out my outfit for the assembly. That got them all laughing and asking if I wanted to be a fur trapper and I said, 'No, I want to win the Iditarod dogsled race.' Do you know they've never even heard of it? I said, like the movie *Balto* where he leads the other sled dogs through the ice and snow? That got them all interested."

It didn't surprise me that middle-schoolers in Virginia hadn't heard about dog sled racing. Jack gave me a thumbs up and a nod when Fern looked down at her plate.

"So," Fern continued, "I need you to come to talk to my teachers to get permission for me to bring Thor for my presentation. They need to see a real sled dog. I'm going to bring some of my other stuff along too."

"Do you think Thor will like going to school?" I asked doubtfully. I didn't want to dampen her enthusiasm, though I worried about him becoming provoked by squealing girls and slaughtering the entire seventh grade.

Jack jumped in. He had a huge grin on his face. "That will be fantastic. Those kids will be awed by Thor." He glanced at me and noticed my look. "I'll go first thing tomorrow and talk to the teachers. I'll also go the night of the assembly and make sure all goes smoothly. Thor is just a big puppy. He'll be fine."

I gladly turned the whole affair over to Jack. True to his word, he went early the next day. At first, they were reluctant, but Jack's enthusiasm won the day. For the next month, he and Fern worked on a facsimile of a sled.

The night of the assembly, Jack and Fern left early with Thor to get set up. I picked up Ivy and we headed to the school. Ivy, at least, was in my corner. She thought it was a bad idea. She'd never warmed to Thor.

"Thank God Jack will be there," I said as we parked. "I'm sure he'll keep Thor under control."

"We can only hope," Ivy replied doubtfully.

Fern and Thor were an unqualified success. Fern walked out on the stage with her dog. She didn't even have him on a leash. He wore some kind of leather harness. Jack carried the sled out and set it down by Fern. Fern explained the harness and how many dogs were needed to pull the sled. Pointing at Thor, she described the important role of the lead dog.

She followed this with a slide presentation showing the map of the 1,000-mile race route. Fern described legs and distances and how many days it took to complete each part. She talked about the women who'd competed, including the first woman to win, Libby Riddles who braved a blizzard and Susan Butcher who won four times. Dramatically, she explained this was not a race for the inexperienced, adding many mushers die while competing. The audience gasped.

Thor appeared to realize he represented all the sled dogs of the world. He stood up on the stage proud and powerful, looking every inch the hero. After the assembly, kids came up to Fern and Thor and asked nervously if they could pet him. Fern allowed one at a time to come up. "Let him sniff your hand and then you can pat him on the head. Sled dogs are not pets, so he's not really used to all this attention."

Several of the kids asked if Thor was a dog or a wolf. Fern didn't answer directly but managed to imply he might be at least part wolf.

The assembly made Fern the star of seventh grade. Fern discovered she didn't need beauty or the right clothes to fit in. And the kids discovered heroes didn't need a bow and arrow or a wand. They just needed to be fierce. Fierce as a wolf dog. Fierce enough to conquer the wilds of middle school.

Chapter Forty

School continued to go well for Fern. Unfortunately, the lack of communication from her father broke her heart. She wrote him every week. William sent short notes once a month. They rarely contained any news.

He did tell us when his cast was removed. After settling with the insurance company, he purchased a new truck. Now he could drive himself to the doctor's and to physical therapy. He said he was working hard to get his arm functioning normally again. Reading between the lines, I could sense his frustration his arm wasn't perfect after the cast came off. He didn't come out and say it, but I got the feeling he was in a lot of pain.

I continued trying to connect with him. As Thanksgiving approached, I sent him an invitation. "We are planning on having a memorial service for Margie since the whole family will be here." I also added a note not to worry about the cost of the plane ticket. "We'll all be happy to pitch in. Fern would be thrilled to see you."

After visiting the cemetery with Fern, we went to a local funeral home and looked through books of headstones. We also walked around the cemetery to see what style might appeal to her. She finally picked out a stone that looked like a boulder that had crashed down a mountainside. It was smooth in the front where the names and dates could be added, but the rest was rough-hewn stone.

"It reminds me of the rocks at home," she said. "Nothing fancy. No flowers or frills."

"What about an inscription?" I asked. "Do you want to add something about your mom?"

Ivy suggested all kinds of poems about mothers she found online. Some were so long there'd be no room to add William's name to the stone when the time came. She read out the list to Fern. "These are some of my favorites," she smiled. They mostly included things about stars and hearts and hugs and kisses and being BFFs with your mom.

"Your mother is your best friend and your first friend."
"My mother was my role model before I even knew what the word meant."
"A mother's hug lasts long after she lets go."
"Mother – the most beautiful word on our lips."

"Thanks Ivy," Fern said, taking the papers.

When we ordered the stone, Fern wanted to add, "My mom, the best mom ever," under Margie's name.

Ivy didn't think it was enough and almost said so, but I gave her a look and she just said, "Beautiful, Fern. Simple and heartfelt."

Despite knowing our plans for Margie's memorial, I didn't hear from William. I assumed he had decided not to come. He probably didn't have the money for a ticket. Maybe he was embarrassed to ask Ivy. I remember him getting mad at us, accusing us of treating him like a child.

I finally received a scribbled note the day before Thanksgiving. "Thanks for the invite. Too much going on." I shared the news with Fern, who was obviously devastated though she tried to hide it. She was always making excuses for her dad. "Poor dad. It's so hard on him trying to get his arm better. Even writing is hard."

Fortunately, the arrival of the rest of the family distracted her. She always enjoyed hanging out with her cousins, who she hadn't seen much of since they moved to Northern Virginia.

Her favorite cousin, Little Ivy, informed us that she had changed her name to Livy and would appreciate that we all call her that. "OMG, I couldn't handle middle school being called Little Ivy like I was two years old." Fern and Livy ran upstairs.

The day after Thanksgiving, we went to the cemetery to unveil the headstone. Fern carried the urn with Margie's ashes. Everyone loved the memorial stone, saying it was perfect for Margie and William. Fern beamed.

A small hole had been dug in front of Margie's headstone. Someone from the cemetery arrived to officiate. Fern read a poem she selected. Then we sang one of Margie's favorite songs, "To Every Season." Fern walked up and placed the urn inside the hole. We walked by in single file, touching the headstone and dropping flowers. It was simple and beautiful, just like Margie.

After the ceremony, we returned to Ivy's to enjoy Thanksgiving leftovers. As I munched my enormous turkey sandwich, I looked around the room at everyone's smiling faces. What was William doing today? What was he eating? I couldn't decide if I was angry or sad.

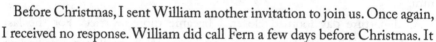

Before Christmas, I sent William another invitation to join us. Once again, I received no response. William did call Fern a few days before Christmas. It was a quick call, which he blamed on the poor phone service. No card or gift or any other communication arrived for Fern from Alaska.

When picture day arrived, Fern insisted on wearing William's old flannel shirt. "I'll send him the pictures with me in his shirt. He'll love it." I made sure the shirt was clean and ironed, which was the best I could do. She framed one of the pictures, and after packing it carefully, sent it to her dad. We received no word from William.

Fern's thirteenth birthday came and went without any note from her dad. If I could, I'd have picked up the phone and yelled at William about missing this important date in his daughter's life. However, he was incommunicado and beyond my desire to rage at him. We threw her a big party to make up for her dad's lack of attention. I learned she'd never had a birthday party before. Or at least not one with lots of kids, pizza, and cake at the local bowling alley.

As the year wound down, Fern talked constantly about going home to Alaska. William, in the few notes we exchanged, didn't mention anything about her coming back. I worried he'd changed his mind. If I'd actually been able to talk to him, I'd have suggested Fern spend the summer with him but return to our house for the next school year. She enjoyed being here and had a lot of friends. I couldn't imagine her continuing her education by herself in a cabin with no one except her father to hang out with.

The last day of school was June fourteenth. We picked July eighth to fly to Alaska, which gave Fern time to finish the seventh grade and have a goodbye party with her friends. We also wanted her to see a real Fourth of July celebration. She had never seen a fireworks display.

We convinced her we shouldn't take Thor with us. "Let's see how things are going at the cabin. See how your dad is doing. Get you settled. We'll send him up later." I could tell Fern wasn't a hundred percent happy leaving him behind, but she realized it would be easier and quicker to get home without him.

As departure day loomed closer, I became more worried. For the last months, there'd been little communication from William. Because he had no computer, and no email, I'd sent him a note listing our travel plans and when we'd arrive. I received no response. I finally sent a note to Zac and Luke and asked them if they could go to the Outpost and call us so we could be sure William was prepared for us to bring Fern home.

I told Fern to pack only what she'd need for a few weeks. We could ship the rest afterwards. Luckily, one of the new young mechanics at Jack's garage happily agreed to stay at the house and watch the dogs. He said he loved dogs, even enormous wolf dogs, and was happy to dog sit.

Two days before we left, Zac called. I knew it was Zac because he identified himself as such. The line wasn't very good, and the news wasn't very good either. Basically, through the crackling wires, I gathered William was struggling. "He often disappears for days at a time. Don't tell us when and where he's goin'. But we stuck a note to the door to remind him you're coming. We're looking forward to seeing you guys. Havin' Fern home is just what William needs." Thanking them, I ended the call. What the hell was going on with William?

I shared my concerns with Jack. "William has never said he wants Fern to come back. He said she'd only have to spend the school year with us, but maybe he was trying to get her to agree to go. And he's never said anything to Fern or me about looking forward to seeing her. Zac said he's often gone into the woods for days at a time. He can't go off and leave Fern alone. I'm worried about Fern's education. I don't see William stepping up. I think she should spend the summer with William but return to us for eighth grade."

Jack grimaced. "Let's not get ahead of ourselves. It doesn't sound good, but we're booked and we're going. Keep your fingers crossed. I'm sure it will work out."

Ivy threw Fern a big, fancy goodbye dinner. Cate and family drove down for the occasion. Fern and Livy cried when they said goodbye and pinky promised to write to each other.

"Maybe you can come to Alaska next summer," Fern said to Livy. "Jack and Rose might visit, and you could come with them."

"I'd love to," Livy said. "Maybe we can all go."

Ivy laughed. "You better bring sleeping bags."

Chapter Forty-One

The knot in my stomach got tighter and tighter with each mile we drew closer to Alaska. When we landed, Fern and I went to get the luggage while Jack picked up our rental. I sat in the front with Jack. Fern jabbered constantly, pointing out things she remembered or recognized. After about six hours of driving, we passed the Last Outpost. Jack asked if we needed to stop. I'd have been happy to but Fern was eager to get home.

"Almost there!" she shouted gleefully. For the last hour, she'd talked endlessly about how wonderful it was going to be to see her dad and all the things they'd do together. It was as if the last year hadn't happened. School, pizza delivery, the friends she'd made and other such modern things as TV, cellphones, and computers were forgotten.

The lack of communication from her father was also forgotten or forgiven. All would be well. I was concerned about what Zac shared about William. Although I'd talked to Jack, I hadn't shared my anxiety with Fern beyond suggesting her father had probably had a difficult time over the last year and she might find him changed. Fern grinned, assuming I meant changed for the better. I worried he'd changed for the worse.

My other concern was Fern's schooling. If she stayed in Alaska with her father, how could she continue her studies? Margie had been in charge of home-schooling and keeping Fern focused. William had never been much of a student. He hadn't graduated high school because he dropped out and joined the army. But maybe he could rise to the challenge. Having his daughter home might be the catalyst he needed to change.

We turned on the final dirt road to William's cabin. Fern bounced up and down on the backseat, squealing in her attempt to contain her joy. A moment later, the cabin came into view. Zac and Luke stood by the front door. They appeared downcast but when they heard the car, they smiled.

Before Jack came to a complete halt, Fern jumped out of the car and ran to the brothers, giving them big hugs. We walked up and everyone shook hands. "We wanted to come over and be part of the welcoming party," Zac (or Luke) said.

I thought it was odd William wasn't part of the group. Was he waiting in the cabin? The homestead looked different. I couldn't quite put my finger on it. It looked messy and abandoned, as if no one lived there.

Running to the front door, Fern yanked it to go inside. It was locked. William never locked his door. The brothers shrugged, looking miserable.

"Why's the door locked?" Fern asked, yanking again as if somehow it would pop open.

"Not sure, honey. Your dad's been gone a lot, and he said he felt better lockin' things up."

"Gone where?" I asked as the brothers walked over to unlock it.

"Don't know," Zac (or Luke) mumbled, fiddling with the key. "Into the woods. On his ATV. He ain't been around much."

The door swung open, and we walked into a scene of total disaster. The cabin stunk. Dirty dishes were piled up everywhere. The smell of rotting, rancid food permeated everything. Dirt, dust, and grime coated every surface. Dirty clothes were thrown all over the couch and chairs. In William's room, the sheets on the bed were almost black from lack of washing. Even worse were the empty beer and whiskey bottles strewn everywhere. We walked around with our mouths open in shock and dismay. There was no sign of William.

Fern started wailing, "Where's my dad? Didn't you guys tell him I was coming home today?"

"Yes, we did Fern. We wrote him. We gave him the date and time," I said, staring at the scene of horror.

"We told him too, honey," Zac (or Luke) said. "We come over last week and put a note on the door since he weren't here and we couldn't tell him directly."

"There wasn't a note on the door when we arrived." I glanced at the door which we'd left open to let the stink out and the fresh air in.

"He must'a seen it then," Zac (or Luke said), walking to the front of the door to check.

Jack began sifting through all the empty bottles, picking them up and staring at them as if the answer to William's whereabouts could be found in the bottom of a beer bottle. Actually, it could be. I wondered how long William had been drinking. Did he start right after we left or did the loss of his wife and daughter and the long, dark winter finally take a toll on his emotions and he cracked?

The appearance of the cabin apparently shocked the brothers as well. "William ain't let us in here in a long time. He'd say he wasn't a real good housekeeper and was best not to visit."

We weren't a hundred percent sure if Zac and Luke knew William and Margie were recovering alcoholics. Were they surprised by all the empty bottles?

"Did you know he was drinking?" I asked.

Zac and Luke looked at each other before staring down at their feet. They couldn't look me in the eye. "Yeah. We didn't think it was a big deal. He'd come with us to The Outpost to get a meal and have a beer with his dinner. Seemed to cheer him up."

There was no point in yelling at them. They weren't his AA sponsors and

154

probably didn't know William couldn't have just one beer.

"He musta been drivin' to Fairbanks to buy this." Zac and Luke looked around in awe at the number of empty bottles. "Can't imagine one person drinking all this by themselves."

Fern ran to her room. I followed and saw her staring around. This area appeared to be fairly clean, other than the inch of dust coating every surface.

Turning to me, she appeared confused. "Rose, where is my dad? Why isn't he here?"

Fern knew Jack and I didn't drink. She knew we went to meetings to talk to other people about not drinking. Did she know her parents were also recovering alcoholics? Did she understand the significance of all the empty bottles? That her father had gone off the deep end?

"I'm not sure, Fern. Let's look around outside. Maybe we can figure out what's going on."

I took her hand and we headed to the main room. Jack opened windows to help let the stink out.

"We're going to check outside," I said. Jack, Zac, and Luke followed us. Behind the house, we found a truck. "William bought that with the insurance money," the brothers informed us. It looked as bad as the cabin, like it hadn't been washed since William bought it. Wherever he had gone, it hadn't been in the truck. Did that limit the distance?

"The ATV's gone," Fern said, sticking her head into a shed. "The dog pens are empty. Where are the dogs?" Fern was obviously distressed to discover the dogs were gone.

I hoped William hadn't let them starve.

Zac and Luke squirmed. They obviously didn't know William hadn't told Fern about the dogs. "He got rid of 'em a few months after you left. Said he couldn't keep up with 'em with a broken arm. Said he didn't want to deal with 'em anymore." I could tell the brothers were reluctant to share this with Fern. William had never said anything about the dogs in his few brief notes.

"Everything's gone," Fern said. "The sled. The harnesses... everything."

She looked at me, anger blazing in her eyes. "He knew I'd be home. He knew these dogs were my team. He knew I wanted to race in the Iditarod." She ran down the length of the kennels, calling each missing dog's name before collapsing in a heap by Thor's old pen.

Zac and Luke looked at me and Jack before glancing down at their feet, which they shuffled back and forth. I couldn't tell if they were embarrassed or ashamed because they hadn't told us what had been going on with William. Still, it wasn't their fault or their responsibility, though it would have been nice to know earlier. If we'd been here sooner, maybe we could have done something?

I led Fern to the house. She shook me off and went to her room. She walked out a moment later, holding the school photo she'd proudly sent to William. "Looks like Dad tossed this on my desk after unwrapping it. Apparently, he didn't care enough to hang it." She threw it down and ran to her room and slammed the door.

I picked up the photo. The glass was shattered. I looked around again at the mess in the cabin. I couldn't imagine spending the night here. I heard Jack saying goodbye to the brothers before walking inside. He shook his head in disbelief. "What... where...?"

"We need to make a dent in the mess. See if there are garbage bags anywhere." Jack found a full box of large garbage bags. Clearly, none had been used in the last year. I wished I had rubber gloves. And a mask. I was reluctant to touch anything. Jack said he'd collect all the bottles while I worked on throwing away old food.

Once we collected and removed the trash, we started to clean. I washed the dishes while Jack scrubbed every surface and swept the floor. We tossed all the dirty clothes into William's room and shut the door. We finally got the cabin cleaned to an acceptable level.

After taking the couch cushions outside and beating them with a broom, we put them on the couch and sat down. I was grateful for the long hours of daylight because we needed it to work by.

156

Jack and I looked around. We'd done a damn fine job. It almost looked livable. I let out a deep sigh and leaned against the cushions. "It's worse than I imagined. Why hadn't I considered William might fall off the wagon? In hindsight, it should have been my biggest fear. He didn't have Margie to anchor him, and he didn't have to worry about Fern because she was with us."

"True," Jack said. Punching the couch cushions angrily, he added, "We should have made him come with us. We never should have let him stay here by himself."

"You're right. But we did try. He was unmovable."

We sat quietly. There were no sounds from Fern's bedroom.

"What now?" Jack asked. "Do we wait for him? Do we assume he got the day wrong? Is there anything to eat here that isn't rotten? I'm starving."

I walked to the kitchen area and started opening cabinets. "Thank goodness for canned soup. It never goes bad." Opening a couple of cans, I dumped them in a pot and heated them on the stove. After I poured the soup into three bowls, I went to get Fern. I found her curled up on her bed, asleep.

"Fern fell asleep, and it's not worth waking her up for a bowl of soup. In the morning, we can discuss our next step."

Jack found some blankets in a cupboard that weren't filthy. He laid on the floor with a cushion and tried to get comfortable. He let me have the couch, which still smelled a little funky.

Fern was the first one up the next morning. I heard her door open and I sat up. "Morning sweetie. Are you hungry?" Jack rolled over and groaned before opening his eyes.

Walking to the cabinets, Fern opened every door, looking for something to eat. She opened the refrigerator, only to find it completely empty. I had thrown everything away, including a few unopened cans of beer. "There's nothing to eat," she said.

"I know. Everything was moldy or out of date, so I tossed it. There's some cans of soup, beans, and vegetables."

Fern wrinkled her nose. "Beans for breakfast? Ick."

We heard the rumbles of engines coming up the road and Fern ran to the door. "It must be Dad. He must have mixed up the days."

More disappointment met her when she opened the door and saw Zac and Luke on their ATVs. "You want some breakfast? Didn't look like there was much food in the cabin." They'd brought a thermos of coffee, a pound of bacon, and pancake mix.

Fern tried to smile at the brothers. Obviously, it was difficult. "Thought you might be Dad," she said, drifting into the house.

"Sorry to disappoint you, honey." Zac and Luke came in behind her. "Wow. You guys did a good job cleaning this place up."

"Don't look in William's bedroom." I helped them arrange the food items on the counter. "Everything we couldn't clean, we threw in there."

Zac and Luke said they'd cook for us. I was most grateful for the coffee. After breakfast, I asked if they knew how long William was usually gone when he took off.

"Depends." The brothers looked at each other as if trying to decide how much to tell us. "Sorry to say we been seeing less and less of him. He stopped going to the Last Outpost with us to get a meal. Maybe he was drivin' into Fairbanks. He had to drive there to see his doctor to get his arm checked. Then he went for a while for physical therapy."

While one brother cooked, the other brought Jack and me steaming mugs of coffee. "That mighta been what sent him off the deep end. Maybe he thought he'd get the cast off and his arm would be all healed." The brothers looked at each other and nodded at the memory. "But his arm was all puny when he got the cast off. He couldn't do hardly nothin' like he used to. When he tried, you could tell it hurt real bad. He stopped going for therapy. Said he could exercise here by himself."

It was the longest speech we'd ever heard from the brothers. It must have been hard for them to see their friend miserable and in pain.

"Do you think he'll be here soon? You said he knew when we were coming," I asked, taking a deep gulp of coffee. It helped.

"Yeah. We told him, but I don't know if he knows what day it is. Might be he don't know you guys are here already."

Which didn't help us decide how long to stay and wait.

Zac and Luke left after breakfast, and the three of us talked. Fern, of course, wanted to stay until her father came home. Jack and I tried to be the voices of reason.

"Fern, we have no idea where your father is or if he's planning to come back. Leaving the cabin a total mess was hardly a welcome mat for us."

Fern's jaw tightened. "He was looking forward to me coming home."

There was no evidence whatsoever of that. He hadn't said anything to Fern about it when he wrote or on the rare occasions when he called. He'd hardly said anything at all.

I decided to tackle the elephant in the room. "Fern, you know what alcoholism is, right?"

"Yeah. I'm not a dummy. I know you and Jack don't drink and Mom and Dad didn't either."

"Yes. But it's not that we simply decided not to drink. We all have a disease, and we are always on the razor's edge of drinking again. Alcoholics can't be social drinkers. We can't say, 'I'll just have a beer or a glass of wine with dinner. Just one.' Because it starts with one, soon it's two or three and then dozens. And people change when they drink like that. They're selfish. They'd literally sell their soul for a drink."

I couldn't tell what Fern thought about this because she wouldn't look at me.

"Did you see all the empty cans and bottles littering the house? There were more outside in trash bags. Your father isn't having a beer with dinner. He's on a full-blown bender, and there's no telling when he will find his way back." Or if, I thought.

A tear rolled down Fern's cheek and fell with a splash on the floor. That one was followed by a flood.

"So, you're saying he doesn't love me anymore?" Fern noticed her school

159

photo on the end table. I'd thrown the broken glass away. The frame and photo survived. "He doesn't care." Her face crumpled.

"Oh, sweetie. Your dad loves you. I know he does. He'll always love you. Unfortunately, drinking is his priority right now. He probably thinks you're better off with us and he's better off up here. Alone." And much easier for him to continue drinking without a child to take care of.

We finally compromised and agreed to stay for two more days. Jack drove to the Last Outpost to get a plane ticket for Fern, since it was apparent she was flying home with us. Even if William, by some miracle, showed up, I wouldn't leave Fern with him. Not now. He'd only get her if he could prove he was sober and, from the looks of things, he was far from that state.

Jack came home with food and our tickets. Over the next two days, I tried to make a dent in the filth in William's room. Cleaned some things and threw others away, including the sheets. At least if and when William returned, he'd come home to a better place than he'd left.

The night before we left, I couldn't sleep. I was worried about William and broken-hearted for Fern. A little after midnight, I slipped off the couch and walked out the door to the edge of the woods. It wasn't as bright as day, but it wasn't black. The sky shimmered with a golden edge. I stared into the woods. The wind whispered through the branches. William could have been five feet in front of me or five hundred miles away. "Where are you? Please come home," I prayed before returning to bed.

We got up early, and Zac and Luke came to say goodbye. They brought a gift for Fern. It was a carving of a dog pulling a sled.

While Jack and Fern loaded the car, Zac came over to talk to me. I'd finally figured out which one of the brothers was Zac and which one was Luke. Zac had a small scar over his right eyebrow and his voice was deeper.

"Sorry this happened," he said, the image of abject misery. "Sorry William ain't here and Fern can't stay. She's already had enough heartache. I guess we didn't think to tell ya William was drinkin'."

Zac looked up, his eyes full of hope of forgiveness. What could I say except it was fine. It wasn't their fault. William was a big boy. He'd made the bad decisions all on his own. Zac grabbed me in a bear hug and I almost suffocated, squashed up into his burly chest. I disentangled myself before I passed out.

"We'll keep an eye on things and let you know if we see William," Zac said, his voice full of unshed tears. I patted him on the shoulder. Next Luke hugged me. Fortunately, not as forcefully.

Fern was the last to climb in the car. She paused, looking into the woods. For a moment I wondered if William might be standing there, invisible behind the deep black of the forest. I knew Fern hoped and prayed with every fiber of her being her dad would come home before we left. It didn't happen.

I rolled down my window as we pulled out, calling out to the brothers, "Thank you. Thanks for everything." It really wasn't their fault.

We drove to Fairbanks in complete silence, lost in our own thoughts. I couldn't wait to get to the airport and call Ivy. I needed to update her.

After we checked in, we found seats by our departure gate. I excused myself and walked down to another empty waiting area. I pulled out my phone. What the hell was I going to say? I pushed her number and waited.

"Hey there," I heard Ivy's cheery voice on the other end of the phone. "I've been waiting for you to call. How was the happy reunion? I'm sure you're sad leaving Fern…" She babbled on as Ivy often does, and I finally cut her off.

"Ivy. Stop. You aren't letting me speak." I continued quickly before she jumped in. "There was no joyful reunion."

I paused. There was silence on the other end of the phone. Finally, she said, "What the hell?"

Filling her in on the details as quickly as I could, I told her William wasn't there. "The house was a complete pigsty, and he's apparently been drinking for some time. Fern is coming with us. Not like there was any other choice."

"Oh, my God. Poor Fern. That must have completely devastated her. She's been looking forward to being with her dad."

"Yes, she was, and yes, it has. We'll figure out the next step when we get home." I hung up and walked to the departure gate. Fern and Jack sat with their eyes closed.

Before we boarded the plane, Fern said, "Good thing we didn't bring Thor. He'd have had to turn around and fly back. Like me."

The lifeboat had been so close to the shore, but it flipped over and sank.

Chapter Forty-Two

Fern sank into a deep depression. She couldn't understand why her father abandoned her. Why he wasn't there with his arms wide open welcoming her home. No amount of explaining the power of alcohol and the hold it had over those who suffered from the disease made any difference. To her, it meant he'd rather drink than be her father. Which, at this point, was true.

We hadn't made plans for Fern for the summer since we didn't think she'd be with us. The summer loomed long and empty. Thankfully, Cate called and said they were going on vacation to the beach and Livy would be thrilled to have Fern come along.

Fern had never swum in the ocean, so a week with her cousin might be what she needed. Cate and family pulled up, and we loaded Fern's things into their minivan. I warned Cate about Fern's moodiness. "Who can blame her?" Cate replied.

"I didn't want you to take it personally."

Cate laughed. "With teenagers, you learn to take nothing personally." And off they went. Fern didn't wave goodbye.

I hated to admit it, but I was relieved. Her mood was beginning to affect me and Jack. Jack usually never let anything bother him but even he found it difficult to put up with the silences, the sulks, the slamming doors, and the rudeness when she was forced to speak. The only punishment we had was to ground her, and she didn't care since she wanted to stay in her room anyway. With Thor.

The next day, I went to Ivy's. Ivy continued to come over to our house for Sunday dinner. It embarrassed me to realize I hadn't been to her house in a long time. I used the typical excuse of work and family.

She wanted to show me the pieces of art she'd been working on since the previous summer. "These were difficult. Usually the images erupt in my head and from my mind, they explode onto the canvas. This time my mind was black and empty. I kept seeing Margie, and so I finally gave in and thought, 'Okay. I'll paint Margie,' since it appeared to be what my muse was saying."

I nervously climbed the stairs to her studio. She used the back bedroom of her house for her studio. It had windows on three sides, and Ivy said the light was perfect for painting.

On the wall hung a huge triptych. Three connected paintings. Quite popular on the altars of medieval churches, according to Ivy. Once again, I knew nothing about altars or medieval churches.

"This is *Fear, Hope, Anguish,*" Ivy announced with a wave. "What do you think?"

I stood quietly, staring at the paintings.

Ivy continued talking. She appeared nervous and tried to fill in the silence. "It's how we felt—well, how I felt, after that phone call. First, we were filled with *Fear*, not knowing what happened. When we got to the hospital and found out everyone had been taken there, for a moment there was *Hope*. And then *Anguish* when we found out about Margie."

She walked closer to the triptych and pointed to the panel on the right. "Do you think *Anguish* is a good title? Or maybe *Despair*? Or *Hopelessness*, but that's too long. Plus, I'm not sure if I like *Hope* and *Hopelessness*." She stared at the paintings. "Might work if there were only two panels."

Finally, she stepped aside and let me walk closer. *Fear* was a mouth open wide. Screaming? With tears raining down. *Hope* was bright and full of light, and a smiling face seemed ghosted under the layers of paint. I could almost see Margie. And *Anguish*, or *Despair*, though personally I preferred *Anguish*, were many mouths of different sizes and shapes open in silent screams. Some bold, some fading into the background. A chorus of agony. It was powerful. Moving.

Tears slipped down my cheeks. Ivy walked up and put her arm around me and laid her head on my shoulder. She was crying too.

"Oh my God, Ivy. How did you paint this? Wasn't it overwhelming?"

"It's why it's taken almost a year to finish. Sometimes I'd quit painting because I'd start crying and I'd almost hyperventilate, and I'd have to wait until the tears stopped before I could continue. I destroyed many earlier versions. I'd get upset and paint over the whole thing with black paint." She pointed at a corner in her studio where several canvases were streaked with black paint.

"It was worth waiting for," I said, hugging Ivy tightly.

We went downstairs and Ivy fixed us some herbal tea. "Now we have to talk about William." I raised an eyebrow. "What are we going to do about him? Which raises the question of what are we going to do about Fern?"

I shook my head. "Sadly, we can't do anything about William. He has to decide for himself to stop drinking, to put his daughter first and to return to the land of the living." I sipped my tea, burning my tongue. "We can't hire a private detective to look for him like we did before. He's disappeared into the wilderness. We may think of his cabin as the wilderness, but it's the height of civilization compared to some parts of Alaska."

Ivy nodded, blowing on her tea. She must have seen me flinch when I burned my tongue. "True. For all we know, he may never come home."

"Zac and Luke have promised they will call the minute he returns. But what then? Do we fly up and kidnap him and forcibly bring him here and put him in rehab?"

"I don't know," Ivy said with a hint of anger in her voice. "I'd do anything.

If not for William, since I am actually furious with him, then for Fern. Her heart has now been broken twice."

"You have to find a way to forgive William. He didn't make a conscious decision. Maybe it was conscious, but he's an alcoholic and it's so easy to slip. Maybe he ran out of pain meds and the doctor wouldn't renew the prescription, for good reasons, and he decided a beer might take the edge off and then it was well, one beer helped, two beers would be better, and it accelerated from there. It's not like he held up two hands and said, 'Would I rather drink, or would I rather see my daughter?' He probably thought he had it under control. Alcoholics are masters of lying to themselves."

"You're the expert," Ivy said and I cringed. I wished I wasn't, but she was right.

"For now, we have to keep Fern busy and occupied until school starts. Hopefully that will help. I'm sure she'll be all right when she's back in school."

"I have a trip coming up to see my agent in New York. He wants to talk about my triptych. How about the three of us go and have a New York experience. The sights, the sounds, the shopping, the shows."

"Sounds great." I smiled. "We'll dazzle her with beaches and big city lights."

Chapter Forty-Three

We tried to keep Fern distracted with activities all summer. I knew Fern loved the trip to the beach. She had never seen anything like that in Alaska. We didn't pester her too much with questions since she shut down if pressed.

She was amazed by New York City. She thought Richmond was the biggest city in America. It was the biggest she'd ever seen. Much bigger than Fairbanks, which was the only other city she'd been to. New York boggled her mind. But it has that effect on everyone. Everything we did was new to her. Shopping in huge stores, going to museums and monuments, Central Park and attending Broadway shows. The view of the city from the Empire State building left her breathless.

Seeing a gallery full of Ivy's paintings astonished Fern. A few fans were there and were excited to meet Ivy Bane Berenstein in the flesh. Fern had probably assumed Ivy painted sweet little paintings as a hobby. Now she appreciated Ivy was a big deal.

A few times, Fern started talking about something we'd seen or done that had been fun. In the middle of gushing over something, she'd realize she was talking to us and she'd slam down and put her grumpy face back on.

When we returned, Fern continued to look blasé and speak in monosyllables.

She was angry with us, apparently blaming us for uprooting her from her home. She believed it was all our fault her dad started drinking again. Often when she erupted, those were the words she yelled at me, how I ruined her life and her dad's. A few times, I worried Jack was going to grab her and shake her until reason returned. If it was only that easy.

Jack spoke to her sternly, saying she wasn't allowed to talk to me that way. I was the one who saved her. Brought her to our home. I was trying to fulfill her mother's dream. Fern never yelled at Jack. She'd just storm back to her room with Thor.

Jack and Fern continued to go to the mountains a few weekends each month. After one weekend trip, Fern actually came racing into the house, jumping up and down with excitement.

"Calm down," I said, laughing. It was good to see her happy. "What's up?"

"Jack bought a cabin in the mountains. It's so cool. Now we can stay for a whole weekend or more."

Turning to stare at Jack, I hoped my face said, "Are you out of you mind? Tell me this isn't true."

He grinned sheepishly, which meant it was true. Fern bounded up the stairs and I tried to stay calm as I asked Jack about this. "What the …? A cabin? In the woods? We can't afford a cabin. We have a mortgage and a child and bills."

Jack grabbed me, swinging me around. "It's going to be great. It was a bargain. A fixer-upper. Well, maybe more of a tear-it-downer and start-from-scratcher. It will make Fern happy. And Thor too. A place we can all go on weekends and hang out. Fresh air. Hikes. Good stuff."

I didn't know what to say. His heart was in the right place. How could I get mad at him? Before school started, Jack, Fern, Thor, Frito, and I went up to see our cabin. We were able to drive right up to the front door, except it really didn't have a door. We sat in the truck for a moment and looked at our "vacation" home. It would have been an overstatement to describe it as a wreck.

"We'll get this fixed up in no time," Jack said, stepping out. He went to the back and pulled out a variety of tools. Fern, Thor, and Frito jumped out and followed him inside. I admired Jack's enthusiasm but found it hard to share his feelings. I didn't want to be the spoilsport, but I've never really been the outdoorsy type. I could imagine being eaten by a bear who could casually stroll in the opening formerly known as the front door.

We spent the weekend at the cabin. Jack was in his element, hammering and sawing. Fern helped by carrying trash outside, mostly branches which had fallen through the holes in the roof. Thor and Frito sniffed around inside and out. I could only image some of the smells they were picking up. I swept and tried to hide my feelings about the mess. When the sun began to set, Jack made a fire in an outside pit, and we cooked hot dogs on sticks for dinner. For a moment, I conceded that it was a bit charming. We slept in sleeping bags on air mattresses under the only section of the roof that remained.

Jack said he bought the place for Thor and Fern. Our wolf dog had begun to slow down, and Jack worried about him. The vet said he was getting old. "Just like people, dogs slow down as they age. None of us are as young as we used to be." The vet prescribed some joint medicine and supplements for geriatric dogs.

The thought of anything happening to Thor terrified Fern. She spent the weekend catering to him. Going with him and Frito on long walks in the woods. Thor no longer took off into the woods by himself, running like the wind. He was happy to stick by Fern's side and sleep near the warm fire at night. And Frito was happy to stick to Thor's side and sleep next to him.

When we left Monday morning, the cabin looked a little better. "I'm going to come up next weekend with some of the guys from the program. I've got a list of what I need and we'll get this place ship-shape in no time," Jack said.

Fern was smiling and talking on the drive back home. Could the answer to our problems be a cabin in the woods? It seemed way too easy.

The long summer finally ground to an end and school was about to start again. I kept my fingers crossed that we'd make it. A routine would be good for Fern. She had friends and she loved learning.

But I was in for another surprise. When I called to get Fern re-enrolled, instead of a human on the other end of the line, I got a recording. "Thanks for calling. Blake Middle is now officially closed." The recording gave another number to call to get further information since the former students were being shifted. Since Fern was no longer enrolled, we might have "missed the memo" about the changes.

What the hell, I thought as I called the second number. This is not what we needed. Another change. When someone picked up, I told them, "I'm trying to re-enroll my niece in Blake Middle School."

The voice on the other end said, "Didn't you get the letter?" Without waiting for me to answer or maybe because I said nothing, she went on, "We've shifted the former students to Peyton Middle on Hanover Avenue and a new school on Magnolia Road. You should have received a letter about this change sometime this summer. It would have also included information on where she'll be attending."

"They weren't expecting her to attend this year, so I didn't get the letter."

The voice asked for Fern's name and address. I heard her typing on a computer. "Fern Bane has been assigned to Peyton." She asked for my email address and said she'd send me further information.

I put the phone down with a groan. Couldn't anything stay the same? Fern didn't need any more changes. Where were her friends going? It would be like starting over again.

When Jack got home from work, I told him Fern would be going to a new school. The smile faded from his face. "Oh no. Have you told her yet?"

I shook my head. "No. We'll have to break the news at dinner tonight."

I showed him the information I'd received about Peyton and the new time and place for Fern to catch the bus. They also sent me Fern's class assignments. For some reason, they didn't have her records from Blake, and she was being treated as a new student. It appeared she'd been placed in all basic classes. I sighed. "First thing tomorrow, I'll have to go there and fix her schedule."

At dinner, we told Fern. Surprisingly, she didn't look too concerned. "Yeah,

I talked to Emma and Hannah, and they said something about it. We're all going to a brand-new school. Sounds nice. Blake was pretty old and crummy."

I tried to keep my face and voice neutral. "Yes. I called the administration today, and it appears they divided up the Blake students between Peyton Middle and this new place. Apparently, because of where we live, you'll be going to Peyton."

Fern's face darkened. I waited for her to erupt, but she just stared at me. "None of my friends are going there. Why do I have to?"

"Because it appears they simply drew a line and divided the kids equally. It's not deliberate. They had to balance the numbers." Fern continued to look at me as if I had requested she be separated from her friends. "More importantly, they've stuck you in all basic classes, so we'll have to take your records from Blake and get your classes straight."

"Who cares?" Fern said before shifting her gaze to her plate.

The next day, I took Fern along with me to Peyton to straighten out her class assignments. She followed behind me like a beaten dog with her tail between her legs. She slumped down in her seat while I talked to the counselor, Ms. Trible. I tried to sound upbeat, but the counselor kept looking at Fern. I'm sure she was wondering why Fern was so shut down. She probably thought we abused her.

"Well, Ms. Bane. I see from these records Fern is quite the student." Ms. Trible turned to look at Fern. "What is your favorite subject, Fern?" Fern stared at her feet and shrugged. Ms. Trible looked back at me with a stern expression. I felt like staring at my feet and shrugging too. I should have called first to explain a bit about Fern's situation.

"I'll get the class schedule straightened out and email it to you," Ms. Trible said, standing up. We were obviously being dismissed. As we left, she put her hand on Fern's shoulder and added, "I'm here for you to talk about anything. Anything at all." She looked pointedly at me when she said this. Fern did not respond. I tried to smile back. It probably looked like a sneer.

Chapter Forty-Four

On the first day of school, I let Fern walk to the bus stop by herself. The stop was in the same place, but the kids from last year weren't there. Fern stood waiting all alone. Was the dividing line right down the middle of the street? Had those kids also ended up at the new school?

When Fern got home, I asked if any of her friends from seventh grade were at Peyton. She slowly shook her head. "Not many. Most are at the new school." Fern's future had been determined by one block. The former Blake kids were now in the minority.

Fern went upstairs to do her homework. Thor followed. He had begun to have trouble climbing the stairs. Hang in there, Old Boy, I prayed. Fern needs you now more than ever.

The few kids who knew her from Blake were surprised to see Fern. I'm sure they asked her why she wasn't in Alaska with her dad. I wondered if Fern told them that her dad had disappeared into the wilderness, and she didn't know where he was or if she'd ever see him again.

Things improved slightly at home. Fern wasn't the warm fuzzy Fern of seventh grade, but at least she spoke to us. She spent a lot of time with Thor since she worried about him.

We tried to get to the cabin at least one weekend a month, though it was beginning to get cold up on the mountain. I was impressed with all the improvements Jack and his crew had made, including fixing the fireplace so we could enjoy a roaring fire on frosty nights. Jack had found some furniture, I didn't ask from where, and we had places to sit and sleep and even a table with chairs. The place was beginning to look cozy and livable. And there was a real front door with a lock on it now. Weekends at the cabin helped us all to get along.

First quarter report card, Fern got straight As. There were a few comments about Fern being quiet. Not participating in class activities. That didn't surprise me. She'd had two terrible shocks in her life. A lot to adjust to. I made the mistake of assuming all was well.

Middle School was still the emotional and social landmine it had always been. Apparently, a cadre of Mean Girls ruled the roost at Peyton. A feeding frenzy erupted from the ruling elite to take down anyone who came from Blake. They decided if you were to be accepted, and if you didn't make the cut, you were banned. Sentenced to total isolation. If you'd been deemed as an untouchable, no one dared talk to you because they were afraid to be banned too. Why the Blake girls didn't form their own clique, I didn't understand. They wanted so badly to be accepted they willingly abandoned their former friends.

Of course, I found out about this later. Too late to help.

The triumph of the year before, being the girl who tamed a wolf, was now considered "not cool". Nothing was worse than being not cool. The first few weeks weren't too bad. Fern was ignored, but not yet banned. As the days got colder and shorter, Fern pulled out her Alaska gear and the mean girls decided the time to put her in her place had arrived.

I happened to be home when she got back from school. The front door crashed open and closed and I heard Fern running up the stairs, followed by the slamming of her door. That hadn't happened in a long time. We reached the point where she'd drop her bags on the steps and come find me or Jack to get a snack and share her day.

With knots in my stomach, I climbed the stairs and knocked on her door. "Hey, Fern. I have cookies for you."

"Go away." I thought I heard a sob catch on the end of her words.

"Is everything all right?" Obviously, it wasn't. I creaked the door open. I saw Fern curled up in bed with Thor, her back to the door.

"Maybe it will help to talk about it?" When do we turn into our mothers with these expressions? I winced at my words.

For a long time, she didn't respond. Finally, she rolled over and looked up and said, "Yeah. Sure. I got called a baby seal killer and worse today. All the eighth-grade girls have decided wearing fur is the worst thing ever. They think I'm some kind of monster because I have mukluks. I told them my mukluks weren't made from baby seals and in Alaska, you have to wear fur or freeze. Much better than man-made materials." The mean girls sensed a weakness in Fern. Vulnerability. A soft spot they could exploit, and they went in for the kill.

Fern wore those same boots last year when she was the hero of the seventh grade. The girl who had a wolf. The girl who could defy the elements and race in the Iditarod. "What are your mukmuks made out of?" I wasn't sure I wanted to know.

"Mukluks," Fern replied haughtily, as if everyone knew what a mukluk was. "Not mukmuks. Seal fur. It's the most water resistant, but they're not made from baby seals, for goodness sakes!"

"Can I see them?" I'd never paid much attention to these boots before.

She stood and picked up one of the boots she'd kicked into the corner and handed it to me. I turned it over, examining what appeared to be short, bristly fur.

"Does kind of look like seal fur," I said. Which was stupid because, let's face it, I really hadn't seen many seals up close. Why did I act as if I was some famous naturalist in these situations where I really knew nothing? "The problem is people, even kids, are opposed to fur. Wearing it, you know. People think killing animals for their fur is cruel. Or using them for experiments. It's... frowned upon."

"They're stupid," Fern said angrily. "They eat animals, don't they? They wear leather, don't they? What's the difference other than they don't have seals down here to eat and use for clothes? They're such hypocrites."

"You're right. People are hypocritical sometimes, which doesn't stop them from getting angry about other people doing things they don't think are right. How about we go boot shopping this weekend for some nice snow boots that will keep your feet warm and are made out of wonderful man-made materials and won't offend anyone."

"Whatever. Sure." Fern said, flopping back down on the bed. "It doesn't matter. It's an excuse to..." Fern didn't finish the sentence.

"To what?" I asked. Fern didn't respond, and I went back downstairs to cook dinner. Jack came in the back door and gave me a kiss before looking in the pots to see what we were having to eat. He stopped and looked at me. He could always tell when I was upset.

"What's going on?"

I sighed. "Apparently Fern is no longer the girl who talks to wolves or is cool in any way. The other kids got after her today for wearing fur. Apparently, her mukluks," Jack looked at me quizzically, "those stupid clunky boots she wears, are made out of sealskin, and she was chastised, though I'm not sure that's the right word, more likely berated and tormented, for wearing them."

"Lesson learned. The ways of the natives are different down here." Jack said and went upstairs to change out of his work clothes.

At dinner we talked to Fern, who continued to rant about what happened. "They're stupid and I hate them. It's really Isabell and all her clique. They think they run everything, and everyone is afraid to go against them. I'm not."

I was angry at myself and even angrier at Ivy, who had a daughter and knew about having to negotiate through all this drama. Why didn't she warn me you can't skate through middle school unscathed unless you kowtow to the powerbrokers? I hoped it would all go away once Fern stopped wearing her mukluks.

I filled Ivy in on the latest drama. She only listened with half an ear, since her agent had called saying the world awaited the unveiling of her triptych and he needed a date from her. She basically told me not to worry about it. "It's just typical middle school nonsense. Next week, it will be someone else or something else."

When I tried to say it seemed worse than that, Ivy interrupted, "I'm sorry I have to get back to my agent. Try not to worry. This too will pass." And she hung up.

I put down the phone and noticed Jack watching me.

"Does it ever make you mad?" he said.

"What?" I was confused. Did he mean the issue at the school?

"Ivy," he said. "Does it ever make you mad all this gets dumped in your lap and she goes about her life with no worries? Alone in her studio between jetting off to see her agent and her fans." He smirked at the word "fans".

"No," I said. "In Ivy's defense…"

Jack threw his hands up in the air in disgust. "I knew you'd defend her. I love your sister and I'm happy you have her in your life, but she takes advantage of you. 'Here, watch my dog.' 'Here, watch my niece.' 'Here, take care of Fern's wolf.' The list goes on."

"Ivy is my dearest and best friend. She didn't offer to take Fern. We did. And she's been very generous with money. We couldn't have flown up to Alaska again without her help."

Jack walked over and hugged me. "I know, babe. I just hate to see you so sad and worked up." He kissed me on the forehead. "We've given up a lot. Ivy could step up a bit more."

I snuggled into Jack's hug. Was he a little right? Sometimes my age-old jealousy of Ivy did rear its head. I squashed the thought.

We went shopping on Saturday and I got Fern new boots made from all kinds of synthetic material. I wanted to be sure no part of them had come within a hundred miles of an animal. Too little, too late. Fern was now labeled as some kind of psycho animal killer.

Apparently, someone had written "murderer" on her locker. Why do they always leave messages on the lockers? And where are the teachers and janitors while people are busy scrawling things on the lockers? I did get a call, without too many details, that a rude message had been written on her locker. I was assured the school was taking care of it.

But they weren't. Things escalated. The kids avoided her and gave her the evil eye. She sat alone at lunch. When she went to sit with her former Blake classmates, they muttered something about being sorry, but it might be better if she sat somewhere else. In gym class, some of the eighth-grade girls cornered her in the locker room and said she better not wear any other dead animal.

We weren't aware of what was going on because Fern didn't tell us, and the administration didn't either. Fern became more withdrawn, like when she first came to live with us. Maybe someone should have let us know she sat alone in the cafeteria. She had no friends. Maybe Ms. Trible should have done her job a little better and kept us in the loop.

In the beginning, I hoped it would pass and the mean girls would move on. Instead, it ramped up. Someone apparently googled Fern and found out about the accident that killed her mother. Hard as it was to believe, kids started teasing her about it. Telling her the moose was a messenger from the animal kingdom punishing her parents. "They got their revenge on your murdering dad."

A few weeks later, I got a phone call from the principal's office saying there had been an incident and I needed to come to school. Immediately. When I tried to ask what happened, the administrative assistant said the principal wanted to discuss it with me in person. My anxiety level shot through the roof.

Luckily, I wasn't at a job. I jumped in the car and drove to the school. When I walked into the office, I saw Fern slumped in a corner chair. I started to walk over to talk to her, but the admin assistant stopped me and directed me to the principal's office.

Walking in, the principal, Ms. Spezzeri, thanked me for coming and asked me to close the door. Ms. Trible was there as well.

"I know you were told there was an incident. I don't have all the details yet. Apparently, Fern was involved in an altercation with a group of kids and in the confusion, Fern punched a boy and …" She paused. "She broke his nose." Ms. Trible looked at me as if to say it was no wonder Fern reverted to violence. What was wrong with that woman?

"What?" I couldn't think of anything else to say. I sat stunned. "Fern punched a kid and broke their nose?"

"From what I've been able to ascertain, there has been some teasing going on. Something about a moose and Fern's parents?" Ms. Spezzeri looked at me questioningly, as if wanting me to fill in some details.

"Fern's mother was killed in a car accident. In Alaska." I thought I didn't need to say anything about the moose. "I shared that information when I first registered Fern." I looked directly at Ms. Trible, who didn't even have the decency to look ashamed.

"Hmmm…" Ms. Spezzeri looked down at some papers on her desk. "As I said, this teasing has been going on for a while; however, Fern hadn't told anyone about it, so her teachers didn't know. I guess she snapped and beat up this boy. I'm not even sure if he was one of the ones teasing her or if he just got in the way. As I said, his nose is broken. Lip cut. A few loose teeth."

"Sounds like he got what he deserved," I said without thinking. I was furious at the school, at the kids, and mostly at myself for being so unaware. And upset with Fern for not confiding in me.

"I'm sorry, Ms. Bane, violence is never the answer." Ms. Spezzeri gave me a stern look, and I blushed. Ms. Trible gave me another one of her self-satisfied smirks. I thought she'd look good with a broken nose and a few loose teeth.

"No. Of course not," I mumbled.

"Fern will be suspended. Depending on the outcome of our investigation, she might even be expelled."

My head shot back up. "Fern is being suspended? What? What about the boy?"

"He didn't touch her. She attacked him from all reports. His parents might even sue. As I said, there will be further investigation. For now, we think it best if you take Fern home. We'll be in touch."

Standing up on legs that felt like Jell-O, I feared I might collapse in front of the terrifying and powerful Ms. Spezzeri and the smug Ms. Trible. I knew how Dorothy felt in the presence of the Wicked Witch. Flying monkeys might appear at any moment.

"Thank you," I muttered as I left. I didn't want to thank her. I wanted to punch her in the nose, too. No one seemed concerned or cared about what Fern had endured. They worried about being sued. Walking up to Fern, I said, "You should get your books. We're going home now."

She nodded and we walked to her locker. Her locker was a mess with words written and painted over. I noticed graffiti and hateful words showing through the paint. Was that all the school had done, white-washed her locker door? Fern emptied out her locker and we walked silently to the car.

Chapter Forty-Five

⟨~⟩

*F*ern was suspended. Thankfully, since it was close to the end of semester, she was allowed to finish her work at home. She came in after school to take her final exams. They didn't want her anywhere near the other students, in case she went psycho again and beat up someone else. I wanted to find this Isabell girl and confront her and her parents about what happened. That wasn't allowed. The boy's parents didn't sue us. However, we did have to pay the medical expenses that weren't covered. Thankfully, as usual, Ivy paid.

Christmas break came as a welcome relief. Ivy and I talked about what to do going forward. I didn't want Fern returning to Peyton. The administration obviously was not in our corner, and I didn't think the teasing and meanness would stop. Maybe the time had come to consider private school. Not a boarding school. A private school close by. Ivy said she'd help with the tuition if we decided to go that route.

Ivy and I visited a Catholic school within driving distance. They assured us during the tour you didn't have to be Catholic to attend and there was no pressure to convert, but statues of Jesus and the Virgin Mary filled the halls, and they celebrated Mass every Friday in the auditorium. Even if there was no overt pressure, there was subtle pressure. One advantage was everyone wore uniforms. Fern wouldn't be wearing fur and mukluks to class. My main concern was that she wasn't going to fit in. Most of these kids started school together in kindergarten, making Fern the outsider again.

Maybe this wasn't the answer. I was torn. Maybe we shouldn't take Fern out of Peyton. Wouldn't it be a win for the bad guys or, in this case, the bad girls? Even if no one else dared to tease her and risk getting their nose broken, she wouldn't have any friends. Could she last until the end of the school year being ostracized? High school might be a chance for a new beginning.

There was always the chance William might get his act together, sober up, and Fern could go home before high school started. Realistically, though, I had to consider that might never happen.

I'd been getting short notes from Zac updating us on William. His latest note included the information that the brothers had spotted the ATV at the cabin but now the truck was gone. They hadn't seen William.

I hadn't shared these updates with Fern. It would only distress her more. She had too much to deal with already. Thor. School. She didn't need to think about her absent father any more than necessary.

Zac called right before Christmas. The phone connection hadn't improved. His voice crackled as he told me that they had seen William. "We went to check on the cabin. We still do that. Not so much for William but for Fern."

They saw smoke coming from the chimney and figured either William had come home or some wandering hiker came upon the cabin and set up there for the winter. "We was surprised to find William there," Zac said. "Sitting there pleased as punch, like he hadn't gone missing for months."

They tried to talk to him about Fern and our visit. "That turned him mean real quick. Said he didn't care, saying Fern was better off with you guys. Saying she didn't need a drunk father, and it would be best if she forgot him."

They went over a few days later and found a note on the door. "He didn't 'xactly apologize, though he said he was sorry he hadn't been much of a friend or neighbor. He wants us to find him a renter for the cabin 'cause he left for Anchorage to look for work. Added he'd probably be back in the summer."

Thanking Zac, I hung up. I thought about the note William had left for the brothers. The summer? Did he want Fern to live with him? I certainly wasn't going to fly to Alaska with Fern until I knew more.

I called Ivy to fill her in. I didn't tell Jack. Our relationship had begun to fray due to Fern. I hated to blame her, but Jack had certainly not signed on to be a full-time father when he asked me to marry him. Her constant moodiness dragged us all down. He also became increasingly annoyed with Ivy "not pulling her weight," as he called it.

At dinner, I tried to get a conversation started but it was like pulling teeth. All I got in return was yeah, no, grunts, and annoyed glances. Since I'd never been much of a conversationalist in any of my relationships, it made it that much more difficult.

When Jack and I first married, I finally got a chance to talk to an equal. It was a pleasant change. Now neither Jack nor Fern talked to me or to each other. Jack and I rarely even went to the same AA meetings. He claimed he went at lunchtime so he could be home in the evening. If I suggested I could meet him at a lunch meeting, he always had a ready excuse why it wouldn't work. I finally gave up suggesting it.

I continued to attend the Tuesday night meetings as often as I could. Gwen asked about Jack. "I haven't seen that good-looking man of yours in a long time. He's still going to meetings, I trust?"

Forcing a laugh that I hoped didn't sound fake, I said, "With a teenager at home, we have to split up. Someone needs to be at home with the kid."

Gwen nodded. "I understand."

I wished I did. Lying in bed at night, I'd sense Jack awake next to me. Was he lying there wishing he'd never married me? Or wishing he'd never gotten involved with my crazy family? Did he miss his one-room apartment over his garage with no ties, no complications, no moody teenagers?

Fern had become a weight, dragging us all down to the depths of despair. Maybe it was comforting to Fern to know we were all miserable.

Chapter Forty-Six

━━━━◦◦━◦◦━━━━

Christmas was a quiet affair. Ivy was going up to spend the holidays at Cate's. Ivy's son Alex and his family were going there as well. Fern didn't want to leave Thor, and he wasn't welcome. Too many small kids, noise, and excitement. Ivy never got to the point where she completely trusted Thor.

"Let's have a small family Christmas this year," Jack suggested. He didn't add that we needed a break from drama and excitement and as much as I loved Ivy and her kids and grandkids, sometimes it could be overwhelming and hectic.

After Christmas, Ivy planned to go to New York for a New Year's Eve show. Her triptych was finally being unveiled, and she wanted to be there when the piece was shown to the world. She wanted me to come too. "This is something we shared. You should be there with me."

"I appreciate that you want me by your side and I would seriously love to be there with you. It's an amazing piece. Sadly, I think we need to hunker down here and lick our wounds. We haven't decided what to do with Fern for the rest of the school year. Sending her back to Peyton seems wrong, but I don't think All Saint's Middle School is the answer either. Might be way too much of a change for her."

"I'm sorry Rose. Sorry this has not worked out happily. For you and for Fern."

For Jack either, I thought but didn't say. "You don't need to be sorry. It's a privilege to have Fern in my care. I wish William had come with us after the accident. It would have changed everything."

There was a long moment of silence on Ivy's end of the phone. I knew she was struggling with how to respond. Finally, she said, sounding unnaturally cheerful, "Well, you know what you always say—everything happens for a reason. It will work out. Right now, we just can't see the bright shiny ending."

I wanted to say that I never say that but decided not to waste my breath. "Thanks, I'll try to keep that in mind." I hung up. It was easy for Ivy. She was off to the bright lights of New York. I couldn't help feel a little bitter that Ivy seemed to end up with the shiny endings a lot more than I did.

The holidays were rapidly coming to an end. A decision needed to be made. One night after dinner, as Jack tried to slink off to watch TV, I asked him to come to the kitchen with me. "I have something I need to talk to you about. Get your opinion on."

He began to protest even before he knew what I wanted to talk about. "What is it Rose? Can't you handle it on your own? You're so good at handling things."

Did I detect a note of sarcasm in his voice? What had happened to the warm, caring guy I married? I worried maybe he'd started drinking again, which explained why he never wanted to meet up at noon meetings. If Jack was drinking, I seriously couldn't handle it. I felt like I was about to have a complete collapse.

"We need to talk. Isn't that what families do? Discuss problems and come up with solutions together?"

He slumped on one of the bar stools and leaned his elbows on the counter. He didn't say anything, just raised an eyebrow as if to say I could proceed.

I tried to keep my anger and fear under control. "I can't decide what's the best thing for Fern." Jack rolled his eyes. I could tell he wanted to get up and leave, so I continued speaking quickly. "We could send her to Peyton for the rest of the school year." Jack shrugged. "Or we could send her to All Saints. I would like to be able to give you a list of the pluses and minuses, but I've concluded there are only minuses at both."

Jack stood. "Make the best decision you can. She's your niece. It's your decision."

"No, Jack!" I almost screamed. "It's a family decision. We are a family. She is our responsibility."

Jack sat down reluctantly. "What are the negatives?"

"If she goes to Peyton, no one will tease and harass her since they're probably a little afraid of her. The downside is, she'll have no friends. She'll have classes but no social activities."

"Okay." Jack drew out the word as if he couldn't really see why this was so bad. Men didn't get how women needed companionship. Friends.

"And if she goes to All Saints, she can start fresh, but will she really fit in there? For one, she's not Catholic, and two, all those kids have been together since forever and would she be able to make friends there?"

Jack stared at his hands. I thought he wasn't going to say anything. He looked up. "I see what you mean. No good solutions."

"It would only be until June. Five and a half months until school ends. Then we have the summer and maybe William will have come to his senses by then and she can return home."

Jack gave me a skeptical look.

"I know. It's probably not going to happen, but it could. If she doesn't go to Alaska, we can fill her summer with stuff and then she'll start high school in the fall. Kids from four different middle schools will go there. The Peyton kids could be eaten up by even bigger and meaner kids. She'll be in advanced classes and away from the crowds."

"That sounds good," Jack agreed. "But you still have the next five and a half months to figure out."

"I know." My voice cracked. I was on the verge of tears.

"Have you asked Fern what she would like to do?"

No, I hadn't. It was a possible solution. Put the decision in her hands. Or at least get her input.

"Brilliant," I replied.

Chapter Forty-Seven

⌐⌐≈⌐

$\mathcal{I}$ had developed a tradition of taking a small Christmas tree to the cemetery for Mom, Lily, and the rest of the family to enjoy. Jack found it amusing. Fern thought it was dumb. I told her we were going the next day.

"I don't wanna go. It's creepy and stupid. They're dead. Dead and gone. They're not there."

"It makes me feel close to them. I think about them and how much I love and miss them, and it doesn't matter if they're there or if they care, since they are all beyond caring, but it keeps them alive in my heart."

Fern huffed and puffed but she knew she had no choice. I carried the tree to the family plot with Fern dragging behind me, hoping to convince anyone who saw her that she was not related to the crazy woman carrying a Christmas tree for dead people. As we walked, Fern noticed all the decorations on different graves. Maybe I wasn't the only crazy person.

When we got to the plot, I put the tree in front of Mom and Dad's headstone. Then I placed a sprig of holly on the tops of everyone else's grave. I'd made a little spruce halo for the angel on top of Lily's grave. Then I sat on the bench. Fern stood for a while, hoping I'd catch the clue and get up and leave. I continued to sit stubbornly on the bench, ignoring her. She finally got tired of standing and plopped down next to me.

I glanced at Margie's headstone. "I know how much you miss your mom, Fern. People always say it's harder around the holidays. I think it's hard every day of the year. There are always reminders. I used to call my mom every day at the same time and for a year or more after she passed, I'd pick up the phone to call her before remembering she wasn't going to answer." A tear slid down my cheek.

"You're angry. Probably at me, your dad, the world, the universe, because your mom isn't here anymore. You want to scream and rage, but there's no one to scream at. No one to get angry at. Just a dead moose far away in Alaska."

Fern's voice was so low I could barely hear her. "I can be mad at my dad. I'm mad at him every day. Why did he leave me? Why doesn't he care?"

Putting my arm around Fern's shoulders, I pulled her close. "I was mad at my dad for years, too. After Lily died, he and my mom fought all the time. When your dad was born, Ivy and I thought it would get better. It got worse. My mom fantasized that she was giving birth to a girl, a new little Lily, and when your dad was born, she couldn't deal with it."

Fern's body shook against me as she cried. I continued. "One day my dad walked out. I saw him put his suitcase in the car and drive away. He didn't even say goodbye. We weren't allowed to ask questions or to grieve. Mom said it would be better with him gone. The only thing that was better was there weren't any fights anymore.

"I went away to college and started drinking. Ivy married some awful rich guy to create the family she never had. Your dad left and never came home."

We sat there, each absorbed in our own thoughts. "Twelve years ago, I came here to visit the gravesite, and I saw my dad standing by my mother's grave. Talk about shocked. I hadn't seen him in like forty years. He asked me to have a coffee with him. I went. We talked. He apologized for everything. It shamed him to hear that your dad had disappeared from our lives. He blamed himself. He wanted to see Ivy and meet his grandkids."

Leaning over, I kissed the top of Fern's head. "That never happened. Before we could all get together, he had a heart attack. We barely made it to the hospital in time to say goodbye before he died. As sad as it was, his death was the reason Ivy and I went to find your dad. We owed him. We wanted him in the family.

"And we found him and you." I kissed her again. "Just a toddler then, and your wonderful mother out in that cabin in the woods. Your dad turned his life around when he met your mom. And now she's gone, and he's kind of lost his way again. I hope that he'll find his way home, back to us, back to you."

"Me too," Fern whispered into my shoulder.

"For now, though, I want to take care of you like your mother wanted. To love you and get you educated. To plan for a future."

Her head nodded against me. "So, we have a decision to make. You have to finish eighth grade. And our choices are either you go to Peyton and tough it out or go to All Saints. It's only five and a half months, which probably sounds like an eternity, but before you know it, the summer will be here. And if you're still here in September, you'll start high school, and it will all be different.

"Can I stay at home? Could you homeschool me?"

If I had said yes, would that have changed what happened or was it inevitable? Did it have to happen? Do all things happen for a reason?

"No, honey. That isn't one of the choices."

189

Chapter Forty-Eight

Fern decided to go to Peyton.

I called Lauren to tell her we, or Fern, had reached a decision. I kept Lauren updated on everything. But I hadn't shared with her the state of my relationship with Jack. I was too embarrassed. Too ashamed to admit the most perfect man and the most perfect relationship ever had lost its glow.

Lauren picked up and after the usual hellos, she asked, "So, what was the decision? Where is Fern going to school?"

"Actually, we let Fern decide. She has so little control over anything in her life, and Jack suggested I let her pick."

"What a good idea," Lauren said. "And what was her decision?"

Even though I was still annoyed with Jack and his mostly hands-off attitude, I agreed it was a good idea. "Surprisingly, she picked Peyton. I guess the evil she knows trumped the unknown."

"I can understand that. We are always more comfortable with the world we know, even if it's painful, than to step out into the unfamiliar. A change might be better but it could be much worse. So why risk it? It's why many people stay in unhappy marriages. At least they know what to expect."

"True," I replied. "People are afraid to make a change. To chance it."

"I hope it works out. Sadly, there didn't seem to be any good options for her."

We chatted some more. Lauren updated me on Miranda, her kids, and her job. It was always exciting to hear what she was working on. I still enjoyed watching her show every week. Lauren made her usual kissy noises and hung up.

I slowly hung up as well. I thought about her saying Fern didn't have any good options. I worried about Fern's future, which appeared to be a bleak slate. Would William ever return? Would life here get better for her? What was the future for the three of us as a family?

I couldn't bring myself to share the news about Jack with Ivy either. When she was in town, she joined us for Sunday dinners. She might have sensed things were a bit off, though Jack always put on a show for her. If she picked up any tension in the house, she probably blamed it on Fern.

When I told her Fern was going back to Peyton, she seemed momentarily confused, as if we'd never discussed this. She finally said, "Oh. I'm glad to hear it. I think it's the right decision." She didn't fill me in on why she thought that, just skipped to her big news.

Her New Year's Eve show and the unveiling of her triptych had been an unqualified success. She'd brought over copies of articles that appeared in the art section of some big-name newspaper. "IBB's Triptych is a triumph!" the headline declared.

I raised an eyebrow. "IBB?" I asked.

Ivy smiled and waved her hand dismissively. "Oh, those art critics love to give us all little nicknames. They probably got tired of writing out Ivy Bane Berenstein."

"Really?" I was trying hard to be nice. I was happy Ivy was a big deal in the art world. I just sometimes wished I could be a big deal in some world. Any world would do.

Ivy and her agent were busy planning more shows and talks and unveilings, so naturally my problems fell a bit lower on her radar. Almost off the screen. I wanted to ask her when I might expect the bright shiny ending she promised, but decided not to bother. She was constantly popping in and out of our lives, dropping off and picking up Fritz between flights.

Jack stopped going to the Tuesday night meetings. Gwen accepted my explanation that one of us needed to be at home to keep an eye on Fern, and she stopped asking after him. I felt so alone. Occasionally, I saw Jack's sponsor, Otto, who was always friendly. He didn't act worried about Jack, which reassured me Jack might actually be attending lunch meetings.

Many nights, as I pulled up to the home of a client, I'd have to sit quietly in the car, trying to get my head on straight before going inside. I'd repeat my mantras over and over. "Let Go and Let God. Forgive and Forget. Let Go and Move On. Let Go and Let God."

I needed to have faith I could leave this all in God's hands. I had to believe there was a plan. God had a plan. It would work out. It might take a while and I was running out of patience. Often as I drove home after my hospice work, I fantasized about stopping by the liquor store and getting the biggest bottle of Merlot I could find. Then I'd drive to a sheltered spot and toast Jack, Ivy, and William with a big "Fuck You" as I finished off the bottle. Why were they all getting to live the life they wanted while I was dealing with the dying? Never mind it was the job and life I chose. Logic doesn't fit in with feeling sorry for oneself.

The only thing stopping me was Fern. No matter how she behaved, I loved her and forgave her. I wanted the very best for her in every way. She didn't deserve what had happened to her. I wasn't going to be one more adult who let her down.

This time, school issues would not get away from me. I drove Fern to Peyton. I'd made an appointment with The Wicked Witch of the West, Ms. Spezzeri and her flying monkey assistant, Ms. Trible. I stopped to look at Fern's locker on my way to the principal's office. All freshly painted. If only emotional scars could be painted over as easily.

When I got to the office, the secretary ushered me right into Ms. Spezzeri's office. Ms. Trible was already there. "Thank you for coming in, Ms. Bane," Ms. Spezzeri said while straightening out various stacks of files on her desk. Maybe I was supposed to be intimidated, thinking those huge stacks were all files on Fern. "I know none of us want a repeat of what happened the first semester."

"No. We don't," I replied, trying to sound confident and in command. Instead, I felt like the little kid sent to the principal's office for talking in class. I wished Ivy was with me. She was good at putting people in their place. However, she was off on an art show tour. As usual.

"We're being pro-active," Ms. Trible said, also shifting a pile of papers in front of her. It was like a parole board hearing. They held all the documents on their side.

"I'm glad to hear it. What is your plan for keeping Fern safe?"

They both winced. I'm sure they didn't think the issue was keeping Fern safe as much as keeping the rest of the school population safe from her.

"As I explained at the beginning of the year," I reiterated, trying to sound firm and in control, "Fern has had to deal with a lot. At a very young age. The death of her mother, losing her father, moving to a new, unfamiliar place and going to school for the first time. And instead of getting kindness and sympathy from her fellow students, she was teased mercilessly. Who makes jokes about the death of someone's parents?" I let that settle over both of them. They should have been ashamed for letting the mean girls rule the roost. Maybe they were afraid of them too.

"I am sorry to say, Ms. Bane, due to social media, kindness is in very short supply. It's not easy to battle that monster," Ms. Spezzeri said before turning to the guidance counselor.

Ms. Trible cleared her throat. "First, we have changed some rules. Any defacement of another student's locker or property will result in immediate suspension. Any inappropriate notes left in lockers, desks, or gym bags will also result in immediate action. We can't do anything about social media. We advise you to talk to Fern and ask her to tell you about any harassment she encounters either online or at school. We can't change things if we don't take immediate action."

I nodded. It appeared they were actually, finally, on Fern's side, but I wasn't letting my guard down.

Continuing, Ms. Trible said, "We know social isolation in the cafeteria is one of the weapons used against students. We have set up an alternative lunch space for Fern and other students who have been singled out by the 'popular' kids." Ms. Trible used air quotes when she said popular. "Some of the other teachers and I will monitor them in a separate area. They can listen to music. The teachers might read stories. We'll change it up as we see what's working."

Maybe this could be a good thing. Fern wouldn't be sitting alone while people threw things at her. Or gave her dirty looks.

"And finally, I have gone over Fern's schedule and none of her previous tormentors will be in any of her classes."

I was stunned. They certainly gave the impression they were taking this quite seriously and were going out of their way to fix the problems. Made me realize Fern wasn't the only child at the school being tormented by the mean girls.

I stood up and shook their hands, thanking them. "I am hopeful Fern will have a good semester with these changes." Ms. Spezzeri smiled, and Ms. Trible stood, waving me out of the office.

It all sounded too good to be true. Was it?

Chapter Forty-Nine

When Fern got home that afternoon, I asked her how things went. She shrugged and said, "It's okay. My classes put me in a different section of the school, so I don't see Isabell and her gang hardly at all."

I waited, wondering if she'd mention the new lunch set-up. Were they pulling the wool over my eyes with that pronouncement? Not wanting Fern to know I'd talked to the principal and counselor, I bit my tongue.

"And I don't go to the cafeteria for lunch anymore. About a dozen of us have lunch in a room by ourselves. Ms. Trible, the guidance counselor, was there with us and explained we were chosen based on some previous issues. She didn't say why we were picked, but I recognized a couple of the other kids who'd been bullied."

I pretended ignorance. "How was that?"

"Not bad, though who knows what will happen when everyone else finds out about it. Like we're being given special privileges or something. They let us listen to music. Play games. Ms. Trible said different teachers would be hanging out with us."

So far, so good. I could hardly breathe. I'd been nervous about how Fern was going to react.

As she left the kitchen to head up to her room with Thor, Fern turned and said, "There's also a new school rule about defacing school property, which means if you write some dumb mean stuff on a locker you could get expelled."

I exhaled as soon as Fern was gone. Only five and a half months. And things appeared to be under control.

For Fern's fourteenth birthday, she only invited one friend to come to dinner with us. Her name was Jessica. Fern met her in the lunch group. I wasn't sure why she ended up there. Whether she'd been victimized by the mean girls or if there was some other issue.

We went to Fern's favorite Mexican restaurant for dinner. Fern loved Mexican food. We picked Jessica up on the way to the restaurant. She was a nice-looking girl, tall, with long unnaturally black hair. It made me realize how pretty Fern was in a completely natural way. Jessica was already wearing lots of make-up. Fern wasn't interested in make-up, and I didn't encourage her to use it.

During the meal, I found there was something about Jessica I just didn't like. It was hard to put a finger on it. She was polite and well-mannered but obsequious was the word that came to mind. And phony. I decided to keep an eye on Jessica. At the same time, I tried not to let my imagination run away with me.

That night, I asked Jack what he thought of Jessica. He looked at me, bewildered. "She's a fourteen-year-old girl. What's there to think about? She seems nice and polite. It's good Fern has a friend." He turned back to the TV.

True. At least Fern had a friend. I needed to focus on that.

Over the next few months, there were subtle changes in Fern. She still wasn't the sweet, easy kid of seventh grade. She still didn't spend a lot of time with us. On the plus side, she wasn't openly hostile and belligerent. On the negative side, she was falling more and more under Jessica's influence.

The first change was make-up. One morning, as Fern dashed into the kitchen to grab her lunch before catching the school bus, she collided with me. She was wearing wild, bright eyeshadow and mascara. I opened my mouth to say something, but she was gone before I could speak.

After school, she took Thor out for his walk. The eye make-up was gone, either worn off over the course of the day or Fern had rubbed it off on the way home. When she returned and came into the kitchen to grab a snack, I said, "Hey did I notice some eyeshadow on you this morning? Thought you didn't like make-up?"

"I'm not a baby anymore. Jessica has been showing me how to use make-up. She says we have to be ready for high school. We can't look like unpopular dorks." Fern looked pointedly at me since I'd told her I wasn't the most popular kid in high school. I didn't want to tell her make-up or the lack thereof had not been the issue.

Fern asked Ivy to take her shopping on Saturday. The way she asked made it obvious she didn't want me to come along, but she didn't want to come out and say it. She believed Ivy was the better person to help her get the right look. I was decidedly not that person. When Ivy came to pick Fern up, she asked me if I was joining them. I wanted to grab my coat and say, "Yes, of course, thought you'd never ask." One look at Fern's face told me I better not.

"No, I need to do some work. Paperwork. Boring stuff. I have a new intake later this afternoon. You two go off and have fun." The bitter part of me wanted to add, "I know you two cool kids don't want me to drag you guys down to my level." I waved them off, smiling until the door shut.

Jack returned a little while later. He'd been out walking Thor and Frito. "Where's Fern?" he asked, hanging up his coat and the leashes.

"She and Ivy went shopping."

"Nice," he replied, not even asking why I didn't join them. I was relieved he hadn't asked. I think I might have burst into tears. How absurd was that?

When Fern came home, she was carrying bags of new clothes. Jessica was with her. Apparently, she'd also been invited along on the shopping trip to advise Fern. Ivy was merely the banker. Fern and Jessica ran up the stairs laughing. It was nice to hear Fern laugh, still I wasn't happy about what was going on. Maybe I needed to take a 'chill pill,' as the kids would say.

Ivy came into the kitchen, and I fixed her a cup of tea. "Weren't you leaving for a new client?" Ivy asked, sitting down on the kitchen stool.

"I switched it to tomorrow." Could she tell I was lying? "How was the shopping trip? I didn't know Jessica was going."

"Me either," Ivy said, blowing on her tea. "When Fern got in the car, she asked if Jessica could come. I said it was fine. I'm glad Fern has a friend. And Jessica's a really nice girl."

Everyone seemed glad Fern had Jessica. Why was I the only one who didn't like her? "Looks like you had a successful day."

Ivy laughed. "Yes, we did. Remember that first shopping trip right before seventh grade started and I could hardly get her to try on or buy anything? Let me tell you, things have changed."

I smiled. It was a bit forced. I wasn't sure I liked how much they were changing.

"The girls got make-overs at the make-up counter at the department store. You should have seen them. They both looked so glamorous. You would never have guessed they were fourteen."

"But they are fourteen," I said.

"It was fun, Rose. Lighten up."

Why was I the only one who was stressed? I wished I could lighten up. Everyone seemed to have completely forgotten about William. Fern didn't even mention not hearing from him on her birthday. Maybe that was a good thing though I couldn't imagine she was completely reconciled to her father dropping out of her life. And feeling Jack had dropped out of my life was an added pain. I wanted to sit down and have a long cry.

Jessica came banging down the stairs with Fern, and Ivy stood. "I said I'd give Jessica a ride home." Ivy gave me a quick hug and whispered in my ear, "Be happy. Things are great." And they left.

198

Chapter Fifty

*M*iddle school finally ended. We survived the five and a half months until the summer. There was a graduation ceremony, which Jack, Ivy, and I attended. Fern's name was called over and over as she won awards for all kinds of things. It was a nice way to end a bad time.

I was not pleased at Fern's reaction to her name being called so many times. She was sitting with Jessica, and she'd stand, shrugging, looking embarrassed instead of proud. Her new friends appeared to be laughing at her. None of their names were called for any awards. I thought how odd it was Fern found this group to be friends with, since it was apparent she didn't have much in common with them.

We were better prepared for Fern to stay that summer, and we'd planned many activities. After the annual beach trip with cousin Livy and family, we'd signed Fern up for a two-week sleep-over science camp, a month-long reading program at the library, and an art program at the local university. Fern, Ivy, and I also went back to New York for a visit to Ivy's gallery, along with more museum visits and Broadway shows. And lots of shopping. Fern had become a shopaholic, which didn't make me happy, but Ivy loved having someone to shop with.

We also took several weekend trips to the mountains with Thor and Frito. Thor was actually doing better. The vet was amazed at his resilience. During the entire summer, those weekend trips to the woods were the only time I saw the former Fern, the little girl I loved, emerge. She was tender and loving with Thor, making sure he enjoyed himself. And since she couldn't get any cell service, she wasn't on the phone with Jessica all day. Jack was happier and easier on those trips, too.

If there was one downside, it was Jessica's constant presence whenever we were home. The old expression—familiarity breeds contempt—certainly applied to my feelings about Jessica. I felt like I needed a bath after she visited. There was something so oily about her. Ivy, on the other hand, adored her, and she loved taking the girls out for mani-pedis, make-overs, and shopping.

I couldn't put my finger on what it was about her that bothered me so much. We'd met her father, a single dad, and he also seemed a bit of a hustler. Was I too judgmental? Ivy thought Jessica was great and Jack was indifferent, apparently not picking up any negative vibes.

At last, high school started and it did seem better than middle school. It was so large that the mean girls of the world were swallowed up in the void. I'm sure they were still there but there were a million cliques and they all stayed in their own circles. There were the athletes, the brainiacs, the nerds, the fashionistas, the goths, and the kids coming out, struggling with their new identities. And there were the druggies. They seemed like hippie hold-overs from the 70s but there was also a darker element there.

I wasn't sure what group Fern was in or if she was even in a group. She and Jessica and their small group of friends seemed to be on the fringes. Without Jessica's influence, I felt Fern would have been drawn to the brainy group. Jessica wasn't interested in grades. She and Fern had no classes together since Fern was in all advanced courses. My secret hope had been that Fern would drift away from Jessica and make friends with the kids she had classes with, but she seemed completely under Jessica's sway.

Before Thanksgiving, I sent another note to Zac and Luke asking them to tell William we would love to have him visit. Of course, we heard nothing back. He was probably still in Anchorage or wherever he had gone. Ivy had suggested hiring another private investigator to track him down again.

"I don't think it would work this time," I said. "Last time, William was living under his own name and not really hiding, since he thought no one cared about him or where he was. This time, he could be totally off the grid, not using his real name and taking jobs where he gets paid in cash. No trail to follow. He might have misled Zac and Luke, telling them he was going to Anchorage to throw them off."

Ivy frowned. She hadn't considered this. "You're probably right. No point in wasting the money. I just can't imagine where he is and what he's doing. I keep getting images in my head of an old skid row scene with drunk bums passed out in gutters."

"Let's hope he's crawling his way out and up." Even as I said this, I didn't believe it.

We got our usual crackly Christmas phone call from Zac. He confirmed that they had not seen or heard from William since he had stuck that note on the door. That was more than a year ago. "We got a good fellow to rent the cabin, and we're putting the money into the bank for Fern when she gets older. Maybe she'll eventually come back." Zac sounded hopeful. "Are you planning on coming again next summer? Bringing Fern for a visit to the old homestead."

"I don't know, Zac. We're trying to get through the first year of high school with a teenager." I said this hoping it sounded like a joke, which it wasn't, but Zac didn't need to know that. "We'll let you know."

Zac hung up and I stared at the phone. William, William, William, where are you?

Fern had not mentioned her father since we had returned from the disastrous trip to Alaska the summer between seventh and eighth grade. The summer that turned her life from triumph to despair. She made it through the next year by the skin of her teeth and now was in high school. Hopefully it would be smooth sailing until graduation.

I felt more and more isolated from Fern and Jack. My only constant companion was Frito, and we often sat on the couch together. I could tell him anything but he had no advice to give. I even felt cut off from Ivy because I couldn't tell her what I was going through.

I was the only one who didn't like Jessica. Ivy and the girls were constantly going off together, doing things. Ivy would invite me but it was so obvious Fern didn't want me to come that I usually declined the invitation.

One time, I told Fern she couldn't go because her room was a pigsty, and she hadn't been helping out around the house. "Having fun is not the only thing in life. You have to pull your weight," I said to her, trying to be stern but not mean.

She flew into a rage. "You just don't want me to go because you're jealous of Ivy. You've always been jealous. Living in her shadow. She was prettier, more popular, dressed better and had more boyfriends, not to mention she had kids and you were an old spinster until you met Jack."

It was like she had thrown scalding water into my face. My cheeks burned and tears pressed against my eyes. I didn't want her to see how much she'd hurt me. "Go to your room," I managed to say, trying to keep my voice steady. Fern stormed off and slammed the door to her room.

I went to the living room and collapsed on the couch. Frito jumped up in my lap and snuggled me. I buried my face in his fur, muffling my sobs. He licked my face and wagged his tail. How pathetic was I? I wiped my tears with the back of my hands and thought about what Fern had said.

Where had she gotten all of that from? I had shared a few things with her, joking that Ivy had been more popular than I was and a better dresser, but the rest of it? Was Ivy telling her things about me? How I couldn't get a guy and the only man I ever loved married her instead? He'd never noticed me and fell in love with her at first sight. My face burned again in shame.

Was I jealous of Ivy? Even Jack said she seemed to float through life without any worries or cares. She never had to work. I was still working. She had lots of money. Jack and I had some struggles. She was a famous artist. I worked with dying people. She had two wonderful kids and grandkids. I had wanted to have dozens of children and never had one. Just my brother's daughter, who seemed to hate me.

Maybe a small part of me envied Ivy. But in life, we make our choices for better or worse. I loved Ivy. I loved Jack. I loved Fern. Hopefully one day the world would right itself and harmony would return to our universe. Who was I kidding?

Chapter Fifty-One

We muddled along the best we could. Fern kept her grades up but her attitude continued to be atrocious. I went between trying to be stern and punishing her and forgiving her because she had lost her mom and dad. Consistency would have been a better choice.

Jack spent more and more time at the garage. He didn't even walk with Fern and Thor in the morning. Often it was left to me to take the dogs for a walk since Jack and Fern seemed to be in a contest to see who could get out of the house the quickest. At least the neighbors had become reconciled to Thor's presence. Some of them stopped to chat as we walked along, even offering Thor a hand to sniff, followed by a pat on the head. Thor accepted it all as his due. Frito pranced around until he got some attention too.

I was no better than Jack and Fern. I looked forward to calls and new clients so I could also be gone from home as much as possible. We were not a happy family. We were hardly a family. We ate dinner together, which was usually a silent meal. Fern would have spent the entire meal staring at her cell phone, but we had a no phone rule at the table. So, she didn't look at her phone but she didn't look at us either.

Jessica and Fern had discovered boys and spent all their time talking about them, texting them, hoping to be asked out. Was ninth grade too early to date? I thought it was. Fern had just turned fifteen. That seemed so incredibly young and vulnerable to me. I imagined if she was still living at the cabin, William would have met any boys that showed up with his shotgun slung casually over his lap.

Boys started coming to the house. They would hang out in Fern's room. The rule was they had to keep the door open. I would listen to the music and laughter float out of Fern's room. When Jack got home, he would announce that "the party was over" and everyone would troop down the stairs and out the door.

"Maybe you should get a shotgun." I smiled.

He didn't smile back. "What are you talking about?"

I turned and walked into the kitchen, not bothering to answer him. Not that he expected an answer.

School would be over in two months. I thought about Zac asking if we might come to Alaska for the summer. It seemed like a waste of money. Fern never brought it up. And I hated the thought of having to go to Ivy again, hat in hand, begging for money for the airplane tickets. Better to just fill Fern's summer with camps and classes and possibly some volunteer work. At fifteen, she could work at the library or maybe with children. Or animals. That would suit Fern.

Jack was getting more and more disgusted with kids constantly in our house. This was not the life he had envisioned when we married. It wasn't the life I had envisioned either, but I joked with him and said, "Only three more years and Fern's off to college."

He would not return my smile or laugh. "Don't know if I can last that long."

That was a punch in the gut. Was he saying he wanted to leave us? Leave me?

I wish I had the courage to talk to Jack, but our relationship was dangling by a very thin string. I imagined if I brought up that he seemed unhappy, which of course made me unhappy, the string would snap. "Now that you mention it, I am pretty miserable," he'd say before walking out. Forever.

Ivy invited me to go to Chicago with her for the weekend. She was having another opening. "You need to get away. Have a little fun. You seem so down."

My attempts to convince Ivy that all was well were apparently not working. Even she saw the cracks in the façade. "I worry about Fern. And I worry about William. Fern never mentions him. She doesn't mention her mom either. I try to get her to come to the cemetery on Mother's Day or her mom's birthday and she refuses. I guess I could force her, but what would that achieve?"

"Maybe she's reconciled to her new life? She always seems to be in a good mood when we go out."

My jaw clamped tight. I wanted to say that of course she's happy when she's with you, you buy her whatever she wants and demand nothing of her. But there was no point.

"I'm glad she has you to have fun with. I think she finds me and Jack to be a drag on her existence."

"That's the way all teenagers think of their parents. Get used to it." Ivy laughed. "And yes, it's nice she has a fun aunt too."

Ivy didn't realize that her words stung but maybe I should just accept that I was a parent now, which meant Fern would be at odds with us until she graduated and moved out.

I talked to Jack about Ivy's invitation. He shrugged. "Sounds fun. You could probably use the break. Between Fern and your job, not much fun going on here."

I should have been happy that he was encouraging me to go but of course I flipped it and was sad he didn't say he would miss me.

Next, I told Fern, whose only response was, "That's not fair. She should take me. I've never been to Chicago before."

That's not fair, the universal anthem of the teenager.

Chapter Fifty-Two

━━━◆◇◆━━━

I had never been to Chicago either, so I was excited. Ivy and I left on Thursday and got to our hotel in time to have a fabulous dinner. I had to admit that it would be pretty damn nice to live Ivy's life. At least I got to live it vicariously when she invited me along. The next day, I followed Ivy while she shopped. We shopped some area called the Magnificent Mile which made me laugh. "I'm more used to shopping the Walmart Aisle rather than the Magnificent Mile."

Ivy laughed. "Live a little." That night was the soft opening for her show, which was by invitation only. Ivy had talked me into buying a beautiful new blouse to wear. "You're my sister. You must be fabulous and glamorous so that everyone will 'ooh and aah' over the Bane sisters."

I agreed that we should both be gorgeous, if that was possible at our age, and I decided I deserved a treat so I bought the blouse. It was more than I would normally have spent, and I couldn't imagine where I would ever wear it again but it made me feel good to own something that nice.

I felt so adult with a glass of sparkling cider (no one knew it wasn't champagne), listening to people talk about Ivy's paintings. I was drawn into conversations which I enjoyed. It was nice to be able to interact with other people about things that weren't about drinking (or not drinking) or dying (or not dying). Or about teenagers moaning about their sad lives. I could get used to this, I thought as I sipped my drink.

When we returned late to the hotel, I noticed I'd missed a text message from Jack. I had texted him when we arrived and when we were leaving for the show but had only gotten a thumbs up emoji in response. This message said that he had to go out because a kid he was sponsoring was having a meltdown. He had to leave Fern alone, but he wasn't worried because she wasn't a child anymore. He told her that no one was allowed over while he was gone.

I texted him that I hoped things went well. A few years earlier, he had lost one of the kids he sponsored to suicide. I knew he worried. Normally he would not have gone out and left Fern alone, but I agreed—she wasn't a child anymore. And Thor would watch out for her. He was still large and intimidating. And he had a very intimidating bark. More like a lion's roar.

The phone woke me early in the morning. I looked at the clock. It was five in the morning, so it was six in Virginia. It was Jack. He was in a rage. "I got home this morning to find a bunch of boys asleep in Fern's bedroom. Fern and Jessica were on the bed and the boys were scattered on the floor. I threw them out, including Jessica, and told Fern she is grounded forever."

"Oh Jack," was all I managed to say before he started up again.

"You need to get that girl under control. You have spoiled her. Well, you've let Ivy spoil her. From now until the end of the school year she is on lock down. No going anywhere. No doing anything." Jack went on and on and on, repeating himself, repeating threats, anger, and accusations of my leniency that had led to this unacceptable behavior.

"Before we know it, she'll be pregnant or on drugs or drinking or worse. I want you to come home. Now. Get the first flight out. I shouldn't have to deal with your niece. She's your responsibility." And then he hung up.

Ivy had been sitting up in bed listening. Even though I didn't have my speaker on, Jack shouted so loudly she could hear almost everything he said.

"Whoa. What is up with Jack? You'd think he found an orgy or worse," Ivy said, standing up and grabbing her robe.

What could I say? How much did I want to say? I didn't want Ivy to think badly of Jack or worse than she apparently already did since he had just accused her of spoiling Fern and turning her into some hedonistic imp.

"Men." I rolled my eyes. "Always turning molehills into mountains. The boys probably came over and they were all up late and fell asleep. Of course, he had told her not to have anyone over so I can understand why he's angry." I got out of bed, grabbed my suitcase, and began to pack.

"You're not really leaving, are you?" Ivy looked stunned. "Tonight is the grand opening for the show. I want you to be here. You deserve a weekend off."

"Ivy, Jack's right. Fern is my niece. Our niece. Jack agreed to take her for a year with the understanding that she'd go home to her father after that. She's been with us almost three years and her father has disappeared off the face of the earth, so it appears we'll have her for at least three more years."

I wasn't even folding my clothes, simply tossing them in my bag. "That's a lot to ask of a person. To put up with a disagreeable, disrespectful teenager. Maybe it's easier if they're actually your kids. But Jack never wanted kids. He's been great but I think he's reached his end."

I got dressed and then went to the bathroom to brush my teeth. Ivy still looked decidedly unhappy. "I'm sorry. You don't know how sorry I am, but I have to go." I hugged her. "Have a wonderful time tonight."

"Stop. No point in going half-cocked off to the airport. You don't even know if you can get a flight." Ivy was right.

She grabbed her laptop and started typing. She waved at me and told me to order breakfast through room service. I thought I'd order heavy. If I even got a flight, chances were that I'd be flying late or making twelve stops with no time to grab a bite.

The food arrived and I began to eat. No point in letting it get cold. Ivy had only ordered a yoghurt parfait and coffee. I suddenly was ashamed of my eggs, bacon, and toast. But it was whole wheat toast. And I had a glass of orange juice. Don't say I don't eat a healthy diet.

Between bites I texted Jack and said I was trying to change my flight. He texted, *Make it happen*. My blood pressure shot up as I typed, *Trying*.

Ivy shut her laptop and collapsed onto the bed. "Damn. I think everyone in the world is flying out of Chicago today. Maybe there's something we don't know? Should we be worried?"

"No time to worry. Did you get me on a flight?"

"Yes. But seriously, you should wait until tomorrow. I got you on a 1:00 flight that flies to Dallas, Texas, where you have a two-hour layover."

"What the hell?"

"Your flight arrives in Dallas at 3:00 p.m. It will be four in Virginia. You fly out at 5:00, 6:00 Virginia time. You fly to Washington, DC, getting in at 9:00. Then you have thirty minutes to make your flight to Richmond. If you miss that, you're stuck for the night unless you rent a car. Best case, you get to Richmond around ten.

"And that's only if there are no complications or cancellations. What's the point? We have an 8:00 a.m. flight Sunday morning, which will get you home by eleven. Six of one, half dozen of the other, but at least you don't spend an entire day flying ass over elbow."

"That sounds much better but I don't think Jack will go for me staying over until tomorrow. He'll think I'm not trying so I can stay for the opening."

"Really? That doesn't sound like the Jack I know." She paused, remembering some of the things he had said. "I guess anger has made him a little irrational? Call him and tell him it's either ten tonight or eleven tomorrow."

I didn't want to call because I didn't want to hear him yelling again, so I texted him the details. His answer was terse. *Do it*.

"He doesn't seem to care. He wants me home tonight even though everyone will be asleep by the time I actually walk in the door."

Ivy shook her head. She had nothing more to say. Ivy got dressed and we went down to the coffee shop and stared out the window. There wasn't any time to do anything. I needed to leave for the airport at eleven at the latest. Traffic was always iffy though better on weekends. We had planned to walk through the parks today and get a photo together at the famous Chicago Bean. I also wanted to do some souvenir shopping for Fern and Jack. Not now. Fern didn't deserve anything, and Jack was too angry at me to want anything.

I picked up my suitcase and we walked out to the taxi stand. Hugging Ivy, I said, "I'm so sorry. Thank you for bringing me with you. I had a wonderful time. Just sorry I had to cut the trip short. Kick ass tonight." Ivy looked like she was going to cry. I hopped in the cab before I started to cry as well.

There was no traffic, so I got to the airport in plenty of time. Sailed through security and had a good two hours to wait. I thought of texting Jack to say I was at the airport, but he'd probably ignore me or make another rude remark.

Finally, it was time to board the flight to Dallas. I had never been to Texas but I wasn't sure if it counted as a trip to Texas if I only sat in an airport. Two hours later, we touched down. It was 3:00 p.m., which meant it was 4:00 p.m. at home. I texted Jack. *I'm in Texas. Leaving at 5 to fly to DC. I'll let you know when I land.*

There was no response for a long time before he texted *OK* in response.

Finally, the flight left, and I arrived in DC in time to catch my flight to Richmond. Jack hadn't said anything about picking me up, so I took a cab. I walked into a very quiet house. Everyone was no doubt asleep. It was almost midnight. Frito came tearing down the stairs, and I picked him up and hugged him before he started barking.

"Hey, little friend. At least someone is glad to see me." I walked up the stairs and into our bedroom. I brushed my teeth and slipped into bed. Jack rolled over and moaned but did not wake. I shut my eyes. It took me a long time to fall asleep.

The sounds from the kitchen woke me up. Jack was obviously not trying to be quiet. Opening one eye, I glanced at the clock. It was eight o'clock, but it felt like I had just crawled into bed minutes ago. I rolled over and opened my eyes. The ceiling looked the same. I was home. My stomach was in knots.

Sitting up, I swung my legs over the side of the bed and searched for my slippers with my feet before I remembered they were in my suitcase, which I had left downstairs. I found an old pair in the closet and walked down to the kitchen. As usual, Frito was the only one who greeted me enthusiastically. Jack stood in front of the coffee pot waiting for it to finish brewing.

"Morning," I said, trying to sound positive. I really wanted to scream at him like he had screamed at me. Or throw something at him. I've always thought bonking a coffee cup off someone's head would be quite soul satisfying.

At the sound of my voice, Jack turned. He looked terrible. "What time did you get in?" he asked.

"Sometime around twelve." I replied.

"Long day, huh? It was a long day here as well. Fern spent the whole day in her room. I've taken her phone away as well as grounding her. She screamed at me and told me I wasn't her father and I couldn't make rules for her. Then she stormed off. Didn't even come down to eat dinner."

I sighed. I had nothing to say. This was not going to be easy. "I guess I'll have to go up and make her come down for breakfast. She's probably starving and then we'll have to have a talk. Set up rules, etc. Hopefully she'll see that she violated your trust by having people over when you told her not to."

"That's doubtful. I'm afraid she's gone too far. She's this person I don't even recognize. Like she's been taken over by a demon. Maybe we need to perform an exorcism." Jack smiled weakly at his little joke. "Did you check on her last night when you got in?"

"No. I was too tired, and I thought Thor might bark and wake her up."

"True. You want to go get her? Probably better than if I go up. She's seriously angry with me." Jack sipped his coffee. "I'll make eggs. Maybe that will help."

I headed for the stairs. Frito danced in front of me. "You're going to trip me up and kill me, buddy. Calm down." I made it up the stairs despite Frito's best efforts. Knocking softly on Fern's door, I said, "Fern. Time to get up.

212

Jack's making breakfast." There was no response, which didn't surprise me. Opening the door, I peeked in. I saw Thor on the floor, which was odd since he always slept in bed with Fern. Stepping into the room, I saw why. Fern's bed was empty. Was she already up and in the bathroom? But why had she closed her door and left Thor in there by himself?

I walked over to the bed, even though it was obvious she wasn't there. I touched the sheets. They were cold. I looked at Thor. "Where's your Fern, buddy? Why did she leave you locked in here?" Thor looked grim. Can a dog look grim? He didn't wag his tail. I walked out to the hallway. "Fern? Jack's making breakfast." No response. I walked to the bathroom and knocked on the door. No response. I opened the door. The bathroom was empty. I glanced in the other rooms upstairs. I was beginning to feel panicky. Had she gone downstairs already?

I quickly went downstairs and into the kitchen. "Jack, is Fern down here with you?"

"No. Of course not. How could she have gotten past you? Isn't she in her room?"

Jack saw the look on my face and ran past me up the stairs and into Fern's room. He threw the sheets back on the bed, looked under the bed and in the closet. "Where is she?" He looked around in confusion. He glanced accusingly at Thor, who laid down with his head on his paws, the image of abject misery.

I'd followed Jack upstairs and watched as he darted from room to room before running downstairs. He went to the front door and looked at the coat rack and shoe rack. Fern's jacket and sneakers were missing. "Oh my God," he gasped. "She left. Where the hell is she?"

My heart was pounding, and I thought I might throw up. I heard a sizzling sound from the kitchen and smelled something burning. I dashed to the kitchen and saw the eggs turning black on the stove top. I grabbed the pan and turned the burner off.

Jack came in clutching the top of his head with both hands. "What are we going to do?" He kept repeating it over and over.

"First things first. We have to stay calm. Don't panic. Deep breaths. We can't come up with a plan if we're not thinking clearly."

We stood there breathing in and breathing out. Despite cautioning calm, I wanted to scream and pound things.

When Jack appeared somewhat calmer, I said, "We need to call Jessica. I'm sure that's where Fern would go. Isn't that what teenagers do when they take off? They go to their best friend's house. Complain about their parents and then come home. It'll be fine." I said that as much for myself as for Jack. It would be fine. It had to be fine. I wouldn't survive if it wasn't fine.

Jack went to grab Fern's phone from where he had hidden it when he confiscated it from her. "Do you know her password?" he said, struggling to get the screen to open.

"It's 1-2-3-4. I told her it had to be something we could use if we had to open her phone. No secrets. Hopefully she hasn't changed it."

We got lucky. The password still worked. Jack fumbled with the phone and almost dropped it.

"Why don't you give me the phone and let me call Jessica? Last time you saw her, you were yelling and threw her out of the house. Maybe it's better if I talk to her."

He reluctantly gave me the phone. He probably thought if Jessica heard his voice, she would turn into a quivering lump and hand Fern over. I doubted it. Jessica was not one to be cowed by adults. She was far too sneaky for that. I had to tamp down my dislike of her so she didn't hear it in my voice though I was pretty sure she already knew I didn't like her.

I found Jessica's number in the contacts and pushed call. The phone rang and rang. She didn't answer. I left a message. "Hi Jessica. This is Ms. Bane. Fern seems to be out early this morning and we were wondering if she's with you. Please call. We'll be coming over to talk to you and your father."

Jack looked confused. "Why did you say that we were coming over?"

"Because girls like Jessica have no qualms about lying. It's just harder to do it to our faces. And maybe with her dad there, she'll be less likely to lie."

We dressed quickly and headed to Jessica's. We knocked on the door for several minutes before Jessica's father appeared, looking like he had just crawled out of bed. After an all-night bender, I might add. He scratched his head and stared at us, confused. "Can I help you?" he croaked out.

"Hi. Maybe you don't remember us. We're Fern's parents. Jessica's friend?" He continued to stare at us blankly.

"We need to talk to Jessica. Now. Thanks." It was getting increasingly difficult to speak to this man in a civilized tone. I wanted to grab him by his dirty, ratty t-shirt and shake him until his teeth rattled. Jack put an arm on my shoulder. He could sense I was about to lose it.

"Ummm…I think Jessica's still asleep. Is Fern spending the night here?"

"That's kind of what we're trying to figure out."

Jessica's father went to the bottom of the stairs and bellowed, "Jessica, get your ass down here. Fern's parents want to talk to you."

He waited a few moments before yelling again. This time Jessica appeared at the top of the stairs. She was rubbing her eyes as if she had just woken up. She was such a devious girl.

"What? What are you yelling about?" Then she saw us and added, "Why are Fern's parents here?"

"Why don't you get the hell down here and they can tell you themselves. I'm going to make coffee." He stomped off in the direction of the kitchen, and we stepped inside and shut the door.

When Jessica got to the bottom of the steps, Jack suggested we go into the living room and sit down. Jessica followed us in.

"What's up?" she said when we were all seated.

"What's up is that Fern is missing. She's not at home. Her coat and shoes are gone. She's obviously taken off. What can you tell us about this?"

"Me?" Jessica almost put a hand to her throat in a dramatic gesture to indicate her innocence. "I haven't seen or spoken to Fern since yesterday morning when you," she nodded at Jack, "threw us all out of the house."

"So, she didn't come here last night?" Jessica shook her head. "And you have no idea where she is or might have gone." She shook her head harder.

Jack and I looked at each other. What were we going to do now? We both assumed that Fern would be hiding out at Jessica's house.

"I'll take a quick look if you don't mind," I said and headed up the stairs. I looked in Jessica's bedroom and glanced in the other rooms. Housekeeping was obviously not a priority. Downstairs, Jessica's father stood in the doorway leading from the kitchen into the living room, sipping a cup of coffee. He did not offer us any.

"You got some nerve going upstairs in my house, poking around." He was angry. I guess he had a right. It wasn't his fault his daughter was a bad child. Well, wait. It probably was his fault.

I said nothing. Jack stood up. "I've got the names of the boys that were over. We can start with them." Jack turned before we walked out the front door. "If you hear from Fern or hear anything about where she is, please call us immediately. We are worried sick."

Jessica tried to hide her smirk. "Of course. I'm worried too."

Chapter Fifty-Three

*W*e sat in the car, lost in our thoughts and fears. What now, what now, what now, echoed through my brain. I had been certain we would find Fern at Jessica's. Now I didn't know what to do.

The phone rang and my heart leapt, thinking it was Fern. I answered without looking at the screen. Ivy's voice came through the line. "Hey, where are you? I thought you were picking me up?" Was it eleven o'clock already?

"I'm sorry. I forgot. Didn't even realize what time it was. Things are not good here. Fern has run away."

"Oh no." Ivy sounded horrified. "Do you know…"

I wasn't in the mood to answer questions. "No, we have no idea. We went to Jessica's house, but she claims she doesn't know anything. We got names of other friends, including the boys who spent the night. We'll just work our way through the list."

"Don't worry about me. I'll catch a cab. Call me when you know anything."

"I will." I hung up and looked at Jack. His forehead was resting on the steering wheel. I touched him on the shoulder, and he sat up and looked at me. "What do you think we should do now?" I asked.

"As you said. Work our way through the list." He pulled away from the curb.

There was no one home at the first house. "It's Sunday. They could be at church." Jack looked doubtful, as if boys who slept on girl's bedroom floors didn't go to church. But maybe their families did.

We got lucky at the next boy's house. His name was Sam. We explained that our daughter Fern had run away, and we thought Sam might know something or at least give us names of more of Fern's friends. The parents were quite distraught and told Sam to tell us everything.

Sam was actually a very nice boy. His parents hadn't known he had slept over at our house. "He told us he was staying with his friend Tyler." They gave him a disapproving look. "We'll talk about that later. For now, please tell Fern's parents anything you might know."

Unfortunately, Sam knew nothing. "I'm sorry. I don't know where Fern is." He gave us the names of other friends, including some of Fern's girlfriends. I thought that was a better lead since Fern would more likely talk to other girls before sharing her plans with a boy.

By four o'clock we had spoken to a dozen teenagers, including the first boy, Ben, who had finally returned with his family. We left our names and numbers with the kids and their parents. Some of the parents were concerned and helpful. Some looked at us like what kind of people were we that our child had run away.

One of the girls, Olivia, seemed quite upset. I got the feeling she was not a fan of Jessica's either. "Jessica's always coming up with these plans of things we should do that I know my parents would freak out about. I try to stay away from her. I like Fern, but she seems to be under Jessica's thumb. Jessica's dad doesn't care what she does." Olivia promised she'd call around and let us know what she found out.

We got home, and I realized I hadn't called Ivy. Surprisingly, she hadn't called me either, which showed a great deal of restraint for her. Jack said he'd make us both a cup of tea while I phoned Ivy.

"Thank God you called," Ivy said. "I've been on pins and needles. Have you found her?"

"No." I paused. I had to collect myself before I continued. "We talked to lots of kids. No one knew where she might be. I'm pretty sure Jessica knows something, but she acted all innocent. I've never liked that girl."

"Have you called the police? Maybe she's been abducted?"

"I guess we'll have to. We were trying to find her before we pursued that route."

We talked for a few more minutes. Jack walked in with the tea, and I said goodbye to Ivy.

"What now?" I asked. "Do you think we should call the police?"

Jack put his head in his hands. He looked like he was going to cry. I was shocked.

"This is all my fault," he finally choked out. "I've been such an ass, letting a little kid get under my skin. I could have done more. Tried harder. Been more of a father to her." He swiped at his face. "Been more of a support to you. I know it's not been easy on you, and I just let you handle all of it."

I was speechless. Surprised that Jack had acknowledged his behavior. Surprised he apologized to me. "It's not been easy for either of us," I said, trying to make him feel better.

"Worse for you. Much worse without any help from me."

I stood up and walked over, sitting next to him on the couch. I hugged him. "You never knew you were signing up to be a dad when we got married. You did as well as you could."

Jack hugged me tightly, and we stayed wrapped in each other's arms for the longest time. At last, he pulled away. "I guess we need to call the police now."

It's always a surprise when you're in a situation you never thought that you'd be in and you have no idea how to proceed. Should we call 911? Or call the general number? Did we go to the station? We finally called the main number and were put in touch with someone who said they would make a runaway report. They sounded less than interested. "Most of these kids show up after twenty-four hours, forty-eight at the most. They're mad cause they didn't get their way. Go to a friend's house and hang out until they decide to come home. We'll put her description out to all the patrol cars. Let us know if she comes back on her own."

So much for the police. It sounded like we were on our own. Neither one of us were hungry but I heated soup and made grilled cheese sandwiches, my specialty. "We need to keep our strength up."

Jack took the dogs out for a walk. The poor guys had been alone all day and had been very good about not pooping in the house. When he came in, Thor walked up the stairs into Fern's room. He looked at the bed and then flopped down on the floor. He was the image of misery. He was missing his girl. How could she have gone off without him?

Chapter Fifty-Four

Neither of us slept well. Jack tossed and turned all night, which woke me. I got up a few times to look in Fern's room, praying she'd be there. Each time, Thor looked at me accusingly. "I'm sorry, Buddy. I'm as upset as you." He didn't appear to believe me.

I got out of bed at seven. There wasn't any point in trying to sleep any longer. Jack's side of the bed was empty, and I could smell coffee brewing. When I got to the kitchen, Jack was walking in with Frito and Thor.

Pouring a cup of coffee, I watched the dogs. Even Frito appeared depressed, not his usual bouncy little self.

"What's the plan?" I asked. "Or I guess I should say, do we have a plan?"

"We should go to school today and talk to Fern's teachers. Explain what happened. Enlist their help."

"Oh my God," I groaned. "How embarrassing. Excuse me, we lost our child. Can you help?"

"They're with these kids all the time. Maybe a teacher can get one of the kids to talk or give us a lead."

"You're right."

We dressed and headed to the school. We went directly to the principal's office. I was glad I didn't have to deal with Ms. Trible and Ms. Spezzeri anymore—the wicked witch and her flying monkey. They'd have been thrilled to call child protective services on me.

Jack asked the administrative assistant if we could talk to the principal, Mr. Carter, about our daughter, Fern Bane.

"What grade is she in?" she asked. We replied she was in ninth. "Oh, that would be Mr. Jefferson. Each grade has their own principal. They move up each year with the class and are with them the whole four years. That way they really get to know the kids."

What a good idea. No doubt I'd heard this at one of the assemblies, but it must have gone over my head. I realized how uninvolved I'd been with Fern and her high school experience.

"Great," Jack replied. "Can we see Mr. Jefferson?"

"Can I tell him what it's about?"

"It's kind of personal."

She could tell from our strained expressions it must be serious. "Hold on, I'll give him a buzz." A moment later, she put down the phone and said, "Go right in."

Mr. Jefferson was a tall black man with graying hair and a kindly expression. I liked him immediately. "So, you're Fern Bane's parents? You should be proud. She's quite the student."

Jack shook Mr. Jefferson's hand. "We're actually her guardians. I'm Jack Frost and this is my wife, Rose Bane. It's usually easier to say we're her parents than launch into a long explanation."

"I understand. How can I help you?"

It wasn't easy but we told him Fern had run away from home. Jack explained about getting angry at her for breaking the rules and grounding her. He told Mr. Jefferson he also took away her cell phone, and in the morning, she was gone.

"We spent all day yesterday going to see all her friends, including her best friend, Jessica Schmidt, and they all claim they don't know anything."

222

At the mention of Jessica's name, Mr. Jefferson grimaced. He looked down at his desk and shuffled some papers before looking up again. "I'm surprised that Fern and Jessica are good friends. They don't seem to have much in common." He laughed and shrugged. "At least not to this old man but young girls are a mystery."

I felt vindicated. He obviously couldn't say much about Jessica, but it was clear he wasn't fond of her. Even he knew what a bad influence she was.

"I will talk to Fern's teachers and possibly bring some of the students into my office to see if anyone knows anything. Have you called the police?"

"Yes, after we talked to everyone, we called. They said they'd alert all the patrol cars to keep an eye out for her, but they didn't appear to take it seriously. They seemed to think she'd come back on her own in a day or two."

Mr. Jefferson nodded. "They get so many calls from frantic parents. Luckily, most of the kids do come back quickly." He stood up and shook our hands. "I'll be in touch if I have any information for you."

We walked out to the parking lot and climbed into Jack's truck. We'd exhausted all our options.

Ivy was waiting on our front porch with Fritz in her arms when we arrived. "I couldn't sit at home by myself. I won't be in the way. I need to be here."

Jack and I both hugged her. "I completely understand. Let's go inside." I knew Ivy was here for the long haul since she'd brought Fritz with her. It meant she wasn't going home until we got some answers.

We let the dogs out while Jack made tea. Fritz never warmed to Thor the way Frito had, but he tolerated him from a distance. Thor, as usual, was indifferent to small dogs. He probably didn't even consider them to be the same species as something as magnificent as himself.

I filled Ivy in on our meeting with Mr. Jefferson. "We hope he'll find out something to at least point us in some direction. We're dead in the water right now."

Jack handed out tea mugs, and we sat silently, lost in our own thoughts. "I still think Jessica is the key to this. She's so smug. She enjoys being in charge, pulling the strings, watching us dangling in her web," I said angrily.

"Wow. I guess you don't like her very much," Ivy exclaimed.

"No, I don't. I never did. I was glad to hear Mr. Jefferson agree with me that she's manipulative and sneaky."

"Now Rose." Jack held up a hand. "That's not what he said."

"He implied it."

"Maybe we could abduct her and make her talk," Ivy joked.

"Don't joke. I'm tempted," I replied.

Ivy looked shocked, as if I was ready to press hot coals to Jessica's feet.

"What day is this?" I pushed my hair off my face. When was the last time I showered? I suddenly felt filthy.

"Monday," Jack said from across the room. "She's been gone for two nights. We're heading into the third night." He sighed in despair. "We have no leads and nowhere to go."

"We have lots of people out there looking. Something will turn up." I stood up. "I'm going to take a hot shower. Maybe it will clear my head. At least I'll feel slightly better." I walked up the stairs.

Standing in the shower with the hottest water I could bear pouring over me, I cried and screamed into my washcloth. Then I scrubbed my hair viciously with shampoo. I was drying off when Jack knocked on the door. He cracked it open and said, "Come downstairs. We might have a lead."

I threw on some clothes and ran down the stairs.

Ivy was sitting, and Jack was pacing. He looked up at me. "Mr. Jefferson called. He said one of the teachers told him Olivia, the girl we spoke to yesterday, approached her in tears, saying she didn't know what to do. She didn't want to get anyone in trouble, but she was worried about Fern."

Ivy picked up the story. "Apparently, at lunch today, all the kids were talking about Fern. There was an announcement over the PA system in the morning asking any student who had any information on Fern to tell a teacher what they knew."

Jack jumped in again. "Olivia said at lunch, Jessica was smirking and indicating she knew where Fern was, saying she'd helped her arrange to run away."

"I knew it, I knew it, I knew it!" I yelled in triumph. "That little bitch."

"By the time the teacher came to talk to Mr. Jefferson, Jessica was already gone for the day. Mr. Jefferson called the police. They are all coming over here." Jack said with a grim smile.

Chapter Fifty-Five

*N*ever in my wildest dreams did I ever imagine my living room filled with police like some scene out of a movie. Maybe there weren't really that many of them, but their radios squawked continuously, and they were in constant motion as they answered calls, so it seemed like a small army. Sergeant Fitzroy appeared to be in charge.

"We went to Jessica's house to interview her but she wasn't home," Sergeant Fitzroy explained. "Or if she was, she wasn't answering the door. We left a note on the door saying we'd be back in the morning to talk to her. Even if we don't scare her, her father will not want to get involved with the police. He's had more than his share of run-ins."

One of the officers came over and whispered something in Fitzroy's ear. He looked up at us. "Jessica's dad called. We're heading over there now." As quickly as they arrived, they all disappeared. Ivy, Jack, and I sat in the silence they left behind.

"We're finally getting somewhere," Jack said. Ivy and I agreed.

Mr. Jefferson called an hour later. "The police got Jessica to give them names of some boys Fern might be with."

"Oh, thank you, thank you, thank you," I cried into the phone. "Are the police going to the boy's houses to see if Fern is there?"

"It's complicated. These two don't live in Richmond. Apparently, they live in Harrison County, so our police have to coordinate with the police there. It's a big rural county and Jessica claimed she only knew the boy's first names, so they don't have an address yet."

I looked at the clock. It was already 5:00. It was beginning to look unlikely we'd have Fern home that night. Mr. Jefferson sensed my despair. "Don't worry. They're working hard on this. They're blanketing the county with Fern's photo and the police are all on the lookout. I'll be in touch as soon as we hear anything."

I hung up. Jack and Ivy looked at me hopefully. "Getting closer," I said, trying to sound optimistic. "They have some names. They think Fern is in Harrison County."

"Why on earth would she go there?" Ivy asked.

I just shook my head in response. Why indeed.

"I'll make more tea," Jack said, heading to the kitchen. "It's going to be a long night." God, how I wanted a drink, a real drink, not another damn cup of tea.

We sipped our tea and waited. Then we switched to coffee. None of us wanted to go to sleep. We were hoping to get another phone call telling us Fern was safe and on the way home. Thor had gone up to Fern's room, with his head and tail hanging low. He was obviously distressed at her absence. Frito was torn between going up with Thor or hanging out with his buddy, Fritz. He stayed downstairs.

When the phone rang at ten-thirty, we jumped. Fritz and Frito started barking. We were half asleep. I grabbed the phone. It was Sergeant Fitzroy. "We have her. We have to coordinate pick up with the Harrison Sheriff's department and then we'll bring her home."

As soon as I hung up, the phone rang again. It was Mr. Jefferson. "I'm sure you've already heard from the police. They've got her. It was a good thing we moved so fast on this. Apparently, around ten, she walked into a 7-11 and asked the cashier if she could use the phone to make a call. He had the flyer with her photo and description and told her to hold on a second so he could get his phone. When he got to the back office, he called the police. Fern had stepped outside, and he started talking to her, asking who she needed to call when the police pulled up. They were there in about five minutes. When they asked her if she was Fern Bane, they said she burst into tears and said she wanted to go home."

"Mr. Jefferson, we can't thank you enough," I said.

"Glad to have been able to help. You're going to have a long night. I suggest you don't send Fern to school this week. Better to keep her from the prying eyes of the other students." After saying goodbye, Mr. Jefferson hung up.

The police showed up around midnight with Fern. She walked in the front door with her head hanging down, the very image of misery. It was obvious she didn't know what kind of reception to expect from us. As soon as she stepped into the house, we were all over her, hugging her and kissing her. Thor came thundering down the stairs, and Fritz and Frito charged out from the living room. They swirled around us, barking and wagging their tails, beating them against our legs. Fern sat on the floor and hugged Thor, tears running down her face. I thought I heard her say, "I'm sorry buddy."

We started to ask questions, but Fern begged us to let it wait until the morning. "I am exhausted and dirty, and I want a long hot shower and then I want to climb in bed and sleep for a week." We reluctantly let her go upstairs with Thor, whose tail wagged fiercely. Fritz and Frito stayed with us, running around happily.

The police stood in the background while we had our happy reunion. "We'll be back in the morning to talk to your daughter. We need to determine if any crimes were committed. And we need the names of the boys she left town with."

We thanked them and shut the door. "We should go to bed too," I said to Jack and Ivy.

"I'm going to curl up here on the couch," Ivy replied. "I'm too tired to even try to go home." Fritz jumped on the couch, snuggling next to Ivy.

I handed her a blanket and an oversized t-shirt to sleep in. "Good idea. We can all be together in the morning." Jack and I climbed the stairs to our room. Even though I was completely exhausted, I couldn't fall asleep. Everything kept spinning around and around in my head. I blamed myself for everything, which is my typical go-to response when anything goes wrong. I finally fell asleep after tossing and turning for hours.

I moaned when Jack said, "Time to get up, sleepyhead. It's almost eight." He made it sound like I'd slept until noon.

"Eight's pretty damn early," I replied defiantly, keeping my eyes shut tight.

"Come on. We have to be up before Fern."

My stomach lurched, and I sat up. "Have you checked her room? Is she there?" I slipped out of bed, my feet searching for my slippers.

"Yes, I have and yes, she's there. Sound asleep."

Jack left the room, and I heard the coffee grinder going off in the kitchen. That would wake Ivy. I walked into the bathroom and put a hot washcloth on my face and scrubbed my eyes. Staring in the mirror, I winced. I didn't look well rested. There were bags under my eyes. I looked old. Old and wrinkled. Remembering the police saying they'd be back this morning, I decided to get dressed before heading downstairs.

Ivy was already up, drinking coffee at the kitchen counter. Despite having slept on the couch, she looked lovely. Sometimes it annoyed me; she always looked good no matter what the circumstances. It wasn't fair. All the dogs were in the backyard. I wondered if we should wake Fern or wait until the police arrived.

Ivy settled the question by suggesting we let Fern sleep in. "She's probably endured an awful time. God knows who those boys were or where she slept. Or what she ate." Ivy appeared particularly horrified over the prospect of Fern existing on Pop Tarts and hot dogs. Maybe that's what led her to decide to go to the 7-11 to call home. Missing home-cooked meals. Not to mention Thor. I still couldn't believe she'd left him. I hoped she missed us too.

Chapter Fifty-Six

At around ten, there was a knock on the door. We opened the door to find a young policeman standing there. Tall and dark-skinned, with bright eyes and a warm smile. Despite obvious differences, he reminded me of the young state trooper in Alaska who told us about the accident. It was odd, but I couldn't remember his name.

He was apologetic. "Good morning. I hope I haven't come too early? I know you were all up late."

"No, it's fine. We've been up since eight," I said as I ushered him in the house. "However, Fern isn't up yet. We decided to let her sleep in."

"I'm Officer Henry Lee," he said, taking a seat.

Jack called from the kitchen, "Would you like a cup of coffee?"

"Thank you. I would appreciate that."

Jack walked out with the coffee and cream and sugar on a tray. They shook hands.

Ivy said she'd get Fern up. I heard her walk up the stairs and knock on Fern's door. "Honey, the police are here. They need to talk to you."

I thought I heard Fern moan, though maybe it was my imagination. Ivy came down the stairs and sat next to me. "She's up. She'll be down soon."

About ten minutes later, Fern came down. She'd dressed before she showed up. A girl after my own heart, my motto being never meet strangers in your PJs.

Fern looked like a whipped dog. Her head hung down and her shoulders slumped. She collapsed into a chair and stared at her feet.

"Hi Fern," Officer Lee addressed the top of Fern's head. "I'm sorry to have to get you out of bed; however, we have some questions that have to be asked about…" He stopped, momentarily stumped by what to call the recent events of the last few days. "…what happened this weekend." He stared at his notes as if the answers to all the questions of the universe could be found there. "Okay?"

Fern shrugged almost imperceptibly. I could feel Jack's temper rising. We wanted answers too. "The sooner you answer the officer's questions, Fern, the sooner this will be over and we can all move on," Jack said in a firm voice.

"True," Officer Lee prompted. "First, we need to know how you got to Harrison County. Who did you go with?"

Fern finally looked up. It was obvious she hadn't considered she would have to explain what happened. I was sure she didn't want to get anyone in trouble, but she had to say something. "Umm…well, I met these guys at the 7-11 on Mason. I'd gone there cause I was mad at Jack cause he yelled at me and took my phone and so I snuck out of the house."

"Help me understand," Officer Lee sounded encouraging. "You're saying you left your house in the middle of the night and walked to the 7-11? And why did you go there? Were you planning on meeting someone? A friend?"

We all suspected Jessica was behind Fern running away, though persuading Fern to admit it would be tricky.

"No. I was on my own. Just walked there. No real reason."

"Must have been kinda scary out there. Walking the streets at night. By yourself? Mason's about five blocks from here, right?"

Fern shrugged again.

"After you get there and you're hanging out, you start talking to some random guys who live all the way over in Harrison County but are at the 7-11 on Mason Street in the middle of the night?"

Glancing up, Fern nodded.

"And you'd never met these guys before?"

Fern shook her head no.

"And you decided to get in a car with these two complete strangers and drive off to who knows where in the middle of the night?"

Fern nodded yes. It was a pathetic response. Her head barely moved.

"Fern, I don't want to waste my time, the police department's time, or your parent's time. We spoke to your friend, Jessica Schmidt, and she told us you were in Harrison County with some guys who occasionally work for her dad. It's a bit of a coincidence she knew you were with these guys since you said you ran into them by chance at the 7-11. And how did she know you were with them since, according to you, she wasn't even involved."

Fern's head slunk down below her shoulders again. She didn't respond.

"Let me tell you what we pieced together. You left home in the middle of the night. You got in touch with Jessica. She met you at the 7-11. And just in case you want to deny it, we have the four of you on the store's security camera.

"She talks you into running off with these guys to teach your parents a lesson. You drive off. Sunday, the Harrison County police get a call from one of these boy's grandmother, saying there's some girl hanging out in her grandson's friend's trailer and she doesn't like the looks of it cause the girl looks young."

Officer Lee glanced at his notepad again before looking up at Fern. "Sadly, at this point, the Harrison County police don't respond because your info hadn't been put in the state missing child website yet. Sound about right so far?"

Fern got smaller with every statement Officer Lee made. If she could have melted away and disappeared in a puff of smoke, she would have.

"On Monday, your parents go to the school and report you missing. Kids start talking and your friend Olivia tells her teacher Jessica knows where you are. The police finally talk to Jessica. She claims she only knows the first names of the boys and says they live in Harrison County. She denies any more involvement. Luckily you showed up at another convenience store and the clerk called the police. You were picked up and brought home."

We all sat silently, staring at Fern. She did not respond.

"I have this written up already. I will give it to you to read. If it differs in any way from what I've said, you have an opportunity to edit and make changes. I want to caution you not to lie to protect Jessica. We know she is in this up to her neck. We've brought both the guys in, and they are being questioned. We're considering charges for all involved."

"Charges?" Fern bolted straight up. "What charges? Am I going to be charged?" Her voice cracked, and tears filled her eyes. "I'm sorry Rose. I'm sorry Jack. I didn't think. I was mad at you and Jessica…" she started and stopped before finally deciding she couldn't or wouldn't protect Jessica, "she said you guys weren't my real parents and didn't have any right to treat me so badly. And I went along with her plan. But you aren't bad to me, and I am sorry for hurting you and…" Fern started sobbing and couldn't stop.

Officer Lee looked at me and handed me the papers. "She can look these over later. After she signs them, call and I'll pick them up."

I walked him to the door. "Is anyone going to be charged?" I asked.

"They could be, though it's unlikely. We had a happy outcome. Everyone learned a lesson. Sometimes it's the best we can hope for."

Chapter Fifty-Seven

Things returned more or less to normal. Fern took the rest of the week off from school. She was a little reluctant to return to school since she was afraid everyone was talking about her and pointing fingers. She was relieved when everyone greeted her happily, telling her they had been worried about her and were so glad she was home safe.

We told Fern her friendship with Jessica was over. Jessica was no longer welcome in our home, and Fern was no longer allowed to go to her house. Shopping trips and mani-pedis with Ivy were done. Fern didn't complain. She finally admitted Jessica had never been much of a friend. "She likes to manipulate people and be in charge. She liked getting Ivy to pay for stuff."

I tried to be kind, which wasn't easy. Forgive and forget, I reminded myself. "I don't think she has a happy home life. Her father doesn't seem to be very loving or caring."

A tentative smile crossed Fern's face. "Yeah. I think sometimes she was jealous of what I had here with you guys and wanted to mess it up. People are weird."

On one hand, everything seemed to be great with Fern. Maybe it was simply because Jessica wasn't around. She had rubbed me the wrong way from the moment I met her. At the same time, something about Fern had changed. Maybe it was learning her good friend wasn't much of a friend. Life had certainly given Fern some hard knocks. She was quieter. Not a sullen quiet. More of a sad, reflective quiet. I convinced myself she was embarrassed by what she'd done.

I was happy to have her and to have our family together. Jack and I were again in a happy place. We even started going to Tuesday night meetings together again. At first, I was worried about leaving Fern alone at home, but Jack said we needed to show Fern we trusted her. We also did family game and movie night every Saturday. If Ivy was in town, she'd join us, and we'd order pizza and play.

The memory of those game nights my mom used to plan for us when Dad was out of town floated up. Sadly, they always ended badly with Mom passed out drunk and Ivy and I carrying little Lily upstairs to put her to bed. Drink certainly ruined our childhoods. Drink almost ruined my life. Drink took William away from Fern. I still prayed he'd return to us.

Talking to Lauren, I told her I couldn't imagine having more than one child. "How do you get through the growing years and the teen years?" I asked. "As soon as you get one straight, the next one goes off the rails! I couldn't do it. Just trying to raise Fern is almost too much for me."

"In truth, most of the child rearing fell to Miranda. She'd only drag me in for the big decisions. Sometimes I felt like I was kept in the dark on a lot of what went on." Lauren was quiet for a moment. "Plus, several of them were in therapy for years. They didn't have a good start in life and needed a lot of help. And remember, Miranda and I did this in our thirties and forties, not in our dotage like you."

"I'm not that old!"

"Yes, you are. You're on the slippery slope to seventy."

"Oh, my God. It's true. How did we get so old?"

"It's better than the alternative. Dying young may sound romantic, but it's sad and a waste of a life." I knew Lauren was referring to my failed suicide attempt, which had brought her into my life.

"I feel guilty. I mean, I must have failed at motherhood for Fern to run away."

Lauren huffed angrily into the phone. "If you ever say you are feeling guilty about anything again, I am going to fly out there and beat your ass. Kids make bad decisions. Some of the best parents in the world have the worst kids and some of the worst have the best. A lot of it comes down to the friends they pick. Friends have a lot more influence than parents do sometimes. Fern sadly fell under the influence of a bad kid."

"I know. But you also know guilt is who I am. I have felt guilty about one thing or another since I was six years old."

"And I have been telling you to stop since you were eighteen." Lauren laughed.

"I'm working on it," I replied, laughing too. "I'm a work in progress."

"You're too old to be in progress. You should be finished by now."

"Agreed."

"Maybe you and Fern could come out here this summer. Show Fern the sights and sounds of southern California."

"Oh Lord, she'd probably start eating avocados with everything and start saying 'gnarly'. I don't think I could handle a beach bunny child."

"Better than a snow bunny."

"Just a regular child is fine." I paused. "And I think the snow bunny life and competing in the Iditarod is no longer in Fern's future plans. It was probably always unrealistic, but it gave her something to aim for. A focus."

"As we grow up, we sometimes have to let go of our childhood dreams. Remember when yours was to be a nun and spend your life in the stone walls of a convent?" Lauren laughed.

"I'm going to stop telling you anything about myself cause you're always turning it on me and joking about it." I pretended to be mad.

"Too late, Buttercup. I know it all now. See you this summer." Lauren made her goodbye kissy sounds and hung up.

Chapter Fifty-Eight

*I*n life, when you think you have everything sorted out and you're on an even keel, you don't realize an underwater earthquake unleashed a tsunami that is speeding toward you. The water surface looks calm. There is no sign of disaster heading your way. Maybe the first hint is when the lifeboat tilts.

About a month after the "incident" as I called it in my mind, not to Fern's face, I got a call from Fern's school. From Mr. Jefferson, actually. I was happy to hear from him and wondered if I'd thanked him enough for all he'd done. Should I have sent him a plant? A fruit basket?

"Mr. Jefferson, it's good to hear from you. I can't thank you enough for all you did. We are so grateful to have Fern back and I think she's learned her lesson and things are going great."

Mr. Jefferson interrupted me. "Ms. Bane. Can you come to the school today? I need to discuss something with you."

A cold shiver went through me. "Oh. What is it? Has Fern been behaving badly?"

Before I could continue babbling and asking questions, Mr. Jefferson interrupted again. "It might be better if we can talk in person. Can you be here by eleven?"

"Um. Sure. Should I bring Jack?"

"No. It might be better if it's just you. I'll see you then." And he hung up.

I put down my phone and stared at the wall. What could possibly be going on? Was Jessica causing problems again? I told myself it was pointless to worry or speculate.

At ten to eleven, I was in the principal's office. The admin assistant looked up and smiled at me. "Hello, Ms. Bane. Mr. Jefferson is expecting you." I walked over, and after a quick knock, opened the door.

Mr. Jefferson sat behind his desk. I went to sit down and noticed Olivia in his office, sitting in the corner. She looked completely miserable.

When I smiled at Olivia, she slumped down, staring at her hands clenched in her lap. I looked over at Mr. Jefferson. He also looked quite unhappy.

"Ms. Bane, there is no easy way to say this, so I will cut to the chase. Olivia came to my office this morning to tell me Fern told her she'd been raped by one of the men she ran away with. She told Olivia because she's worried she might be pregnant, and she doesn't know what to do."

The tsunami flipped the boat over and the anchor was around my neck, dragging me down to the depths of the sea. The roaring sound in my ears blocked out the rest of what Mr. Jefferson was saying. I wanted to cover my eyes and ears and scream, *stop talking*. I couldn't take any more.

Chapter Fifty-Nine

When I was a kid and something unpleasant occurred, I'd pretend I was in a play or a movie. That "this" wasn't really happening to me. It was merely a part I was acting out.

I tried to pretend this wasn't happening to us. To Fern. It was just a story. An act in a play and soon we'd all be bowing to the audience as they cheered our brilliant performances.

Mr. Jefferson suggested we call the police. I nodded numbly. I thought we were done living out a scene from some police drama. Unfortunately, we'd only made it through part one of the series. Now for part two.

Mr. Jefferson asked Olivia to wait in the conference room outside his office. She got up and walked out, pausing briefly to whisper, "I'm sorry," to me as she passed by.

I heard Mr. Jefferson talking to someone on the phone, though I couldn't concentrate on what he was saying. I kept hearing those words screaming in my head, "*Fern was raped. Fern was raped.*" What more could happen to this child?

Mr. Jefferson put the phone down and told me Officer Lee and a social worker were coming to the school to talk to Fern. I couldn't even imagine how Fern was going to react to being interviewed by the police again. And about something so incredibly awful.

Walking into the conference room, I found Fern and Olivia already there. Olivia was crying. Fern was staring down. She wouldn't meet my eyes. I sat next to her and put my arm around her shoulders. She flinched away. "Oh Fern, why didn't you tell me?" She didn't respond.

Finally, we were all together. Officer Lee looked quite distressed. He'd been happy to have "saved" Fern and thought nothing bad had happened. A woman introduced herself, but I didn't catch her name. The roaring in my ears was diminishing, but words still sounded distorted like I was under water.

Mr. Jefferson took charge of the meeting, which was odd since I assumed it was now a police matter. But he had such a calm, forceful demeanor, everyone naturally deferred to him. I was happy he was there. He cared so much. He was talking to Officer Lee and the woman. They appeared to be trying to come up with a plan of action. Mr. Jefferson finally turned to me and said, "Ms. Bane?" I stared, not comprehending what he was saying. He stopped and began again.

"Ms. Bane, unfortunately, you will have to talk to the police and the Commonwealth's attorney in Harrison County. The police here would love to be able to help, but the crime took place out of their jurisdiction. Ms. Lockley will call and make an appointment for you and Fern to meet with them."

He glanced at the woman who I realized must be Ms. Lockley. She jumped in, "I'll call as soon as I get to my office. After I have a date and time, I'll get in touch and tell you when to be there."

I nodded, not moving. Finally, Mr. Jefferson stood up and thanked Officer Lee and Ms. Lockley for coming and they left. He turned to us. "I'm sorry Fern. We'll do whatever we can to support you through this." And we left.

I drove home in a daze. Part of me wanted to ask Fern what happened. At the same time, I didn't want to know. Plus, at some point I'd have to tell Jack about this, and I didn't want Fern to have to tell the story twice. When we got home, Fern asked if she could go to her room. I could hardly hear her, she spoke so low.

"Yes. When Jack comes home, we're going to have to talk about this." I'm sure she knew that. Was it a good idea to tell her? Did she have to be told beforehand? She'd probably agonize about it until he came.

I went to the kitchen and made a cup of tea. I was hungry. It was way past noon. I'd missed lunch. Did Fern have lunch? Probably not. No doubt she wasn't hungry. My stomach clenched in sorrow and anger. Hopefully, the tea would take the edge off my hunger.

I needed to talk to someone, though at the same time I didn't feel I could form the words needed to explain what happened to Fern. Unluckily (or luckily) Ivy was out of town. Not only out of town, but overseas. Her agent believed there was a market there for her paintings and she'd gone to "test the waters." I wasn't going to ruin her trip. There was nothing she could do.

I considered calling Lauren, but I didn't want to tell her. After Fern came home, I was happy, assuming she had emerged from this episode unscathed. But she was scathed. Possibly for life. How would she, could she recover? I chastised myself. People did recover. Fern would recover. Jack was in my corner, and we were a family again. We'd circle the wagons and take care of Fern.

I made a pot of tea and put the pot and two cups on a tray with the cream pitcher and sugar bowl and carried it up to Fern's room. I knocked and opened the door. Fern was in bed with Thor. She sat up.

"The English make a hot cup of tea with lots of sugar when things go wrong," I said as I walked in. "It's always made me laugh, but maybe they have the right idea."

Setting the tray down, I poured two cups of tea and carried one over to her. I pulled the chair closer to the bed and picked up my cup. "Be careful, it's hot," I said, blowing on it.

We sat quietly blowing on our tea. Thor put his head on Fern's lap. She absentmindedly stroked his ears.

"Do you want to tell me about it?" I asked gently.

After a long silence, she shook her head and said, "No."

"When we go to Harrison County, you'll have to tell the police and the Commonwealth's attorney what happened."

"I don't want to. Do I have to?"

"Don't you want this guy to be punished? To… I don't know… pay for what he did?"

"Maybe he didn't think he was raping me."

"What do you mean?"

Fern started crying. "These guys helped me run away, and they were hiding me and feeding me and maybe he thought I owed him or that I wanted to…" Fern paused before whispering, "…have sex with him."

"Did you?"

"No! No! I've never had sex. I didn't want to, but I didn't say no. I just let him do it." She was sobbing now.

I put the teacup down and managed to squeeze next to her on the bed. I hugged her and rocked her. "It's going to be all right. You didn't do anything wrong," I muttered and murmured and rocked her. I rubbed her back until she fell asleep with Thor stretched out beside her. "Watch her Thor. Guard her." Where was he when she needed him? I shut the door and went downstairs.

It occurred to me there was one more visit we had to make. Fern needed to be checked out by a doctor. We needed to know if she was pregnant or had a venereal disease. I shuddered, imagining what awful things she could have contracted. Any friend of Jessica's was no doubt unclean.

What would we do if Fern was pregnant? It was too awful to consider though it would have to be confronted at some point. I didn't want Fern to have a baby at fifteen, but did we want the first grandchild of William and Margie to be aborted? I'd call my doctor first thing in the morning. For now, I pushed it all to the back of my mind.

I must have dozed off because I started when I heard the door open and

Jack's voice call out, "hello." Our world was about to fall apart again. I could hear him looking around for me since I was usually in the kitchen at this time of day.

"I'm in the living room," I said. "Can you come here? I have something I need to tell you."

As his boots clumped toward the living room, my dread built.

"What's up?" Jack said, sitting next to me and taking my hand. "Is Fern all right? Everything okay?"

I told him. I could tell he wanted to jump up and drive to Harrison County and hunt this boy down and hurt him. Hurt him badly. It was a good thing we didn't know his name or where he lived.

Squeezing Jack's hand, I said, "I understand how angry and upset you are. I'm seething with rage. We thought we'd dodged a bullet. We thought everything was fine. I knew something was wrong. I kept telling myself she was ashamed of what she'd done, but she was ashamed of what was done to her."

We heard a noise on the steps and turned to see Fern and Thor. "Come here baby," Jack said, and we sat in a group hug for a long time. Thor squeezed his head in between us and Frito jumped up on the couch, trying to find a spot to wiggle in.

Fern actually smiled and laughed. "Dogs are so silly."

"Best medicine." I smiled at her while patting Frito and Thor.

"Is there anything for dinner?" Fern asked. "I'm starving."

"Breakfast for dinner," Jack declared, "including my world-famous pancakes."

Chapter Sixty

Ms. Lockley called first thing the next day and said the Harrison police were available to talk to Fern on Friday. We drove over and Fern went in by herself to talk to them. It distressed me to have to sit outside and wait. When they came out of the interview, they announced they'd be charging Mr. Dale. Fern looked completely exhausted.

Monday, we received a call saying we had an appointment the next day with the Commonwealth's Attorney of Harrison County. I scribbled down the address and time. After dinner, Jack said he'd take off work and come along. Fern started saying she didn't want to go. "Can't we just forget the whole thing?"

"Let's see what he has to say," Jack said. "Then we can go from there."

The address was a few blocks from the police station. The office was in an ancient building, and the entire Main Street appeared to be the same, with little shops and restaurants. Under different circumstances, I'd have found it charming.

The old building seemed somewhat lopsided. Jack struggled to open and close the door. I worried the entire structure might give up and collapse on top of us. We gave the secretary our names, and she clicked on her computer and said, "Please have a seat. Mr. Singleton will be right with you."

No sooner had we sat down, when the old wooden office door behind her desk swung open and a man in a charcoal-gray suit stepped out. "I'm Mr. Singleton. Do come in. I hope I haven't kept you waiting."

We filed in. Jack in front, me in the back, and Fern wedged between us. Mr. Singleton offered us chairs with a sweep of his hand. "I'm sorry we're meeting under such difficult circumstances." He smiled at Fern sadly. He was the epitome of an old Southern gentleman. Long, wavy white hair flowed down past his ears. An angular nose graced his ruddy face and bright blue eyes stared out at us. He wore a suit with a vest, and I could see a pocket watch chain.

We sat down. "I know this is not easy, Fern, to tell an old man what happened, but I need to hear the facts to know how to proceed."

In a small voice, Fern told about getting angry with us and running away with these two men who her friend Jessica knew. She said the plan was to blackmail us into certain concessions before she came back home. "It was Jessica's idea. She said it was foolproof. I could get whatever I wanted from Rose and Jack because they'd be frantic for me to come home." Fern hung her head when she related how she agreed to go along with the plan. "After Jack fell asleep, I snuck out and met Jessica. We went to the 7-11 near the house where these guys were waiting."

"And these men would be Brandon Dale and Devon Brown?" Mr. Singleton said, reading from a notepad.

"Yeah. I didn't know their names then. They introduced themselves as Brandon and Dev. No last names. We drove to Brandon's trailer, which was parked next to Dev's grandmother's house. I didn't know, like, who lived where and with who."

Mr. Singleton nodded encouragingly while making notes.

"So, when we got there, Dev left, Brandon went into the bedroom, and I fell asleep on the couch."

Some of these details we were hearing for the first time.

"The next day was pretty boring. Jessica texted and told Brandon my parents had shown up and things were working out great. There was nothing to do. I sat and watched TV. At one point, I went outside to get some fresh air." Fern grimaced. "It was stinky in that trailer. Cigarette smoke, rancid food smells, and BO. I saw this old woman staring at me out of the window of the house, so I went back inside."

"Ahh, yes. Mrs. Brown, Devon's grandmother." Mr. Singleton said. "She called the police because she didn't think you should be there, but unfortunately, they didn't respond."

Fern nodded sadly.

"What happened later?"

"Devon came over with some leftovers from his grandmother. I'd hardly eaten all day, so I was grateful to get some food. I overheard Devon telling Brandon his grandmother was not happy about me being there and she wanted me gone. Brandon blew him off, saying it'd be fine and Dev needed to get his grandmother to calm down."

Fern took a deep breath. "After Dev left, Brandon sat next to me on the couch to watch TV. Then he, like, began getting closer and putting his arm around me. And I was trying to move away, and he was joking and saying stuff like come on, let's party. I thought I was gonna be sick. And he pushed me down and started pulling my pants off and I froze. Kinda blacked out what was happening."

Mr. Singleton looked up. "Did you say no? Or tell him to stop."

Fern was quiet for a long time. "No." She spoke so softly I could barely hear her.

"And why not?" Mr. Singleton asked gently.

"I thought I owed him. And I was afraid. I worried if I screamed or pushed him away, he might beat me up." Her voice faded again. "Or kill me."

The only sound in the room was Mr. Singleton scribbling away. The memory of Ivy's first wedding flashed through my mind. I remembered Franklin, the best man, suggesting we go outside and party. I knew if I'd let myself get dragged outside, I'd have been raped even if I said no. I understood how Fern felt. Powerless. My face flushed and I thought I might faint or vomit.

Mr. Singleton glanced up. "Thank you, Fern. I know that was difficult. I believe the police are quite familiar with Brandon Dale, which is another reason they should have gone to his place when Devon's grandmother called.

"We'll be scheduling a preliminary hearing hopefully for next week. You will have to tell your story again in front of a judge. This is not a trial, but Mr. Dale will be there with his lawyer. His lawyer can ask questions too. From there, we'll decide how to proceed."

"Please, no." Fern moaned. "I don't want to. I don't want to see him again. I don't want to tell anyone else what happened. I want it to go away. I want to forget it."

"I know you don't believe this now, but you will feel much better, empowered, if you confront this man. Hopefully, he will be punished. You'll save the next girl from this predator."

We all stood up. Jack and Mr. Singleton shook hands. "My office assistant will be in touch to give you the date of the hearing." He leaned down and looked Fern in the face. "Be brave. You can do this. I know about you. You're the girl who tamed a wolf."

Fern's eyes widened. "How do you…?"

"I know things. I hear things." Mr. Singleton smiled, tapping the side of his head. "If you could wait outside, I need to talk to your parents for a moment."

Nodding, Fern stepped out and Mr. Singleton turned to us as he shut the door quietly. "I want you two to be aware that these cases are very difficult to prosecute and get a conviction. But it's important that we try." His smile slipped, and he suddenly appeared old and tired. "I don't want to give you false hope, but I will do everything I can."

We thanked him and walked out of the office. I wanted to scream or cry or throw or hit things, but I needed to be brave. For Fern. Jack's face was locked in a grim mask of anger.

Chapter Sixty-One

⚬⚭⚬

$\mathscr{F}$ern didn't go to school the rest of the week. I scheduled a visit with the doctor for Fern. She didn't want to go. "You have to go. We have to know if you're pregnant or if you contracted some kind of disease." She grimaced.

At the doctor's, I let Fern go in by herself. I offered to go with her, but she declined. I imagined her under the sheet, naked, bright lights, feet in the cold stirrups. Another assault, in a way. At least my doctor was a woman. I hoped it helped.

Fern walked out, looking humiliated and defeated. The doctor said they'd have the results in a few days. She glanced sorrowfully at Fern and me.

On Friday, Mr. Singleton's office called. The hearing was scheduled for Monday. I told Mr. Jefferson Fern would miss another day. He said not to worry. He also said Olivia wanted to go with us. To offer Fern moral support and even testify if necessary. There wasn't anything she could testify to, but I appreciated she wanted to be there for Fern.

I went up to Fern's room. She was on the floor with Thor, listening to music. She looked up when I walked in. "Do we have a date for the hearing?"

I nodded. "Monday. So, we have the weekend to prepare."

"Okay."

"Olivia wants to come with us. With you. Is that okay? I know you're kind of upset with her for telling Mr. Jefferson what happened. But she was looking out for you."

"I know she was."

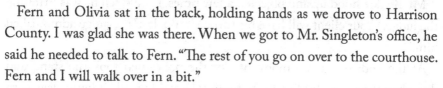

Fern and Olivia sat in the back, holding hands as we drove to Harrison County. I was glad she was there. When we got to Mr. Singleton's office, he said he needed to talk to Fern. "The rest of you go on over to the courthouse. Fern and I will walk over in a bit."

We went to the courthouse, another ancient building seemingly on the verge of collapse, and found our seats. Olivia sat between us. She now held my hand.

A few minutes later, Mr. Singleton walked in with Fern. She looked transformed. Not afraid. Determined. Mr. Singleton must have given her a pep talk. She sat behind him in the front row. A moment later, the door banged open and a scruffy young man walked in wearing an ill-fitting suit that looked like he'd borrowed it from a relative or found it at Goodwill. This was the man who'd hurt Fern. Brandon Dale. There was another man with him who I assumed was his lawyer, since he carried a file and a briefcase. They sat at the table opposite Mr. Singleton.

There were several policemen in the court, but no one else. Mr. Singleton told us it was a closed court hearing. The bailiff told us all to rise, and the judge walked in and sat down. The judge looked kindly at Fern as he glanced around the courtroom.

The judge nodded at Mr. Singleton, who rose and announced he was there representing the Commonwealth. He outlined the basics of the crime, reminding the court the defendant was not someone Fern knew. They had no relationship at all. And he reiterated Fern was only fifteen, below the age of consent. Then he sat down.

The judge looked at the defendant and said, "Mr. Boxley, how does your client intend to plead?"

Mr. Boxley stood, buttoning his suit coat. "Not guilty, your Honor." No surprise there. I foolishly hoped he'd simply confess and save Fern the embarrassment of testifying. No such luck.

Mr. Singleton put Fern on the stand, and she told her story. She spoke in a soft, clear voice. Mr. Singleton prompted her.

Mr. Boxley stood up and objected a few times. I could tell he was irritating the judge. "Your client will have his turn, Mr. Boxley," the judge admonished him.

At the end of her testimony, one of the policemen took the stand and described the events leading up to finding Fern. He made it quite clear Fern was so desperate to get away from Brandon Dale, she'd walked several miles to find a phone to call home.

There were no more witnesses. Mr. Boxley stood again, claiming this was a basic difference of opinion. A he-said, she-said case and it had no merit. Since Fern hadn't gone to the hospital until a month later, there wasn't any evidence there'd even been any sexual activity.

The judge thanked Mr. Boxley before quietly looking down at his notes. He called Mr. Singleton up to the bench and asked him a few questions. After Mr. Singleton returned to his chair, the judge glanced around the room, saying, "Based on evidence presented, the court finds probable cause and certifies the charge to the grand jury."

Everyone filed out of the courtroom. Mr. Singleton was smiling. "I believe that went quite well. We have that rascal right where we want him. I have a few tricks up my sleeve he won't be prepared for."

We thanked Mr. Singleton and drove home. The girls were quiet on the drive. We told Fern she'd done a wonderful job. She'd been so brave. "Yeah. Mr. Singleton told me before we walked over I needed to channel all the guts it took to win the Iditarod, and I did."

Tuesday, the doctor's office called. Fern was not pregnant and did not have any kind of venereal disease. If there was a silver lining in this terrible event, that was it. I did not even want to think about having a conversation with Fern about what to do if she was pregnant.

The grand jury found probable cause, and a trial date was set. A week before the trial was due to start, Mr. Singleton's office reached out, asking if Jack and I could come in the next day. Was this good or bad news? "Not Fern?" I asked but was told she wasn't needed. Mr. Singleton had some news for us.

My mind was jumping through hoops. I tried to go over all the possibilities with Jack, but he didn't want to talk about it. "Waste of time. We don't know anything. Let's just wait and see." I hate it when he's logical. It took me a long time to fall asleep.

We were shown into the office the minute we arrived. "I'm sorry if I worried you," Mr. Singleton said after looking at my face. "It's actually good news. Brandon Dale has decided to plead guilty. To a lesser charge but still guilty. I convinced his friend Dev to testify against him and the grandmother, Mrs. Brown, was also going to testify. He probably felt the noose tightening."

"So, there won't be a trial?" Jack and I asked at almost the same time.

"No. I would have liked to send him away for a very long time, however we didn't have an airtight case, so I took what I could. As I told you, these cases are hard to prosecute. And the best part is, Fern won't have to testify in front of a room full of people and describe all the details. Again."

We agreed that was a good thing. Fern was dreading going to trial.

"We'll call this one a win for the good guys. Tell Fern Mr. Singleton sends her his best. It was a pleasure meeting her. I'm sorry this happened to her." He paused. "These are the kinds of things that can make or break a person. I believe Fern will emerge from this stronger. But give her time."

Fern was happy the trial had been cancelled and Brandon Dale would be punished. It was time to look forward, not back.

Chapter Sixty-Two

When Ivy came home, we told her what had happened to Fern. We all sat together and hugged some more and cried some more. Ivy apologized to me later for not being around. "Rose, all this got dumped on you. I feel terrible."

"Don't stress about it. What could you have done other than sit here and hear the horrible details?"

"I could have been here for you. Held your hand. Hugged Fern. Made tea."

I laughed. "The tea would have been great. And it would have been wonderful to have your support. It's fine. Jack was here. We pulled through."

I also called Lauren and told her. She was enraged. She thought we should have held out for a stiffer sentence.

"Sometimes justice isn't quite an eye for an eye," I replied. "Yes, I'd have been happy if he was sent away for years, but what if he was acquitted because it was basically a he-said, she-said, and he got away completely?"

"In a perfect world, women wouldn't have to prove they were violated or coerced or manipulated," Lauren fumed. "They wouldn't have to answer to police or lawyers or judges who ask, 'What were you wearing? How much did you have to drink? Did you say no?' As if the burden is always on the woman."

"True. Sadly, we don't live in that world yet. Things are better than they were. Not perfect yet. However, Fern did not want to go through with the trial. It would have been humiliating to have to tell what happened to her in a room full of people. And maybe this guy didn't go away for life, but now he has a criminal record. If he does it again, they can throw the book at him."

"Being involved with the criminal justice system, I see way too much of this kind of thing," Lauren said sadly.

"I'm sure you do."

"It's always harder when it happens to someone you know. We never think it will happen to someone we love. Crime is for other people. Strangers."

I sighed. How true. Even though our family had been visited by death, divorce, alcoholism, disease. This was the first crime.

"Tell you what," Lauren said. "How about you let Fern spend the summer here? She'd really love it, and we'd love having her. I think we have a couple of grandkids around her age who are still around. I'll check with Miranda. She always knows the names and ages of everyone." Lauren laughed.

"Sounds great. I'll talk to her about it."

"I could set her up with an internship. Might give her an idea for what she would like to do in the future. She'd make a wonderful lawyer. She has the brains and the grit." Lauren made her kissy-sounds and hung up.

Fern and I developed a new routine for bedtime. She and Thor would come to our huge bed, and we'd all curl up together and read. Of course, Frito was there too, snuggled up with his huge buddy. We bought Thor a ramp to get up and down into bed. His joints were getting stiff.

"I know how you feel, Thor." I'd say after he climbed up and plopped down next to Fern. "Old age isn't for the weenies. You've got to tough it out."

For story hour, we were going back to childhood classics. I thought they'd be comforting. We read through all the Winnie the Pooh stories, The Wind and the Willows and before we tackled Alice in Wonderland, we were reading some shorter illustrated classic books.

I'd just finished reading "The Velveteen Rabbit" and Fern and I were in tears. "Oh Rose, that is the saddest book ever. Why did you read it to me?" Fern snuggled into my shoulder, wiping her tears on my nightgown.

"I always loved that book. Best book ever. I've read it many times and every time I am sobbing by the end, which shows the power of the story and the power of the message." I kissed the top of Fern's head.

Fern looked up at me. "I guess it had a good ending, but so many sad things happened."

I wiped away her tears. "Life can be hard and full of pain, as you well know. And love can hurt, but it's worth it. It's worth it to love someone with every part of your being."

"Like I loved my parents." I could hardly hear Fern, she spoke so low.

"Yes, just like that. You loved them so much. Which is a good thing. They were wonderful parents who loved you too and gave you an amazing life. Your mom may not be here on earth with you, but her love is still with you. And your father, he still loves you and eventually love may bring him back."

"You think he will? Come back?"

"I hope he will. I know you've been terribly hurt by what happened. When my baby sister died, it broke me. I couldn't imagine life without her. At the same time, if someone said to me, 'We will make it as if Lily was never born. You will never miss her because she won't have ever been a part of your life,' I'd have said 'No! Never!' because knowing and loving her was such a big part of my life. I never want to forget her. You should never regret loving or being loved.

"And loving Lily made it easy for me to love you the moment I met you because you were part of my brother and part of me and part of Lily. And by extension, part of my parents, who were damaged individuals, but I loved them too. You were like a promise that love goes on."

Fern smiled. "Really?"

"Yes." I tucked her hair behind her ear. "When I was younger, I wanted to have dozens of children. I wanted to fill my life with love, the love I had for Lily."

"Why didn't you get married, Rosie?"

"I fell in love and the boy broke my heart. That happens often with first loves because sometimes one person loves more than the other one does. I let it hurt me and I was afraid to try love again. I kept missing my chances." I didn't think I should mention that Aunt Ivy married the love of my life, Terry. Some stories don't need to be shared.

"I'm sorry, Rose. You'd have been a great mom."

"Thanks, but don't be sorry. As Ivy and Lauren always tell me, everything happens for a reason. Actually, they claim I always say that, but I don't remember ever saying it!" I laughed.

"If I'd married and had a dozen children, then I wouldn't be here with you right now with a huge wolf laying on my leg, putting my foot to sleep, and I wouldn't have that odd little creature, Frito, but most importantly," I glanced up and saw Jack leaning on the doorjamb, "I wouldn't have met and fallen in love with and married the best guy ever on this earth. The guy I'd been waiting for my whole life."

Jack jumped on the bed with us, scaring the dogs. Fern squealed as Jack tickled her. "Yes, indeed, sometimes you have to wait for the best things in life to come your way," he said in a deep, growly voice.

And at long last, we were a family. A mom and a dad, a wolf and a dog and best of all, a daughter to center our world around.

Chapter Sixty-Three

It was time to retire. I was sixty-five. I had spent my entire life dealing with other people's problems, which was my way of paying the universe for my mistakes. But in hindsight, what had been my mistakes? Lily's death led to William's birth which led to my parent's getting divorced which led to Mom drinking which led to Ivy's terrible first marriage. I could go on and on.

But those weren't my mistakes. I wasn't responsible for Lily's death. I wasn't responsible for what happened to my parents. I was partially to blame for how Ivy and I treated William, but she led the charge on that. Now I was switching from blaming myself to blaming others.

I was responsible for my drinking. My isolation. My lack of relationships.

Maybe that's why I chose to be a therapist and a hospice worker. It made me feel good to help others. Or to feel I was helping others. But now I had one specific person to help and take care of. That person was Fern. I probably should have quit my job when she first came to live with us. Would things have turned out differently or do things actually happen for a reason?

Jack continued to work at the garage. We weren't rich, sometimes I felt we were slipping below middle class, but we had food on the table and a roof over our heads. And a cabin in the woods.

Now that I was a full-time mom, I joined the PTA. Kept up with local school politics. All that stuff I never had time for before. I supported Fern in all her activities. Sports, drama class, field trips.

The summer after that terrible ninth grade year, Fern spent a month with Lauren as her intern. I flew down to pick her up when she was done. She couldn't stop talking about how wonderful it had been. "I got to go behind the scenes. I met famous people. I served coffee to Zane Alexander!" She said this with such breathless excitement I didn't have the heart to tell her I had no idea who that was. "I went to the beach almost every day." The list never ended. I was afraid she was going to want to move to California immediately.

The last night before we flew home, Lauren and I went out to dinner together again. Just the two of us. She couldn't stop raving about Fern. "She is so bright. So exceptional. I know it was terrible what happened to her family, but it would have been awful to leave her up in the wilderness of Alaska. That girl can go anywhere. Be anything."

"I'd like to take all the credit but Margie was a wonderful teacher who opened Fern's eyes to the world even in their remote setting."

Lauren laughed. "You can take some credit too, Rose. Give yourself a pat on the back. You deserve it. You and Jack and Ivy too. You know I was never a big fan of your sister because I thought she took advantage of you, but I think going to New York with Ivy was another great experience. Museums, art, Broadway, and good food. Let's not forget the good food!"

"When we get home, Ivy, Fern, and I are finally going on that trip to Chicago. I didn't really get to see much the last time I went. That weekend when everything went to shit." I glanced at Lauren, "And don't even say, 'everything happens for a reason'. It may be true but I will seriously punch you if you say that one more time."

Lauren laughed and laughed.

The rest of the summer went well. We had our trip to Chicago. Fern loved it, though she still thought New York was the best big city in the world.

Right before school started, we all went for a whole week to our cabin in the mountains with Thor and Frito. Jack continued to make improvements. Having guy's weekends with his AA buddies. They had done such an amazing job fixing the cabin up that I hardly remembered how bad it had once been.

Each time we went to the mountains, we thought it was Thor's last time, but the woods invigorated him and gave him new life. I began to hope that he would live forever. I had gone from fear and loathing to loving Thor as the most wonderful dog ever. He had been the one constant in Fern's life. On Fern's next birthday, they would both turn sixteen. My fingers were crossed that he'd reach that milestone.

A week before school started, Mr. Jefferson asked us to meet with Fern's guidance counselor. A new program was available for a select number of students. Fern had to take a test to see if she qualified to attend the Governor's school for arts and sciences. Of course, she passed easily.

I was living my best life ever. I never imagined when I was a snarky drunk that I would enjoy being a wife and mom but then I remembered my dreams when I fell in love for the first time. I had absurd notions of living in a cottage in the woods with dozens of children and pets while my husband went off to work at the university. The dream included me growing all my own fruits and vegetables and making everyone's clothes. We would never watch TV but would read stories and play games like Scrabble and Chess.

I didn't quite achieve that level. We only had one child and two dogs. I did cook fresh and delicious meals but only a bit of it was grown in our small garden. I never learned to sew, so we had to buy our clothes at the store. And while we did have game and story nights, we also loved to watch movies and documentaries on TV.

When not traveling, Ivy spent a lot of time at our house. She never married again. She liked being our "third wheel" as she called it, though actually she was our fourth. Life was good.

Chapter Sixty-Four

Given our history, I should have been more prepared for another upheaval in our lives. Nothing with the Banes went smoothly for very long.

One day, there was a knock at the door. Frito flew down the stairs barking, followed by Thor, moving slower but reaching the door before I did. I opened the door and stared out the glass partition at a filthy, shaggy man. What was this obviously homeless creature doing at my door? Before I could speak, Thor began to whine, and his tail wagged. I looked at the man. I could barely see his face, it was so covered in a shaggy gray beard but then I looked into his eyes.

Could it be? I threw open the door and grabbed him. "William! Is it really you?" I yanked him into the house and stepped back for a better look. The dogs circled around, barking. Frito had picked up on Thor's good mood so he was yipping happily.

The man laughed and kneeled down to hug Thor. "Thor, old buddy. Good to see you again." He stood up and hugged me so hard I thought my ribs would crack. "Oh Rose, you're a sight for sore eyes."

"What the hell... Where have you been... why are you...?"

"Rose. Stop. At least let me in the door before you give me the third degree.

I'll tell you everything. I promise."

"Before that, I have to ask you to shower and change your clothes. You smell a bit ripe."

William laughed. "I bet I do. I'm coated with weeks of grime. It will feel good to stand under hot running water."

We walked upstairs. His only luggage was a small duffle bag. "Unfortunately, I don't have any clean clothes on me or in my bag."

"Never mind," I said, handing him some towels. "I'll find something of Jack's that you can wear. Then I'll wash your clothes."

Grinning as he shut the bathroom door, William said, "You might just want to toss them in the trash."

I knocked on the door when I heard the water turn off. William had been in there for over thirty minutes with the water running full blast. "There are clean clothes on the bed. Come downstairs after you're dressed."

Fifteen minutes later, William came down the stairs. He had combed his hair back but I could still barely see his face. "Come in the kitchen. I have a chair set up. That beard and hair have to go."

I trimmed the beard as close to his skin as I could. William rubbed his face. "Haven't felt my skin in a while. I'll shave the rest of this later."

"Now for a haircut." I was no expert but I used the old bowl cut method and at least got his hair cut above his ears. I stepped back. "Not great." I winced. "But better. We'll go for a real haircut later this week."

William stood up and walked into the small downstairs bathroom and looked in the mirror. "Yes. Much better. Not great, but much better."

"At least you look like a human being and not a bear."

He laughed. "It's safer to look that way when you're on the road. No one tries to rob you because they think you're crazy and broke." He paused. "Well, the broke part was and is certainly true."

Flopping on the couch, he said, "You just don't know how good this feels to be clean." Thor climbed up on the couch next to him. "And Thor. Oh, my goodness. I wasn't expecting you to still be around."

"I think he was watching over Fern until you returned." My eyes began to fill with tears.

William buried his face into Thor's fur. "Thanks buddy."

We sat quietly for a moment.

William looked up. He had a huge smile on his face. "Before I begin my tale, can you please get me a little something to eat and drink?"

"Of course. Sorry, I should have asked." I ran to the kitchen and made a huge turkey sandwich with chips and a pickle. The works. I poured him a Coke, remembering he liked Coke. He joined me at the kitchen counter and sat down. He swallowed the entire Coke first. "Ahhhh… that tastes so good," he said, setting down his glass before biting into his sandwich.

After he took the last bite, William stretched. "Now for a nap."

"Absolutely not! Now you tell me what the hell has been going on for the last four years."

"Do I have to?" He pretended to whine.

"Yes. You have to."

We walked out to the living room. William sat quietly, as if gathering his memories. "I know you guys came the summer after Margie died. I was a coward. I couldn't face you. I'd started drinking again. I kept telling myself I could quit any time. Then the week before you were set to arrive, I realized I'd been lying to myself. I couldn't quit. I got angry and said to myself, 'Why the hell do I have to quit. If I want to drink, it's nobody's business but my own.'"

William stared down at his hands. He didn't speak for a while. I waited. "You know how good alcoholics are at lying to themselves," he said, looking up at me with a sad smile.

"I do indeed."

"So instead of feeling guilty, I convinced myself I owed nothing to nobody. Even my own daughter." He winced.

"After you guys came and left, I snuck back to the cabin. I was angry you'd cleaned it up, though mostly angry you'd thrown out my leftover beer. I wasn't sure what you might be planning to do, like come and grab me up and take me to rehab…"

"That's exactly what Ivy wanted to do," I said.

"I decided before the white-coated men arrived on my doorstep I would take off for Anchorage and change my name and live the life I wanted." William shook his head. "Apparently that life included working low-paying jobs and passing out drunk in the streets."

"Which is exactly what Ivy envisioned. She said you were probably laying in a gutter somewhere with an empty liquor bottle in your hands."

"She wasn't far wrong." William stared off into the distance before he continued. "But one day, something happened. When I woke up, I wasn't in the gutter, I was in a hospital. Again. Another damn hospital. This time in some kind of ward. Someone found me half frozen to death and had dragged me to the hospital. I was told if this person, a good Samaritan as they called them, hadn't done that, I would be dead. My second brush with death."

William was quiet for a moment, lost in memories. "It was a wake-up call. Why was I doing this? I started going to meetings and began to rethink my life." William ran a hand through his hair. "You know that story of the prodigal son? The kid who's an asshole and takes off from home with his inheritance, spends all his money, and ends up living in a pigsty cause that's the best job he can get?"

"It does sound familiar." I smiled.

"I realized that I had a family who loved me and a daughter who needed me… well, maybe didn't need me but who might still love me and want me in her life."

I nodded. "Seems like you lived two Bible stories. The Good Samaritan and the Prodigal Son."

William grinned. "True. I decided I needed to come home but I wasn't just going to call and ask for money. I still had stuff to work out. So, I decided to hitchhike home."

"From Alaska?" I was incredulous.

"Yes. For the last year or so, I've been hitchhiking and working my way from Alaska. I've had some adventures, believe you me."

"I believe you."

"And now I'm back with my family. I hope to be welcomed. You have my permission to kill the fatted calf to celebrate my return."

"Sorry, all out of fatted calves but we can probably order pizza," I laughed. "I have to say, I'm surprised anyone gave you a ride, considering your wild appearance."

"AA helped with that too. At truck stops, I'd try to find a 'friend of Bill's.' There was always one, and I'd bum a ride." He smiled. "Some days I didn't look quite this bad or smell so ripe."

I glanced at the clock. "Your daughter will be home from school shortly. I don't know how to break the news to her. She might hug you or punch you."

"I deserve a punch or worse. I hope I'll get a hug."

Chapter Sixty-Five

Fern did not punch her dad. Instead, she fell into his arms, weeping. She hugged him, and I thought she would never let him go. She kept saying, "Why and what and how?" William kept saying sorry over and over again.

We went through the same emotional upheaval when Jack came home though not quite as kissy-huggy. I called Ivy and she arrived shortly after Jack. She tried to be a bit more standoffish and angry with William but quickly started hugging him and crying too.

We ordered pizza and William told his story over and over again until he finally said he was done. "You know everything I've done for the four years since the last time I saw you guys. Now, I need to catch up with what's been going on here. Especially with Fern, who I barely recognize. She was just a gangly little kid and now she's all grown up."

We caught him up. We weren't sure whether to tell him what had happened to Fern when she ran away but she actually brought it up. "I was so mad at you, dad. For abandoning me. For not caring. For not loving me. I took it all out on Jack and Rose. I made bad friends. Made bad decisions and ended up in a bad situation." She sat quietly. I could tell William was afraid to hear what had happened.

"I got raped." She spoke softly, looking down at her hands. "But I got lucky. Rose and Jack and Ivy were on it. Looking for me. They had everyone out looking. The school. The police. I made it home and it was a wake-up call."

William's face turned red with anger. "Where is this guy? I'm going to kill him."

"No. You're not. If that had been the solution, Jack would already have done it. There was a trial. He pleaded guilty and he was punished. I don't know where he is now but it doesn't matter. I've moved on."

William pulled Fern over to him, buried her in his chest and cried. I knew he felt guilty that he had not been there. Had not protected his little girl.

That weekend, we visited Margie's grave. William sat for a long time on the bench with his head in his hands.

"Do you like the headstone I picked out?" Fern asked. "It reminded me of Alaska." She paused. "I can't believe it's been three years since I've been there."

"Maybe we can go back this summer," William said, and my heart sank. Was he going to take Fern away from us? Glancing up at me, he added, "Just for a visit. I think I'm done with Alaska. I went there originally to lose myself. I'm ready to rejoin the family."

A few weeks after William arrived, we celebrated Fern's sixteenth birthday. It was mostly a family affair. Fern hadn't made many friends at school, preferring to study and read. Olivia was there. They'd remained friends. We made reservations at the best restaurant in Richmond. Cate and family came down and we had a giant cake that said *Happy Sweet 16* and a smaller cake that said *Return of The Prodigal Son*. William got a good laugh over that.

Two weeks after the birthday celebration, Thor passed away. We were gratified he'd made it to sixteen.

Fern and William had taken him and Frito for their morning walk. When they got home, Thor collapsed on the kitchen floor, struggling to breathe. William picked him up and carried him outside and placed him on the ground. Fern tried to remain calm so she didn't upset him. We all sat around him, stroking his fur and telling him what a good boy he was. I remembered how terrified I had been of Thor. He really was the best dog ever. Frito curled up next to his big buddy. He seemed to know what was happening as well.

Fern said, "He was waiting for Dad to return. He felt he had to watch over me until then." After he took his last breath, we went inside, leaving Fern with Thor for her last goodbyes. We decided to have Thor cremated so we could sprinkle his ashes on the family plot. We sprinkled the rest in the woods by the cabin. It had been a happy spot for him and for Fern.

A few weeks after the end of the school year, William and Fern flew to Alaska. William had let Zac and Luke know they were coming. Both brothers had married since William had disappeared, and Zac was the proud father of a little boy.

They spent a month in Alaska, and William decided to sell the cabin where he and Fern and Margie had begun their lives together. He got a job at Jack's garage. It didn't pay much but it kept him busy. Ivy offered to let him move into her spare room. She was gone more than ever, traveling the country to galleries and openings. When she was home, she was often in her studio painting. But William decided he'd rather squeeze in with us. Ivy was a bit miffed but understood William had missed too much of Fern's life, and he wanted to be with her as much as he could.

The three of us also went to AA meeting several times a week. On weekends, William often went up to the cabin, either with Jack or Fern or by himself. "I like going there. Reminds me of my early days in Alaska."

"Wish you could have been here to help make it livable when we first bought it. At least you would have known what you were doing." I laughed. "You should have seen the place. To call it a wreck would have been an over statement."

Jack bristled at the suggestion he needed William's help. "I think I did a pretty damn good job."

"You did an amazing job."

Life was good. The ship had righted itself. We had reached the shore. We were tucked into a safe harbor.

Chapter Sixty-Six

I can't say that William became a second father to Fern, since he was actually her real father, but he did try to become the best father ever. And he became a better person, too.

He often deferred to us because we had raised Fern since she was twelve. But he was there for every occasion, discussion, and moment. At least once a month they went off to the cabin together. Fern missed Thor the most when they were in the mountains. We asked her if she wanted another dog and she thought about it before saying, "No. It's probably not a good idea. I'll be going to college soon and the dog would be confused and depressed since he wouldn't know where I was."

We had many lively discussions about what Fern should study at university. How did she envision her future? She asked each of us what we had wanted to do at her age, which led to many laughs.

Ivy said, "All I wanted to do was find a rich guy and live a life of leisure. I had no interest in college. Or having a real job." She smiled ruefully. "My wish came true but it didn't turn out to be the dream ending I thought it would be."

We all knew the story of Ivy's first marriage to rich-boy Preston. "But I don't regret a minute of it." Ivy continued. "If I hadn't married that jerk, I wouldn't have my kids and grandkids. And I never would have met Terry."

"So, everything does happen for a reason?" I teased.

"Yes, I think it does. Though at the time when we are in the midst of sorrow and turmoil, we don't see it. If I had gone to college and studied art, I'd probably have ended up marrying some nice boring guy and moved to the suburbs and had Tupperware parties. I don't think I'd have become the artist that I did."

William spoke next. "I didn't even graduate high school, so I never had any thoughts of college or what I wanted to be." He was quiet for a few minutes, remembering his arrest for drugs and subsequent enlistment in the army. "I was a bit of a loser. No. I stand corrected. I was a total loser. I had an after-school job at the local grocery store and if I hadn't joined the army, I'd probably still be there. Maybe still living with mom and eating canned ravioli daily."

William smiled at all of us. "Or I'd be married to some woman who'd also have a dead-end job. We'd have a bunch of kids and live in some crummy apartment. I never would have ended up in Alaska. I never would have met Margie, and I would never have had the best kid ever." William leaned over and hugged Fern, rubbing his knuckles on the top of her head.

"Ouch! Stop." Fern laughed. "How about you Jack?"

"Same. I had no plans. No thoughts of the future. Couldn't wait to get out of high school cause I hated following rules and all the classes bored me. I figured I'd work at my dad's garage forever." He smiled a bit sadly. "Alcohol, the demon rum, changed my life. Not for the better. My dad threw me out and then one day when I decided to get sober, I met an angel in a cemetery who changed my life."

"So sweet," Ivy said.

"Gag me," William said.

I leaned over and kissed Jack.

Fern turned to me. "And now I want to hear from the only member of our family who actually went to college. What did you want to be when you grew up, Rosie?"

"I'm not sure I considered what job I might enjoy. I just knew I wanted to get away from home and getting a degree and a good-paying job seemed like the best way to achieve that."

William piped up. "Funny how we all just wanted to get away from home and the different directions we took to achieve that."

"True. Poor Mom. She would have been so hurt to realize that the only motivation she created in us was a desire to escape."

I thought about what I had dreamed of as my future career way back in the day. "I actually wanted to be a librarian. Seemed like a great job. I could spend all day reading. It would be quiet, and I wouldn't have to interact with too many people, annoying co-workers, or mean bosses. I'm sure that's not true. I think every job has a potential downside."

"Why didn't you become a librarian?" Fern asked.

"I was afraid of Ivy. I thought she'd laugh at me."

They all hooted and roared, slapping each other on the back.

"Me?" Ivy finally managed to choke out. "Why did you think I would laugh? Though I probably would have. What a dorky job. I always thought librarians were the lamest."

"I was convinced you'd tell me just that, along with saying I'd be an old maid forever if I became a librarian. You were off living a glamorous life in the big city. And I would be wearing my hair in a bun with thick glasses, wearing a dress out of *Little House on the Prairie* telling people to 'shush'. I couldn't face your ridicule!"

Ivy's face contorted, trying to suppress her hysteria over that image. Everyone joined in the merriment.

Fern looked disapprovingly at the others. "How did you end up becoming a therapist?"

"I kind of fell into it. I have Lauren to thank—or to blame. After she and I became friends, she convinced me to study psychology to help me with my issues. I was a bit annoyed she thought I had issues but of course, I did. So, I switched my major.

"I thought it would be easy just listening to people talk and muttering the occasional encouraging word. After I graduated, I realized I had to have a master's degree to actually get a decent job. Not sure I would have studied psychology if I knew that from the get-go. Plus, since I was broke and jobless, I had to move home with Mom. Ugh." I grimaced.

William jumped in, "And me too. I was still at home. Still in high school. Thank goodness Rose was there when I got busted. Mom was pretty useless. She was hysterical so Rose took care of everything."

I gave William a mock bow. "Glad to be of service." He bowed back.

"And you all know that it was mom's death that gave me the idea to switch to hospice work. It was a good job. Tough but ultimately satisfying."

Ivy rolled her eyes. She always thought it was awful to spend your life dealing with death.

I turned to Fern. "But now comes the really important question. What do you want to do when you grow up?"

Fern smiled. "I want everyone to guess."

William jumped in first. "I know you had to give up on your original dream of competing in the Iditarod, but I still think you want to do something with animals? A vet?"

"I'm not sure if my dream of winning the Iditarod was ever realistic. But it did give me something to focus on," Fern said. "Any other guesses?"

"I agree with William. You love animals so much I think a vet would be a perfect career," Jack said.

"I'm not sure. Vet seems like a good choice but I'm not feeling it," Ivy said. "But I don't know. Of course, I recommend being a famous painter. It has a lot of perks."

We all got a laugh out of that. "I agree it does, but I think it requires some talent which I decidedly don't have. Never made it past stick figures." Fern smiled wryly. "Now your turn Rose."

I stared at Fern, tilting my head to the side, scratching my chin. "Hmmm... I'm not sure. You could be anything you want, but the question is, what do you want?"

Fern grinned at me.

"I'm thinking maybe a reporter? Like Lauren. You had an amazing time in Hollywood."

"I did. Lauren has a fabulous life and fabulous career, but she has like eight different degrees. Way too much schooling. If you thought just getting a master's was a lot of work, imagine going to law school and getting two or more master's degrees. I think the best thing is being a perpetual student and never actually working at all."

"I could see you teaching at university like Terry," Ivy said.

We all agreed that Fern would make an excellent teacher.

"So, don't keep us in suspense any longer! What do you want to be?" We all shouted.

"To tell the truth, I don't know. There are so many choices. I'll hopefully narrow in on something when I go to college."

We all groaned and threw the sofa pillows at her.

When you're young, a year is an impossibly long time. From Christmas to
Christmas seems an unbearable wait. As you get older, the years zoom by
with hardly a chance to catch your breath.

Chapter Sixty-Seven

When you're young, a year is an impossibly long time. From Christmas to
Christmas seems an unbearable wait. As you get older, the years zoom by
with hardly a chance to catch your breath.

It felt like William had just arrived and now we were sitting in the high
school auditorium waiting for Fern to walk across the stage to get her
diploma. She was the valedictorian, having achieved some astronomical
grade point average that wasn't even possible when we were in high school.

In her speech, she mentioned all the positive influences in her life, starting
with her mom and dad. Ivy, Jack, and I were mentioned as her second family.
She also talked about Thor and how someone once told her that she could do
anything because she was the girl who had tamed a wolf.

"At a very low point in my life when I felt completely worthless, someone
said those words to me. I realized I was the same person I'd always been. I was
the girl who could do it all. My dream had been to compete in the Iditarod
sled dog race. I never got to do that, but there are many other challenges out
there waiting for me."

Fern went to college. Ivy stopped traveling. Jack and William continued
to work at the garage though Jack only went in a couple of hours in the

morning and was always home by lunch. William spent a lot of time up in the cabin. Sometimes Jack went too. And sometimes Fern would meet her father there since her college wasn't that far away. Once, we even managed to drag Ivy along for a family weekend.

The four of us continued to have family dinner together on the weekends. We talked about buying a huge house but never got around to it. Ivy said it was a good thing after spending the weekend up at the cabin.

"I don't know if I could put up with all of you living with me." She sniffed.

Since Fern graduated high school with all kinds of college credits, she started school as a sophomore. She graduated in three years with a degree in communications. We told her that she now had to make a career decision. She had to either start looking for a job or continue her schooling.

We all made it to her graduation ceremony, which was held on a beautiful spring day. Someone asked us if we were Fern's grandparents. Awkward. Well, no surprise, we were all in our seventies, except for William. We joked about how did we get so old and what happened to us and where had the time gone. Even Ivy laughed about it, which surprised me. She'd always been so concerned about her looks, but she accepted growing old gracefully. Of course, she was still beautiful.

After graduation, Fern took a year off. She traveled all over Europe. When she returned, she surprised us all by saying she had taken the LSats before she'd left on her tour and applied to law schools and was waiting to hear back. Part of me was surprised, but it made perfect sense.

Of course, she was accepted by all the schools she applied to. She picked one in California. That summer with Lauren had convinced her that is where she wanted to live. "It's like the three bears," she said, "Alaska is too cold, Virginia too hot, but California is just right."

I felt like Jack and I were living our second honeymoon. Or was it our third? Those years when Fern had been so disagreeable and we had become estranged were distant memories. Maybe everything does happen for a reason because in our case, our lives had turned out great.

One weekend after Jack and William had gone up to the cabin, William pulled me aside and said he was a little worried about Jack.

"What do you mean? Worried? About what?" I asked.

"He gets tired and winded easily. We walk to the stream to fish, and he's huffing and puffing by the time we get there and can barely make it up the hill on the way back."

"We all slow down as we get older. I remember Thor…"

William interrupted me. "I think you should get him to the doctor for a check-up."

I suggested it to Jack, and he put me off, saying he was fine. "I can still outwork a lot of guys half my age."

"I don't doubt it," I said trying to mollify him. "But it doesn't hurt to have all our parts looked at as we get older. Think about cars. You can't run them forever without an oil change or a few new parts. You at least have to get new tires. Let's make appointments together with Dr. Francis. We both probably need a good check-up."

Jack laughed. "You're right. Probably a good idea."

I made the call but the soonest they could see us was six weeks away. "I'm sure that will be fine. We need the complete works."

The receptionist laughed. "I'll tell Dr. Francis that. You'll need to come in the week before for all your tests."

I told Jack we had to go in for all our lab work a week ahead.

"Oh no." Jack moaned. "Not lab work. I hate all that. My blood pressure shoots through the roof just being there."

"I believe you are a coward, Jack Frost." I laughed.

"I don't like doctor's offices," he retorted.

Two weeks later, Jack went out for a walk with Frito, who was quite ancient now. Lately, I'd been more worried about Frito than Jack. I came in from the garden to find Jack sitting in his favorite chair, with Frito curled by his feet. I thought he was napping. I laughed and shook his shoulder to wake him, and he slumped over.

No. I couldn't comprehend it. He was still warm to the touch. Maybe there was a chance. Some hope. I pulled my cell phone out and dialed 911 with trembling fingers. "My husband… something's wrong… he's not breathing…"

"We'll be there in a moment…" a voice said. "Stay calm."

I tried to remember how to do CPR. Most of my patients had been DNR—do not resuscitate—so there was little need for me to use it. As I fumbled loosening his collar, part of my brain was saying he'll be fine. The logical part that had seen hundreds of people pass away told me it was too late.

Jack was too heavy to move. I collapsed on the floor, holding his hand. Sobbing. Frito climbed up in my lap and licked my tears.

I heard a knock at the door. The paramedics came in. The house went from silent to hectic. They pulled Jack out of his chair and laid him on the floor. They ripped his shirt open. I wanted to scream, "You're hurting him. Give him some dignity."

They loaded Jack onto a stretcher and headed for the door. They were doing CPR. I prayed and prayed as they loaded Jack into the ambulance. I saw one of the paramedics look at the other one and shake his head slowly. I knew it already but didn't want to believe it.

A few hours later, William came home from work to find me still sitting on the floor by Jack's chair. He knew immediately what had happened. "Oh my God, Rose. Is it Jack?"

I held up my hand to stop him. "He's gone," I whispered. "Gone."

Later, Ivy arrived. William must have called her. I was now sitting on the couch, staring at Jack's chair. I wanted to drag it out of the house and burn it as if somehow it was to blame for what happened.

Ivy gathered me in her arms as well, crying with me. Someone had made tea and put a cup in my hand. Tea. The answer to all the world's hurts. Not this time. Fern had come in at some point. No doubt she was the one who had made the tea like I'd done for her so many times in the past.

"What hurts the worst is I wasn't there for him. I've been with so many people as they took their last breath, but I wasn't there when Jack passed.

What was he thinking? Did he say my name?"

Ivy shushed me as if I was a small child. "I'm sure he was thinking of you. The doctor called and said he probably went so quickly he didn't feel a thing."

The words we say to each other to comfort in moments of pain, grief, loss. Are we really supposed to feel better that our beloved didn't suffer? Yes. I suppose it's some small solace.

The funeral was huge. Jack had been a popular guy at all the AA meetings. Guys from AA hugged me and told me how Jack had saved them, kept them sober and on the straight and narrow.

Many of his customers from his garage also came. They told he was the only honest mechanic they'd met. "He always had time for a chat, not just about my car but he could somehow sense if something was wrong and give me good advice."

The burial service was reserved for family. Me, Ivy, William, and Fern. Ivy's kids Cate and Alex came with their spouses but most of the family was scattered to colleges and jobs across the country. I had hoped Lauren would come but she couldn't.

By the time we got home, I was exhausted. My feet hurt so badly I couldn't wait to take my shoes off. I could hear Jack's voice in the back of my head, chiding me for choosing fashion over practicality. I responded that I wanted to look my best for him. *You always looked great in my eyes*, Jack's voice replied. Collapsing on the couch, fighting tears, I kicked my shoes across the room.

Fern broke down completely when Jack died. He was the father who raised her from the age of twelve to sixteen, seeing her through some very tough times. Even after William returned to us, Fern continued to consider Jack her dad. She managed her grief at the funeral but it had been a struggle.

Fern went to the kitchen to make a pot of tea. "Remember how you always brought me tea when I was upset?" She smiled as she set the tray down on the table. "You said it was an English custom."

"Yes. Quite civilized, those English. They have lots of good ideas. If I remember correctly, I believe you made me some tea the day Jack died." My voice suddenly thickened with emotion. I sipped my tea.

Fern's eyes brimmed with tears. She sat next to me and took my hand, looking into my eyes. "I'm not going to law school this year. I'll take a year off and be here for you. I don't want to leave you on your own. Without Jack."

Hugging her, I said, "Fern, you don't know how happy it makes me to know you're willing to give up everything for me. But I can't let you."

"Why?" she said through her tears. "I want to. I don't think I can leave."

"I know you don't, but you have to get on with your life. If Jack was here, he'd agree. He wouldn't want you to stay." I took her chin and lifted her face so I could look at her directly.

"I'm old." Fern started to shake her head. "Yes, I am. Old. You are young. You have your whole life ahead of you, and you don't need to derail it by staying here and holding my hand. Doing my shopping. Taking me to doctor's appointments. Cooking me dinner. Making me tea. And whatever else it is that you imagine I will need you for."

"For emotional support," she said a bit testily, swiping the tears from her face. "I know you can still manage on your own."

"Yes, I can, and I have Ivy for emotional support. We've been through a lot together." I grabbed Fern in a tight embrace. "And I have your father too. It's like the old days, us three kids against the world."

I let Fern go and looked her in the face. She turned away and bent down to pick up Frito, who could no longer jump up on the couch. "I worry about what will happen when you lose Frito." Frito had outlived both of his buddies, Thor and Fritz.

"That's not going to be easy either. But life is filled with losses. We have to accept that. Some losses are harder than others."

I could see Fern nodding. "And you, young lady, need to get on with living your life. Seems to me all you've done for the last seven years is study. Have you even been on a date?"

Fern looked at me, annoyed. "Really, Rose, get with the times. People don't date anymore. I have guy friends."

"Friends." I rolled my eyes. "I'm not talking about friends. I'm talking about love. There is nothing like being in love."

Fern looked down and scratched Frito on the top of his head.

"I'm serious Fern. The best thing about Jack was we loved each other. Might have taken me more than half my life to finally find love but it was worth it. I wish we'd had more time together. But if you haven't experienced it, you don't know what you're missing."

No reply.

"Think of your mom and dad and how happy they were together because they were in love. You never met Ivy's husband Terry, but the years they were together, those were the happiest years of her life."

"Yeah, but look what happened to my mom and dad and Ivy and her husband. Love causes pain and heartache. I'd rather read a book."

"Oh Fern. You only say that because you haven't felt what it's like to love someone. It's the most amazing feeling ever. It changes everything. And yes, when you lose the person you love, it hurts very, very badly, and for a while all you think about is the pain of losing them but then you start remembering the good times and all those happy memories fill your heart back up."

Fern looked dubious.

"Trust me on this one. Education is great. A good job is great. Friends are great but nothing beats sharing your life with the person you love."

"If you say so, Rosie," Fern finally said, but she still looked doubtful.

"You might not know this, but before I was a world-class hospice worker helping people transition from this life to the next, I was an amazing world-class therapist helping real live people with their everyday struggles."

A hint of a smile began to tug at Fern's lips. "World class, huh?"

"Ivy thought so. She always told me I was brilliant. And my advice was brilliant. Of course, that was before Ivy became a world-class painter and decided she no longer needed my advice."

Fern laughed out loud. "You mean there was a time when Ivy listened to you? Took advice from you?"

"Hard as it is to believe, it's true. I advised her on all her relationships."

"What did your clients think of your world-class brilliant advice?"

"I think they thought I was competent."

Fern howled with laughter. "Competent?"

Tickling her, I said, "Yes. Competent. I think I helped a lot of people. It's easy to see the solutions to other people's problems. Much more difficult to see it for yourself."

"You left being the world's most competent therapist to help people die?"

"Geez, you make me sound like the angel of death. I helped them accept dying. To reconcile themselves to the life they lived. Letting go makes the transition easier." I thought about my two careers. "It's basically the same advice that I gave my living patients—you can't change the past. You have to accept what happened and then forgive, forget, let go, and move on."

I took Fern's hands in mine. "I'm worried you haven't moved on from what happened, which is the reason you haven't had any serious relationships."

Fern ducked her head so I couldn't see her face.

"You can't change what happened, Fern. You can't change your past, but you can change your future. And let me tell you, no one wants to end up at the end of their lives alone. I've seen too many people realize that when it's too late."

Fern looked up again. "I'll have to think about what you're saying since you are a world-class brilliant therapist."

"You should. Trust this old woman. Now get upstairs and finish packing. Your plane leaves early tomorrow."

William got us up at dawn. He was so nervous Fern would miss her plane. We swung by to pick up Ivy on our way. We walked Fern as far as security and then stood and waved until she was out of sight.

"Call when you get there," I yelled. I thought I saw a hand raise in the air and wave.

Chapter Sixty-Eight

"*I* know how you feel," Ivy said as we sat in front of the family plot. "I thought Terry and I would be together forever as well. We only had eleven years before he got ill."

I nodded. I couldn't speak. I stared at the stone with Jack's name engraved on it. It said, "Jack Frost has melted." It was his little joke. I had added, "Missed and loved by his wife Rose." There were only three blank spots on the headstones now. For me, Ivy, and William.

We sat quietly for a long time, staring at the headstones of our beloved spouses and family members. "It's so wrong we didn't get a lifetime together," I said. "You and Terry didn't get a lifetime together." I paused. "William and Margie didn't get a lifetime. Jack and I only had fifteen years. I thought we'd be together into our nineties."

Ivy squeezed my hand. "I know. I thought the same way about Terry but think about all the people who didn't even get as much time as we did. Or who were married to someone they really didn't love. I'm happy to have had eleven wonderful years."

"You've become so wise in your ancient years." I grinned and then winced when Ivy dug her nails into my hand.

"Watch it. Don't be calling me ancient."

"You are the eternal Fountain of Youth."

Ivy stared straight ahead while tears ran down her cheeks. "I'm a year older than Mom when she died. Remember we thought she'd lived a good long life."

"You're a year younger than our wicked-witch grandmother Meemee when she died. I think she made it to seventy-four."

Ivy snorted. "Old Meanie. What a horrible person. It's no wonder mom had some serious issues. Didn't Pawpaw live into his eighties?"

"I think so, but we kind of lost touch with him after Meanie died. Mom said he spent the last ten or twenty years in an old folks' home. Meemee probably dumped him there as soon as she could."

"How would you have liked to have been a hospice aide to Meemee and Pawpaw?' Ivy smiled wickedly.

"I'd probably be in jail for giving Meemee an 'accidental' overdose of some kind."

"I would have testified in your defense."

We sat quietly, staring at the blank spaces on the headstones.

"I wonder which of us will be next?" I said.

"Don't be so morbid. We're still young." Ivy sniffed.

"Young? We're in our seventies." I shook my head. "Did you ever think we'd be this old?"

"You're only as old as you feel."

"Well, then I feel old. My joints ache. My feet hurt. I have to get up in the middle of the night to pee. Isn't that old?"

Ivy didn't answer.

"Remember when you were fifty and you were on that dumb website—Find Your Forever—looking for love and you told me that fifty was the new thirty? I sure got a good laugh about that. Do you think seventy is the new fifty?"

"No. I think you're right. We're old. Except William. That young

still in his sixties. Well, mid-sixties, so he's almost over
e slippery slope to seventy."

d someone young to take us to all our doctor's appointments
a.   oceries, because they'll probably revoke our driver's licenses
soon."

Ivy chuckled. She'd been using Uber for the last three years. She liked the
convenience. She'd given her car to William.

❦

Early the next year, I sold my house and moved in with Ivy. Seemed silly
for us to be living in houses by ourselves. I enjoyed sharing a house with
Ivy. It was comfortable. Our differences had been worn down by time. Now
we fit together well. I rose early. She stayed up late. But during the day we
coasted along happily. It was nice to have someone to be with again. To talk
to. To share things with.

We offered a room to William who'd retired from the garage at last. He
thanked us but declined. "I think I'll move up to the cabin. I guess I miss
Alaska more than I thought I did. Plus, I seriously can't live with the two of
you in the same house," he joked. "I'm always worried you guys will prank me."

"I thought you were going to stay around and drive us to our doctor's
appointments and do our shopping," Ivy said, trying to appear unhappy with
William's abandonment.

"Sorry, Miss Daisy. You'll have to stick with Uber."

William offered to pay me for the cabin but I turned him down. "Jack
brought the cabin for Fern. Well, for Fern and Thor. To give them a little taste
of home. I don't think he paid very much since it was basically falling down.
If Jack had written a will, he would have left it to her, so you're welcome to
live there until Fern moves home." Our secret wish was that Fern would tire
of life in California and return to Virginia after graduating from law school.

After William settled in, we went for a visit. To be sure that he wasn't
completely alone, we brought him a present, a Husky-Malamute puppy.

When William visited us, he complained the puppy, Odin, was the worst dog he ever owned. "This damn dog couldn't ever be a lead sled dog. Hell, I don't think he could even be in the pack. He is out of control."

We watched Odin tear around the house. "Maybe it's because you spoil him rotten? Your other dogs all slept in kennels," Ivy said, arching her eyebrows. "Where does this one sleep? In your bed and practically eats at the table with you."

William looked at her sheepishly. "I'm too old to be a disciplinarian. Truthfully, Margie was always the tough one. She bossed me and all the dogs around."

Ivy and I had both lost our dogs. Fritz, who had brought Jack and me together, lived until almost twenty. Frito was fifteen or sixteen when he passed away. We had sprinkled all their ashes, along with Thor's, at the cemetery and up at the cabin, but I also had three tiny urns with their ashes that I kept at the house.

I missed having a dog but Ivy and I decided not to get another. "I'm over men and dogs," Ivy said. "They're both too demanding."

Chapter Sixty-Nine

When Fern graduated from law school, Ivy, William and I flew out for the ceremonies. We stayed at Lauren's house, which was convenient.

Lauren was also a widow now. Miranda had passed the year before. I was shocked by Lauren's appearance and tried to hide it. We were both in our mid-seventies, but Miranda's death had taken a toll. Lauren had always been tall, but she appeared to have shrunk. The house seemed too large and empty. Miranda's laugh no longer brightened the place. The kids, grandkids and great grandkids had all moved on to their own lives.

We sat in the living room drinking sparkling water. Lauren caught me looking around at the changes to her beautiful home. "I know," she said. "It seems so big and empty now. Not a home. More like a mausoleum or the tomb of some ancient emperor. I don't know why I stay here." She gazed around sadly. "I still feel Miranda will pop out to ask about my day and tell me about the kids."

"It's hard," Ivy said. "After Terry died, it took me forever to sell our huge house and move to some place more suitable."

"I haven't been able to go through her clothes. The kids are pushing me to start clearing things out. They've already taken what they want."

"As hard as it is, when you finally do it and move to a new place, you'll feel so much better. You think it's disrespectful to let go of all their things but you'll feel lighter. Happier. Things aren't what make the people we love. It's the memories."

"Thanks Ivy." Lauren smiled at her. "I'm planning on retiring this year. I've been given the hint that I'm not quite the raving beauty I once was, and younger women are taking over in the ratings. I picked an industry which is all about youth and beauty." She ran her hands through her hair. "It will be nice to stop coloring my hair and worrying about my appearance."

"Where do you think you'll go?" I asked. "Will you stay in California?"

"I'll probably move to San Francisco. A couple of my kids live in the Bay area so I'll be close to family. None of them stayed in LA."

We sat quietly for a long while. Each of us lost in thoughts of what the future held for us.

"Enough gloomy thoughts." Lauren proclaimed. "Fern should be arriving at any moment. I have a great dinner planned and tomorrow is her law school graduation. Let's focus on her and her future. Which will be bright."

Fern soon arrived. It was wonderful to see her. Visits had been reduced to two weeks at Christmas while she'd been in law school. She didn't come home for the summer anymore because she was always working or interning.

After a scrumptious dinner, all catered of course, since Miranda had been the chef in the house, we moved back to the living room with cups of tea.

"Any plans on what kind of law you want to practice after graduation?" I asked.

"Graduation is only the first step, Rosie." Fern smiled. "I still have to pass the bar before I'm officially able to practice law. It's like only the hardest test on earth. Two days of non-stop torture. And then three or more months until you get your results. There's like a fifty percent fail rate."

"You will not be in that group," William declared. "You'll probably pass with one hundred percent on all parts."

Fern laughed. "I don't think that's ever happened. But I do hope I pass.

I'll be cramming all summer. If I fail, I don't know if I'd have the strength to take it again."

"I have faith in you, Fern. You'll do fine. Have you thought about what kind of law you're interested in?" I asked again.

"I hear corporate lawyers make really good money," Ivy said.

Lauren spoke up. "I've tried to talk her into going into broadcast law. She's done an internship with my studio, but shockingly, she doesn't seem interested."

Fern blushed. "Lauren, you've been wonderful to me. Such a great mentor, but I want to work in criminal law. All aspects. I plan to start out as a public defender. And then maybe work for a private law firm before switching to the other side and becoming a prosecutor. I think that will give me a clearer vision of all the aspects of the criminal system. My final goal is to one day be a judge."

"A judge? Very impressive," William said. "Your momma would be proud."

Fern smiled. "I hope so, but that's years from now. I have to pass the Bar first."

"A public defender?" Ivy asked. "Don't they defend people who can't afford lawyers?" She almost curled her lip.

"Yes, Aunt Ivy. Lots of people can't afford a lawyer and thankfully they are provided one. It's not only the rich who should get good representation because they can hire the best lawyers. Everyone needs an equal chance."

We didn't want to put any more pressure on Fern, so we talked about the graduation ceremony the next day.

"Get there early to get good seats. And don't forget how bad the traffic can be," Fern said.

"I think Lauren is well aware of the traffic in LA."

Fern laughed. "You're right. She's been here a while."

Chapter Seventy

William got us all up early to avoid an LA traffic jam. Lauren had arranged for a car and driver so we didn't have to worry about parking. After getting dropped off a few blocks away, we wended our way through the crowds and found our seats. We had at least an hour until the ceremony started. Luckily it was a perfect southern California kind of day. Beautiful blue skies, a few wispy clouds and warm but not hot.

I sat with my eyes closed, thinking about Jack. It wasn't right he wasn't here to see Fern walk across that stage to get her law degree. He had been a good father to her. Life wasn't fair, I reminded myself as I fought back tears. Margie wasn't there either to share in this moment. Her early influence was responsible for Fern achieving this dream.

Ivy nudged me to point out someone in the crowd. A movie star or a well-known politician, perhaps. I smiled at her. She was a celebrity in her own right and so was Lauren, so I wondered why she was so excited to see someone famous. Ivy laughed. "Always loved people watching." She took my hand and squeezed it. "I know it's hard not to have Jack here."

"It is," I whispered. "I miss him every day."

William leaned over and said, "What are you two whispering about?"

Ivy and I laughed. "We're plotting against you."

"I thought as much." William snorted in mock disgust.

Lauren glanced over. "You three." She rolled her eyes. "I feel sorry for your mother."

The music started, and for the next two hours we listened to speeches and saw Fern walk across the stage to get her JD degree. As she said, she still had to pass the bar, but it was quite an achievement to get this far. William, Ivy, and I cried and laughed and hugged each other. Luckily when the ceremony was over, we quickly found Fern in the crowd. Lauren took us all out to some incredibly fabulous restaurant to celebrate.

Fern spent the summer at Lauren's house studying for the bar exam. She said it was the most intense time of her life, and she was grateful to have some place to stay and food to eat while she studied. Her persistence paid off. She passed on her first attempt.

When she told us that she had landed a job as a public defender, we were less than thrilled. I think we all hoped she'd change her mind about her career path. "Fern, you could do so much better than that. Start at a prestigious law firm and work your way up," Ivy said. "You'd probably make partner in record time."

I chimed in, "Lauren said she could make contacts for you. Set you up with interviews."

"No. I've already planned it all out. I'm going to spend five years as a public defender, five years in a private practice as a defense attorney, and then I'll get a job with the State as a prosecutor. I want to do criminal law and I need to see it from all sides. Eventually, I'm sure I'll be the youngest judge ever elected." She laughed.

There was no changing her mind. Fern got an apartment with a few lawyer friends. Lauren sold her mansion and moved north.

Fern continued to come home for Christmas visits, but she often was working on her laptop. She didn't seem to ever be able to get away from work completely. On her last visit, I told her she had to plan to take time off in the summer, without her laptop. We were secretly planning a big blow-out for Ivy's eightieth birthday. Her father would also be turning seventy that year, but the big party was for Ivy.

"I can hardly believe I have a sister that old. Eighty! Where did all the years go?" I said to Fern while thinking, why couldn't all our loved ones live that long?

A week before the celebration, Fern called and asked if she could bring a friend home with her. "A friend? Are they going to want to hang out with a bunch of old people?"

Fern laughed. "Actually, most of my friends think old people are way cool and a lot of them know about Aunt Ivy's art and are impressed I'm related to her. But this is a special friend that I want you to meet. Thomas, who I've mentioned before."

Chapter Seventy-One

Fern came for the celebration and brought Thomas with her. She had been sprinkling his name into conversations for the last year. They both worked for the public defender's office. He was an idealist too. Fern's motto was: "Justice should not be only for those who can afford a top lawyer. The poor need good representation too."

We were all excited to meet Thomas. Fern had never dated in high school or college, and I worried constantly she'd end up old and alone.

We spent a wonderful week catching up with Fern and getting to know Thomas. Even William liked him. Thomas appeared perfect. He was soft-spoken, polite, easygoing. He was also handsome. I told Ivy that and she said, "Rose, you should not be thinking about young men that way." She tried to look stern before bursting out laughing. "But you're right. He is rather cute."

Fern took Thomas to the cemetery during their visit and told him all about the people buried there. "I'm sorry you never got to meet my mom and Jack."

Before the surprise party, Fern brought Thomas to the cabin. Fern told him Jack bought it for her because he worried about her. And he wanted to give her something a little more like the home she had left. Even at Fern's worst times, she was always happy at the cabin. When she was with Thor.

The day of the party arrived. Fern suggested to Ivy they go to a spa the morning of the party by saying she really needed a mani-pedi. As soon as they were out the door, we headed to Ivy's favorite restaurant. We were expecting around fifty people. Of course, Ivy's children, Alex and Cate, were coming with their children and grandchildren. I think there might have even been a great grandchild by now. Ivy's side of the family didn't seem shy about having lots of babies.

I'd also invited Ivy's art buddies. She didn't paint professionally anymore but I think her agent always hoped for one more amazing Ivy Bane Berenstein painting. Ivy would joke that she had already painted every disease known to man, except the Bubonic Plague. There were also friends from yoga, book club and all sorts of other groups Ivy was involved in.

We told Ivy that we were all going out to Renaldo's, her favorite restaurant, for dinner that night and that they should join us after the spa. When they arrived, Renaldo himself apologized, saying they were full, but he might have a table in the back. When she walked into the room, we all screamed "surprise!" Balloons fell from the ceilings, flashes went off. For a moment, I thought we'd given Ivy a heart attack. Her face froze—in fear, horror, amazement? Her hand flew to her chest before she broke into a huge grin and laughed, walking around the room, hugging everyone and thanking them for coming.

Everyone commented that she didn't look a day over sixty, which was true. Ivy just got better with age. She wore her now silver hair in a pixie cut, which was perfect for her. If I had cut my hair that short, my nose would have dominated my face. Her skin was also still smooth and almost wrinkle free.

A reporter from the local paper wrote a huge article about the famous local artist celebrating her eightieth birthday with family and friends. It made the front page of the weekend section. I caught Ivy reading it several times. A small article even appeared in some of the larger national papers.

Fern and Thomas left a few days later. We were fantasizing about wedding bells in the future.

Chapter Seventy-Two

*F*ern and Thomas joined us for Christmas. Over breakfast on Christmas morning, they announced they were engaged and planned to get married in the Spring.

"You can't possibly get married that quickly," Ivy said. "Weddings take time. You don't have a venue or a dress yet."

Fern laughed. "Calm down, Aunt Ivy." She turned to look at Thomas and he took her hand. "We're not interested in a huge wedding with all the bells and whistles. We're going to fly here, get married at a park, the cabin, or maybe your backyard. No dress. No ceremony. Just the family.

"After the wedding, we'll go to California and have a small gathering with friends and co-workers. Not only to celebrate our wedding, but to say goodbye, because we're moving to Alaska."

All of our jaws dropped simultaneously. Even William looked stunned.

"Alaska?" I finally managed to squeak out. "Why? What? How?"

"According to my five-year plan, it's time to move on in my career. I know it's only been four years but Thomas and I are ready." She turned once again to smile at Thomas, and he beamed back at her. "Last summer, during our trip up there, Thomas fell in love with it. We took a trip to the old homestead.

Zac and Luke still live there, and they each have a passel of kids who all look like miniature versions of them. Even the girls!" She laughed. "Everyone in matching flannel!"

"Yes. Alaska is amazing. It feels so different from California." Thomas chuckled. "Probably because it is. It still has that wild untamed frontier spirit. And we decided to move there. Not to the old homestead," Thomas added, "It's a bit too remote, but to Alaska. There are so many legal issues involving the native population. Especially the women. So many crimes and so little good representation. We want to help."

"I've already lined up a job with a private law firm, and Thomas is going to continue in the Public Defender's office. And Dad," Fern continued, "we'd be happy to have you join us. Return to your roots, so to speak."

"Alaska…" William said and got a faraway look in his eyes.

<hr />

Fern and Thomas returned in May and got married in Ivy's backyard. It was a small wedding with immediate family and a few friends.

Thomas had no family. Fern told us his mother got pregnant at sixteen and was thrown out of the house by her family. I have never understood people who are perfectly willing to abandon their own child and grandchild because they're worried about what the neighbors will think. His mother died when he was six, possibly from a drug overdose. Placed in foster care, he was eventually adopted by an older couple. They were wonderful and were responsible for his education but sadly they passed away while he was in law school.

The ceremony was short and sweet. Fern wore a long white cotton dress she bought at a fair trade store. Thomas wore a white shirt and gray linen pants. It reminded me a bit of Jack and my wedding. Though we had a wild party after the ceremony.

William walked Fern down the aisle, which was the only traditional moment in the ceremony. Tears caught in my throat. Jack should be here, I thought. He should be on the other side, walking Fern. We had the reception catered. It was a beautiful wedding. Perfect for Fern.

They went on a honeymoon to the beach, laughing it would be the last time they'd be able to stick a toe in the ocean since the water in Alaska was too cold. Then they flew out.

Ivy and I went to the cabin to help William pack. He was only taking clothes, some personal items, and of course, Odin. The rest we would store at Ivy's or take to Goodwill. I flashed back to that day so many years ago when we were at the cabin after Margie's death. We went through some dark times, but it had all come full circle.

Since the cabin was quite cozy and fully furnished, we decided we'd start renting it out. That would be a little extra money for William.

A month after they arrived, Fern and Thomas found the perfect house. "It has a separate apartment over the garage for Dad and Odin."

The next year, Lauren passed away. One of her children called to inform me. We hadn't spoken in a while. She had sunk into dementia. It was hard to believe the powerful woman I knew and loved for all those years had been reduced to that state. It broke my heart.

I turned eighty the year after Lauren died. My party was not quite the blowout affair that Ivy's had been, nor did I get a write up in the paper. After all, I wasn't a famous artist. But Fern and Thomas and William all came and those were the only people I really wanted to see. Ivy still looked about ten years younger than me, but I'd long ago reconciled myself to the fact that she would always be beautiful. At least I had all my original parts and good health. That was quite the achievement for eighty.

After everyone flew home, Ivy said she thought it was time for the "next step."

"Okay, and what might that be?" I asked.

"It's time to move into one of those places—retirement communities, I think they're called. I'm tired of having to cook and clean and walk up and down stairs. Let's face it, Rose, we're not getting any younger."

"I can't argue with you, though I don't remember you ever cooking a meal or cleaning your own house."

Ivy snapped, "Oh stop. Whoever cooks and cleans is hardly the point. We don't need a house anymore. It's time for both of us to move on."

We toured several places and talked to our friends who had taken the "next step" and found a perfect place.

When we moved into our retirement community, we had to laugh since Ivy had never worked, at least from a job she "retired" from, and I had quit work over ten years ago. Most of the people there were at least ten years younger than us, which was fine because we considered ourselves young at heart.

"We certainly aren't ready for assisted living," Ivy pronounced. This was the in-between step. We got a three-bedroom apartment to share. We talked about getting one-bedroom apartments right next to each other, but we had grown used to living together. We had maid and laundry service plus two meals a day. The food was delicious. They had entertainment and transportation to take the residents wherever they had to go. It was like a cruise ship that was permanently docked.

I kept hoping that the Alaska winters would drive Fern and Thomas, and William too, back to the milder climate of Virginia, but they all seemed enchanted with the place and their jobs. "We're doing important work," Fern told us on her weekly phone calls. "We're making a difference, which is what I've always wanted to do."

When Fern turned thirty-five, she finally had a baby. I had been biting my tongue since they got married, trying not to ask, badger or cajole them about becoming parents. Fern seemed like she was on a slower track than most people her age. She didn't get married until she was twenty-nine. I remembered when I was still single at twenty-nine, I thought I was an old maid. Was that term used anymore?

I was a grandmother at last. Maybe not biologically a grandmother, but I felt like Fern was my daughter. Jack and I had raised her through some harrowing years. Sadly, Fern and family lived so far away I couldn't snuggle Isaac and read him bedtime stories.

It turned out to have been perfect timing for Fern to have a baby. William passed away the next year when little Isaac was only one. At least he had lived long enough to meet his grandchild, but it was heartbreaking. He was only seventy-nine.

The family came with William's ashes, and we buried him at the family plot. I was sad at the reason for their visit but so happy to finally have Isaac in my arms. Thomas left after a week, but Fern stayed a month to spend time with Ivy and me.

During her visit, I asked her how her career timeline was going. "You said, five years, five years, and five years. You spent four years in California as a public defender and now you've been in Alaska six years, almost seven, as a defense attorney. Have you given up your plans of being a prosecutor?"

"I'm thinking about the next step, Rose. We're considering moving from Alaska. It's one of the reasons I took a month off. I'm exploring opportunities here in the lower forty-eight."

I was so excited to hear that news but didn't want to say anything or beg her to come home to Virginia. I didn't want to jinx it. I just smiled and hugged her and said she had my support. And Ivy and I would help in any way we could.

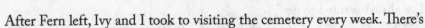

After Fern left, Ivy and I took to visiting the cemetery every week. There's not much to do when you get to your eighties. It made us feel closer to all the departed.

"There's only two empty spots on the headstones now," Ivy said. "I wonder who will be next. Shocking that we outlived our little brother."

"He lived some rough years. Which you certainly never did, my dear sister. Which is probably why you still don't have any wrinkles at the advanced age of eighty-nine," I said.

"I suffered," Ivy said in a low voice. "After Terry passed away, I was an emotional wreck for years."

"I know." I squeezed her hand. "It was a terrible time. Terrible for us both.

Worse for you." It had taken me years to get over feeling I was responsible for Terry's death. I could hear Lauren's voice in the back of my head berating me, "Stop feeling so damn guilty about everything, Rose."

"Okay, Lauren. I will."

"What did you say?" Ivy turned to me. "Were you talking to Lauren? You know she's not here. I hope you're not going all senile on me."

"I am as sharp as a damn tack," I retorted. "You would be lucky to be as sharp as me."

Ivy and I often teased each other, asking in confused old lady voices, "Was I the pretty one and you were the smart one?" while staring into each other's eyes. Then we'd laugh and laugh. Ivy usually said, "I was both. The pretty one and the smart one."

As we left the cemetery, I looked back at the two empty spots. Which one would be etched in next, I wondered. For some reason, I was convinced I was going to be the last one left.

Chapter Seventy-Three

*I*vy left me a few weeks after her ninetieth birthday. She had been going downhill for the last year, ever since William passed. There was one health scare after another and then she broke her hip, developed pneumonia and was gone. We didn't even get to throw her a huge party, which she would have loved. Ivy never stopped enjoying being the center of attention.

Fern and Thomas had planned to come for the big party we never had. Instead Fern came alone with Isaac. She understood how hard it was for me to lose Ivy.

"I don't know how I'm going to go on without her," I told Fern as she made tea for us. Little Isaac played happily on the floor. "Ivy has been my constant companion for eighty-seven years. She was the only one that I could talk to about our childhoods, our parents, our family, and our baby sister Lily."

"I know, Rose. I feel so bad that I haven't been here for you. But when I came for dad's funeral, you and Ivy looked so amazingly healthy. And of course, Ivy still looked beautiful."

I snorted. "Yes. Beautiful to the end."

"It never occurred to me that Ivy would be gone in a year. I was convinced you two would live forever. At least until one hundred. Or more. Of course I thought Dad would make it into his nineties as well, if not a hundred. I was looking forward to the big birthday bash for the two of them."

"I thought we'd all live forever too. No one can conceive of dying and the world going on without them."

"Well, I do have some good news to share. I wish we hadn't waited so long. Remember last year when I visited and you asked about my timeline? I'm finally ready to make the move. We're coming back to Virginia."

I squealed in excitement and squeezed Fern in a rib-cracking hug. Isaac looked up from the floor, confused. I leaned over and scooped him up. "Don't be afraid, baby. Your gramma is so excited to have you move here."

Fern flew to Alaska a few days later with a promise she'd let me know when they were moving. "I think I have a job lined up with the prosecutor's office right here in Richmond."

I stayed on in our three-bedroom apartment. I didn't need the room, but I didn't want to leave. I left everything the way it had been when Ivy was there. Her paintings on the walls. Her bed made up with her favorite duvet. All her clothes in her closet. It helped me imagine that Ivy was still there with me. That she had stepped into her bedroom and would be right out. Sometimes I caught myself talking to her.

"Ivy, I'm making a pot of tea. Do you want black tea or one of the herbals?" She didn't answer.

"Ivy. They're having shrimp for dinner tonight. I know you love shrimp." I waited for an answer that never came.

"Did you see that story on the news about that young actress and her awful…" I didn't care about those kinds of sensational stories but Ivy did. But she made no comment.

"Ivy, your favorite awful reality show is on. The one where the girl dates a hundred gorgeous guys trying to find her husband… hurry, you don't want to miss a minute." But Ivy didn't come out of her bedroom and plop down in her chair, ready to soak up every minute of young buff men showing off for the girl.

I talked to Ivy a lot when I was alone in the apartment. She just never responded. I went down to breakfast and dinner and sat with other residents and interacted with them. Sometimes I even went on the activity bus to a play or shopping trip. But I was happiest in our apartment. I would sit quietly with my eyes closed and if I tried hard enough, I could hear Ivy laughing and telling me she was the smart one and the pretty one.

Fern called and said they would be back in a month. I wouldn't be alone anymore. She said they wanted to buy a big house and I could move in with them. I thought about it but wasn't sure if I wanted to. It could be nice to wake up with Fern again every morning, but it might be too much excitement. I liked Ivy and my apartment. I felt her presence here so strongly.

Epilogue

A voice said, "Yes, I'm the hospice nurse, Betty."

That made me so angry. Who was claiming to be the hospice nurse? I am the hospice nurse. I struggled to open my eyes to see who this person was. It was so difficult. I just wanted to sleep.

A different, younger voice said, "How is she? She went downhill so quickly. A few weeks ago, we were out for her birthday dinner, joking and talking about her turning ninety next year. We were making plans for a big bash."

I wondered whose ninetieth birthday party she was talking about. Ivy's? No, Ivy didn't have a party for her ninetieth.

The young voice continued. "Then she called a few days later and said she wasn't feeling well. I wanted to take her to the doctor, but she refused. She said it was time."

I heard someone crying.

"That's sometimes how it happens. People know," the other voice said.

Know what, I thought irritably. I wished these two would go away. I wanted to sleep.

"It has been quick but some are like that. I think she's close to the end."

"I was so worried I'd be too late. I've been so busy. We moved back here last year, and I've been setting up a house and getting my career up and running."

"And having a baby, it looks like?" I heard someone laugh. Who was having a baby? Who was talking?

"Rose? Can you hear me? I've brought little Rosa to see you. Named after you. My second-best mom."

Why did this voice sound so familiar? I struggled to open my eyes and saw a beautiful young woman with a baby. Was it Mom? Holding Lily?

I reached out to the baby, who took my finger. "Mom?"

"No Rose. It's Fern."

I closed my eyes. Who was Fern? Wasn't that my brother's name? No, his name was William. I saw William and Margie and reached out to them.

"Who do you see, Rose?"

I forced my eyes open again. "Fern? Oh, it's so good to see you."

"Yes. Fern and Rosa, your granddaughter."

"I thought it was Lily," I whispered. Sweet babies. I got them jumbled up.

"It's close now," the other voice said.

"No. I need more time," Fern cried. Time for what, I wondered? I felt fingers on my wrist.

Ivy floated toward me, and I smiled. "Oh Ivy, I've missed you so much."

"We're all here, waiting for you, Rose. Look."

Terry stood slightly behind Ivy. I saw Lily and Mom and Dad, and oh my goodness, there was Jack looking so handsome with a big smile on his face. He reached out toward me, and I reached my hand out to his.

I heard soft weeping and a baby gurgling. I smiled. Jack was standing in front of me on the shore of a huge lake. There was a boat behind him. Everyone was in the boat waiting for me.

"Is that our lifeboat?" I asked Jack.

"Yes." He put out his hand to help me in. "We're all here. We're all safe."

I thought I heard woofing in the back of the boat.

Fern sat by the family plot. Rosa was asleep in her arms. Four-year-old

Isaac wiggled on the bench between her and Thomas. She looked down and smiled. "We'll be leaving soon. You were a very good boy today."

Isaac grinned up at her. Thomas smiled and squeezed her shoulder over Isaac's head. "It was a lovely service."

"Yes, we've come full circle. In some ways, this is where it all began."

Thomas looked momentarily confused. "It began in a graveyard?"

"Not exactly." Fern smiled at Thomas. "It began with Lily. The death of a child. A terrible tragedy. Rose used to say that everything happens for a reason." Fern paused. "Actually she said Lauren and Ivy claimed she always said that but she denied it." Rosa stirred in her sleep and Fern bent to kiss her head.

"If Lily hadn't died, my dad would never have been born. And if he hadn't been born, we wouldn't be here with our babies, because I never would have been born."

Thomas looked at her. Isaac knelt by the headstones, running his fingers over the engraved letters. "My dad felt he wasn't loved because he wasn't Lily. He joined the army and decided never to come back home. And he ended up in Alaska because that was the last place he was stationed and he liked it because it was as far away as he could get from his family."

Fern paused, thinking about the past. "And he drank too much because he was unhappy but also because it's the family curse. He met this wonderful woman, my mom, Margie, and she helped him quit drinking and they got married. And had me."

Thomas smiled at that. "Well, I'm glad he ended up in Alaska, because you are the best thing that ever happened to me."

"That's not the end of the story. I could have stayed in Alaska forever, and Rose and Ivy never would have even known about me. But one day Rose came here to the cemetery and saw her father for like the first time in a zillion years. And she thought it was a chance to reconnect the family, but he died before they ever got to really talk."

"Sad." Thomas said.

"Yes. Very sad, but it was that meeting that made Ivy and Rose decide to try and find my dad. And they did. And when my mom was killed, I came to live with Rose and Jack. And met Lauren and spent a summer in California and went to law school there and met you."

"Best decision ever." Thomas smiled.

"It was. And we fell in love and got married. And had Isaac and Rosa. I mean, what are the chances? All those things had to happen before we were even born."

"It's a lot to think about. How random all our lives are. That A and B happen, which leads to C," Thomas said.

Fern stared at the headstones, a tear slipping down her cheek. "All the blank spots have been filled in. Everyone is with their loved ones now and for eternity. My grandparents, who I never met, Ivy and Terry, my mom and dad, and now Rose is reunited with Jack forever. Even Thor and Fritz and Frito and Odin are here. Rose sprinkled their ashes on the graves.

"Only Lily is alone," Fern added sadly. "I think Rose was so sad that she never got to experience any part of life."

"From the stories you told me, she was much loved by her big sisters. That has to count," Thomas said.

"Yes. Being loved is everything. I wish I could add a small tombstone that would have Lily, Ivy, and Rose somehow together. It seems so appropriate. While Ivy and Rose met and married their forever loves, I feel it was the love between the sisters that meant the most."

"Makes me sad I never had a sibling," Thomas mused, staring at Lily's grave.

"Me either," Fern said. "But at least I had Thor." She laughed.

"A dog brother?" Thomas rolled his eyes.

"Don't be that way," Fern teased. "Dogs are important." Fern looked down at Isaac. "We should get a dog for the kids."

"A small one," Thomas joked.

They sat quietly watching Isaac hide behind the headstones, popping out to give them a huge grin before ducking down again. Rosa slept on, snoring softly.

"Thank you for agreeing to move back to Virginia," Fern said, staring at the headstones. "I wish we could have managed the move sooner. So I could have spent more time with Rose while she was still alive."

"Me too."

"I want our kids to grow up knowing their family, even if they are no longer here. To hear the stories. Hear about the circle that connects all of us to each other and to the past. I want to tend the family plot and decorate for Christmas and share things with everyone."

"Like Rose did?" Thomas asked.

"Yes. This place was important to her. These people were everything to her. I want us to be part of that."

The End

Life is short
And we do not have much time
to gladden the hearts of those
that travel with us
So,
Be swift to love and
make haste to be kind...

Henri Frederic Amiel 1821–1881

About the Author

Patti Gaustad Procopi is a former army brat who lived all over the world before settling in the rural community of Gloucester, Virginia, with her husband, Greg. There they raised three daughters and numerous cats and dogs.

After retiring from working at two area history museums, Patti finally had time to do the things she always wanted to, including writing. Moving constantly made it difficult to make friends and form lasting relationships. Her writing is about emotional connections, friendship and family.

In addition to writing, Patti fills her days with rescuing raptors and other birds and researching her family's past on Ancestry. She and Greg also love to travel and have been busy checking off their bucket list.

Patti can be found on Facebook, Twitter, and Instagram. She loves hearing from readers and is available to meet and talk with book clubs and other organizations.

Patti.pro@cox.net

Pattiproauthor.com